Spiteful Village

Joy's Trouble

Jo Kemrich

Author, Jo Kemrich, lives in the West Country. After working as a solicitor and legal writer for many years, Jo retired to concentrate on writing fiction of another sort. *"It's just pleasure. I put the characters on page one; they get on with writing the story they want to be in. I sit back and let them do it. What could be easier? Well, quite a lot of things really; now, brain surgery for example ......"*

*In memory of my great friend John Avent
and the trees of Levanstrice*

Four people: one pure white - all seeing, all loving.
Another, green as his fields. The third, rich golden red.
Last, one with the colours of a stormy sky.

And one spiteful village.

Itinerary:

PROLOGUE

The warm familiar comfort of English village life.

As everyone living in London knows, that great city is the busiest place in the country, if not the world. Whether you have a paid job or not, simply being there is enough to keep anyone toiling from daybreak to night, just to stay with the flow. And it's all a fight; a fight to grab the shower, a fight to get your latte, your panini, your train to work; a battle to find a table for lunch, to have your ulcers treated…

And there's still paid work to be done - a living to earn.

By contrast, country living's quite the opposite in every way, bar one.

Take the county of Exshire for instance. All those pretty cob and thatch cottages. Such a pleasant, easy-going life; everyone friends with everyone else; no squabbling for bathroom or seat on the train. Just get up in the morning and have a full English breakfast when it suits you; take a leisurely swim in the sea or a little wander on the moor before your nice pub lunch.

Naturally, earning a living in the countryside is no hardship at all. Do a little basket weaving or make the odd oak hurdle in the afternoon and the day's work is done. Then it's time to relax and enjoy a couple of pints and an evening meal in your local with the neighbours. Have a game of dominoes; win a pound or two off the silly villagers and off to bed by twelve.

And all the time surrounded by such warm-hearted people; people who would do anything for you, just because they like you. Money means nothing to them; they just need to see you smile.

No surprise therefore that so many "outsiders" have moved to Coldstow in the last ten years or so. The only wonder is that an exactly similar number of houses has become so conveniently empty to accommodate them.

The one thing that's common to both City and country life? Crime, of course.

* * *

INTRODUCTION

HOMECOMING

Switch on a light when it's dark.

The weather forecast was wrong yet again. That September night was almost as hot as the day had been, and still no relief. The two open bedroom windows let in a very slight flow of warm air, and occasional rumblings, teasing the sleepless with hints and unfulfilled promises of wonderful cool rain; better still, a full-on thunderstorm to freshen air, clear the mind and bring the gift of a cool bright morning.

The day's travel had made her tired and she had been glad to reach home after a week away caring for her aunt. Death had been a release, but she would miss the old lady – her dear friend and the last person who had known her all her life.

She lay on the bare mattress, desperate for sleep after hours of frustrating wakefulness and quite determined not to move. Still partly dreaming but now more than half awake, her mind refused to ignore the sound that had troubled her.

And the same sound, or something very similar, came again; closer perhaps, a little louder, inexplicable and unnerving in that low point of the night which belongs to spirits of the dark, and ought to be left to them while humans sleep in safe ignorance.

Alarmed, and rather angry at falling out of her kindly dreams, after sleep had been so hard to get, she was now fully conscious. Lying there for a few moments she waited to gather enough energy to rise and investigate.

Another sound came from somewhere in the garden - front or back, she wasn't sure. This was different; a sharper noise, like steel striking stone and it was very close to the house. For a moment, fear overwhelmed her curiosity; she wanted to close the windows without looking out, go back to bed and escape back into her quiet dreams.

A coward's way – that wouldn't do. She rose and walked, steadily and deliberately, to the further window which looked over her small front garden and the village lane.

"I'm not afraid. It's just a night noise - something quite normal; a cat, or a hedgehog maybe"

Comforted by that thought, she looked out.

She saw nothing wrong there. To the south, a solid bank of approaching cloud threatened heavy rain. But here, a nearly full moon riding high in the night sky, lit flowers and shrubs in surprisingly strong definition and left only a few areas of deep shadow; none large enough to hide anything she might have reason to fear.

Soothing garden smells of dew, damp soil and roses drifted into the room. Several fields beyond the road she could just hear farm machinery working and see lights from a couple of tractors, probably some farmer desperately trying to gather in drying silage before the expected storm. Strangely the fact that others were working there in the near distance made her feel more isolated and alone.

Otherwise there was silence. Everything seemed normal, commonplace; a typical hot late summer night.

With diminishing fear, and even thoughts of a possible cup of tea, she turned, successfully negotiated the end of her bed and fell heavily, swearing, as she tripped in the duvet she had tossed half onto a chair and half to the floor in her sleepless struggle with the stuffy heat.

Sitting upright, she felt her scalp crawling as she heard again the same sound that had woken her. It was clearer now and close, very close, to the back of the house. She stayed there, frozen, for perhaps a minute; or maybe it was ten – in her present state time meant nothing.

Fear was back in full charge now, wiping away all thought of soothing tea and renewing that earlier temptation to hide. She wanted to bury herself under her bed cover until a new dawn sent night thoughts back where they belonged and cooled the overheated imagination that created them.

But though she feared the unknown (and in some measure, surely we all fear it), she hated the thought of skulking on her bedroom floor, waiting for the next strange noise and fighting whatever horrors her troubled mind might make of it.

She stood, welcoming support from the chair as she disentangled duvet, legs and feet. Now upright, she listened for any further sound, straining to hear it and longing not to. For the moment, there was nothing. She walked the few short paces to the second window and there it came again, close as before, but now very soft and quiet. For some reason that softness was horrible, suggesting somehow that whatever made it was aware of her nearness; playing with her; completely confident in itself. Whatever it was, the night belonged to it, not to her.

The moon's welcome light faded, returned to its full brilliance for a brief moment, then suddenly vanished as the long-promised storm clouds took charge of the entire sky.

Sheet lightning flashed behind the wooded hills. A wait, then a long roll of thunder, at first far off but growing nearer and ever louder. The power of it shook the house; something crashed downstairs. Then brooding silence.

Heart beating wildly, she forced herself to take the last step toward it and look out of the open bedroom window. The sounds had been clear and seemed horribly close, but she saw nothing in the deep shadows below. Suddenly the night was ripped to pieces by continuous flashes of day-bright sheet lightning. The silence ended with another long roll of thunder apparently from every direction. The house seemed at the very centre of the storm.

With a deafening crack, fork lightning struck a tall hemlock in the nearby woods, instantly setting the tree alight from tip to root. Another strike hit the roof of her neighbours' barn, tearing a great hole in the slates and leaving the dry, rotten roof timbers blazing, but no one appeared to tackle the fire. The village might as well have been empty of people.

There was a vile, sulphurous smell, a brief period of silence, then ear splitting thunder, more frightening than anything before as it shook the old house, its contents and occupant with the violence of an earthquake. Something else fell in the kitchen downstairs; she thought of the open windows everywhere and realised with a shock how easily the house might be entered. Why hadn't she thought of that before?

She remained standing, unable to move, looking out from the open window but seeing nothing, one moment blinded by searing light, next unable to see anything in the sudden blackness. The thunder died away. Rain started; first with a few large drops, then in torrents, instantly reminding her of rainy seasons in her beloved Hong Kong when drains are overwhelmed and roads can melt away in a few hours.

Her thoughts far way and calmed for a moment, she almost missed what she looked for, yet feared to see.

For a few seconds a continuous series of lightning flashes illuminated the garden and the edge of the neighbouring woodland in brilliant light and there, in the centre of that lurid scene, was something – no, someone. A person standing, but bent, as if lifting something from the ground.

What it held was unclear. As she watched in those brief seconds of flickering light, the figure looked up and stared directly at her as if it had known she was standing there and now marked her for its attention.

When the next flash of light came a few seconds later, the figure had vanished, but the image of that brilliant scene was seared onto retina and into memory. She remained there, desperate to know more, hoping to see nothing.

The lightning flashes came at longer intervals, then stopped. The heavy rain continued, filling her world with constant noise as it beat on roofs, poured from overflowing gutters and gurgled away down half choked drains. She closed both windows, then sat down, shaking slightly, on the bed and waited for her mind to clear.

* * *

Whether she slept or not, for the next hour she was unaware of her surroundings. Shocked into a dreamlike state, her mind struggled with what she had heard and seen; the dreadful noise, the lightning and fires, the quiet sounds that brought more fear than anything else and the dreadful figure in her garden.

It was two hours before dawn when she pulled herself together. The night was still oppressive; the storm had done nothing to freshen the atmosphere. The wind had died away and the rain had stopped. A cloudy sky allowed a little early light into her room. Remembering the open windows in the rest of the house and the crashes from her kitchen, she cleared her mind and set about doing practical things to help bring her fear under control.

First task: close windows; next: check the kitchen, then mop up.

But, even as she dressed and formed her little plan, she knew it was a sham. Broken crockery and wet carpets were not matters that concerned her now. If she was going to overcome her fears, the house wasn't the place to start.

As if some other power had taken control of her, without further thought, she passed downstairs and through her kitchen to the small rear hall without noting, or attending to, anything at all on the way. Automaton-like she put on boots and her old gardening coat and opened the back door. The fact it was unlocked made no impression on her, although a locked door would have been small protection with so many windows wide open.

The small, paved courtyard was set below the rear garden; four stone steps led up to a neatly mown lawn bordered by vegetable beds. During the day it was a colourful and quietly domestic place but, that night, the woodland behind seemed to loom uncomfortably over the silent garden and the darkened house itself shut out from the courtyard any early light from that side.

Thinking more clearly as she stood there, she wondered why on earth she hadn't switched on any lights, and more importantly, what, if anything, she was going to find by blundering about in a dark garden, most of which lay in heavy shadow.

But, despite her fear, she was strangely determined to complete the venture; going back, even to switch on a welcome and companionable light, was unthinkable. So often we humans act in this irrational way; half way through a task, we realise the need for something overlooked; a forgotten coat in the light rain, the knife missed when laying the table or perhaps our scissors to cut that so-tough plastic wrapping. But we soldier awkwardly on, without fetching these necessary aids, and somehow get by, using a lot more effort than we needed.

The short flight of steps was plain enough to see and, when she reached it, the wet lawn lay shining slightly beyond the shadow of the house. A strong smell of woodsmoke hung in the air but, apart from occasional hissing sounds, the fires seemed to have burned themselves out.

If it hadn't been her own familiar garden, she would have been unable to find her way. Without the outside lights it was difficult to make out any detail, save for the clear silhouette of the woods against a slightly lighter sky.

But it was her garden, and she knew it so well. Walking slowly along the edge of the nearest border, she could make out the row of tall runner beans, lower growing kale and cabbages, the old cherry tree with the children's rope swing hanging there in the shade. And, with the recognition of familiar things, she became a little less fearful and more at peace with herself. Such is the power of a garden.

She walked a little more quickly along the far border with its little tool building at one corner; the trees behind made her uneasy and this wasn't helped by seeing the shed door ajar – she supposed the storm had sprung it open but hurried past, not wanting to risk further enquiry; excusing her weakness on the grounds that could be done better in daylight. Too dark now to poke about in there.

She turned to follow the edge of the third border that would lead her back to the house. She felt easier now, there was just a little more light from the sky and working her way homeward on the last stage of her little inspection tour was almost comforting.

Feeling less fearful, she peered into the flower border, thinking now about her plants and quite forgetting for a moment her search for signs of the intruder. There were the dahlias for cutting and next to them…

She expected an area of bare soil, cleared by the gardener ready for new planting, but it didn't look like the neat level space she expected. She peered into the darkness, more puzzled than anything; what was she looking at?

The closer she came, the harder it was to make things out but it looked to her as if there was some sort of trench running across the bed toward the fence behind. She bent forward, peering through misted spectacles and trying to make sense of this strange excavation. It was far too large to have been dug by any animal and far too neat. About half a metre deep, narrow and long.

Apart from a soft sigh, she made no sound as she slumped forward under the massive blow. She was already dead by the time her body landed cleanly in the shallow grave. Ten minutes later she was buried out of sight, at peaceful rest in her beloved garden.

* * *

He arrived home on the following morning. A tiresome journey from the Scottish shipyard where his clients were modifying a drilling rig. A few hours asleep in a noisy lay-by had done very little to ease his exhaustion

Above all he wanted to see his wife, then something to eat and real, refreshing sleep – twelve hours of it if possible.

But he wasn't going to get any of those things. As he turned into the lane and the house came in view, he saw the driveway full of vehicles – police cars, vans and an ambulance; more cars in the lane itself and, most horrid of all, crowds of people, including most of his neighbours. His arrival triggered attention from everyone, none of it pleasant – well that was nothing new, as far as his neighbours were concerned, he simply didn't belong.

He parked the car and walked toward his front door; it was wide open. Something was being carried out on a stretcher. The body was covered; he felt sick.

The interrogation started immediately. The DCI in charge was already more than half convinced that this was another case of the husband did it.

So began his nightmare; a terrible dream that would last a full year, eat him up and ultimately spit him out, leaving him lonely, lost, without friends, family, job or home.

ANOTHER HOMECOMING

Taking the early train.

A team meeting to discuss the cover design for her new book *'Medieval Ship Building Skills'* had finished successfully, and a little earlier than expected. With luck she might just catch the eight fifteen from Waterloo and be home that evening rather than stop overnight in their London flat. She decided to try.

For once she found an empty taxi within minutes of leaving her publisher's offices in Southampton Row. From then on, everything went perfectly; the traffic was slight, the train was late leaving and she caught it with minutes to spare. Settling back in her seat, she let go of work at last and welcomed thoughts of a quiet weekend at home with Peter. It was a long while since they had been free to spend time together; too long – there was a lot of catching up to do.

She dozed for a while, then slept more deeply, waking suddenly with her heart thumping as the train slowed and she saw the station nameboard sliding past the window – her stop and she had nearly missed it! She started to gather her bag, briefcase, overnight bag and coat – so much paraphernalia and she had nearly overlooked Peter's present, collected excitedly that morning as she imagined his pleasure opening it.

The train had been standing for a full minute by the time she reached the door and prepared to step down onto the platform.

A familiar voice was speaking very close to her:

"I'll call you when I get home, darling. Don't phone me; not tonight at least, he's bound to ask who it is and I hate lying to him. He'll be away next week; we can be together again then."

And another voice, even more familiar:

"......can hardly wait that long......"

She heard no more, indeed could bear no more. She stepped back in the carriage, and without thought, hurried blindly along the corridor to the rear of the train where she got out onto the platform and waited, trembling, hiding in the dark. A few minutes passed, like so many hours, and at last the train pulled away; the platform was left half-lit by patches of cold white light, clear of people and silent, and still she stood, incapable of thought, lost and hopeless.

Setting her bags down, she sat on a platform bench and waited for her mind to recover sufficiently to decide what she would do. Twenty minutes of her life passed without any sensation, then her brain started to work again.

One thing was certain: she was not returning to their home or to him. Not ever. Half dreaming, she walked along the deserted platform, over the footbridge and out to the station entrance and, for the last time in her life, bought a ticket from the friendly clerk. Then she descended the stairs to the up platform and waited, empty of mind, for the next train.

She left her neat, gift wrapped parcel containing the gorgeous red leather case and its engraved watch to lie on the platform where she had last heard his voice.

* * *

Chapter 1

***Old country saying: Places and people take their
character from the soil; if you have bad soil...***

He looked down sadly from his bedroom window. The
neighbouring house and garden seemed closer and uglier than
ever. He wondered how much the value of his home had fallen
since these people moved in and whether his aching desire to sell
up and leave the village would ever be realised now.

The Siptacs had arrived about two years before, buying the
rather boring three bed house and its pretty garden from the
elderly man who had lived there alone for a few years after his
wife died.

Despite his age, Arthur kept the building smart and clean, but
the garden was his great love. His lawn would have done credit to
a golf course greenkeeper. Filled with border plants grown from
seed in his modest glasshouse, the formal flower beds at the front
of the house were a constant pleasure; there was always something
to see and enjoy, whatever the season.

Arthur wasn't just green fingered, he was a champion grower
and easily lifted most of the prizes at local flower shows. Unusually
for Coldstow, no one resented his success; he wasn't just good at
what he did, he was also a thoroughly nice man. Yes, Arthur had
been a friend, a Coldstow rarity, and he missed him.

The housing market had been at one of its lows and the place
stood unsold for some time. He had worried about what sort of
people would buy it and felt obliged to keep the grass cut, partly
for his old friend's sake and partly because he wanted the new

owners to be gardeners. This was quite irrational, and he knew it, but he ran his mower over Arthur's lawn and picked out the weeds in his flower beds every week just the same.

There were rumours about the new owners long before they appeared. He hadn't seen anyone viewing the property but, inevitably, others had. Apparently it was a middle-aged couple with a new car, or perhaps it was the two foreign looking women, no, on good authority it was a local farmer wanting a holiday cottage to add to her letting portfolio.

On balance, he rather hoped the couple and their car would be the ones, that is if any of the stories were true.

And his hope was fulfilled. It was the couple, and their car was new (and, incidentally, bright red and large).

Which just proves the correctness of the old saying *"Be careful what you wish for."*

The newcomers didn't waste a moment getting down to their destruction. They started with the house itself. Inside he could only deduce what was happening by what came out and landed in the skips that kept coming and going. He had known the house well when Arthur lived there and it pained him to see the old man's life being systematically erased.

The Siptacs began with the fitted furniture, followed through with the kitchen and bathrooms, and finished their vandalism by tearing up the nice polished wooden flooring that had given Arthur and his wife so much pleasure when they had it laid.

Before the internal sterilisation was over, a local builder began the external attack. This he could watch from his window, hating to see it but unable not to.

The house had a single neat brick chimney serving an open fire in the lounge. Having few other features, this gave the building some sense of scale and a slightly welcoming appearance. The Siptacs, evidently having no time for such architectural flippancies, had the chimney cut down to ridge level and substituted by a length of thin black pipe topped with a curious brown cowl. The structure was held in place by a number of wires tied back to the roof itself. He had seen something similar before; it had a crude steel box that burned wood pellets at its lower end. Pellets that cost a fortune in energy to produce and to dry.

Entering his gate on the day following the appearance of the black pipe and its saucy brown hat, he spoke under his breath:

"Very trendy, but did it have to be so brutally ugly?"
He hadn't intended anyone to hear and thought he was alone.

"It, as you call our global warning initiative, is something you will have to install yourself. It's going to be law soon; then you'll have to obey, or pay a £10,000 fine. I've sent a list of all the houses in this village to the Council so they can check if anyone doesn't comply."

He hadn't expected a hedge to speak. Annoyed with himself and embarrassed, he stayed silent and walked on to his house for a soothing cup of tea.

But he hadn't got beyond the thought of making it when the doorbell rang and there was Mrs Siptac.

She didn't bother with any conventional niceties such as *"Hallo, I'm your new neighbour"* or *"I'm Joy from next door. Do call round for a drink later today"*.

Instead, she started straight into what the visit was all about; that is, dominating her new neighbour from day one:

"I've brought you a copy of the Government leaflet on Cutting the Cost of Heating Our Homes and the Council's Rules on Chimneys. You've only got six months to comply. Is that your dog? Why isn't it wearing a collar? Is it micro-chipped?"

Wilting under this, his first, encounter with the new neighbour, he struggled to deal with the onslaught.

His natural reaction was to say:

"Hallo to you too and you know what you can do with your pamphlet."

But he had just sufficient self-control to stop short of slamming the door on all possibility of future good relations.

"Good morning, so glad to meet you at last. I'm most grateful for your advice but I don't think I shall be having my chimney knocked down this month. It'll have to wait. My dog is microchipped, thank you. Oh, and she doesn't of course need her collar in the house."

The woman had steel armour; nothing got through to her:

"Well, I shall have to check up on that; I suppose there's a register of microchipped dogs that anyone can look up. I'm sure it's a legal requirement for dogs to be on leads when there are strangers about."

"Well, that's only if the strangers have been invited and as you're not, she can do as she likes in her own home. Goodbye."

He opened the front door very wide and glared at her. Apparently she understood that much because she swept up her pamphlets and went out, stopping briefly to have the last say in her clothes peg voice, "I know your sort; you think you can get away with anything. I shall be watching you. By the way; do you have a television licence?"

He said nothing and she left.

But it was the destruction of Arthur's beloved garden that hurt most.

The Siptac's builder wasn't the most sensitive of an essentially insensitive breed. Removing soil to create a wide path around the house and a vast turning area in front, created a good deal of mess. This was, eventually, cleared away but not the spillage in the lane. The Siptacs evidently took the view that once their clay reached the public highway, it was no longer any concern of theirs.

By then, there wasn't a trace of either lawn or flowerbeds. What wasn't gravelled over was covered with ugly concrete paving slabs in pale shades of pink and grey that clashed with everything else about the place.

The Siptacs were very pleased with the results of their labours and Arthur turned painfully in his grave.

Mr Siptac (Reg to his few friends in the past, but they have all forgotten him now) was christened Harold and that is how his wife addresses him when she feels so inclined. He is not the driving force in his family. If he ever had any enthusiasms, they evaporated long before he arrived in Coldstow. But he does work hard at doing the things he has been told to do. And he does it all without skill and with absolutely no sensitivity whatsoever.

About sixty five years old, he is heavily built and, in fact, quite tall, but a permanent stoop hides that fact and also makes him look older. He has no obvious hair above ear level and it doesn't look as if he has ever needed to shave. This makes him appear rather childlike. Enhancing this impression, he bears a permanent and rather disconcerting smile. At first this suggests he is constantly tickled by some secret joke. However, longer acquaintance corrects any thought that he has intelligence enough to be amused: he is in fact completely stupid.

Harold likes to believe that he is still attractive to the opposite sex and he dresses accordingly. There are some styles that really don't add sex appeal for the wearer, but Harold doesn't know this, so he continues to wear trousers that are tailored for a figure he doesn't have and jackets to match them. He generally wears his long-tailed shirts outside his trousers and hanging just below his rear end, but not quite as far down as his colourful designer shoes.

Unsurprisingly, Harold almost always addresses his wife as "*Mrs S*". Well, he would, wouldn't he?

By contrast, Mrs Joy Siptac is a very small woman.

Slightly younger than her other half, she is yet far too old for the almost, but not quite fashionable clothes she likes to wear. It's all very well being size zero but not quite such an attractive asset after the age of, say, twenty five, as it was in one's teens. Inevitably, some parts of the body age a little faster than others and slimming off a pound or two every now and again to regain that sylph-like figure tends to leave behind some unwelcome surpluses here and there. Maybe the body retains all that extra skin because it knows it will be wanted again later.

So it is with the Siptac. Pursuing her teenage look, she has to cut out the calories from time to time and her appearance shows it. For her sake we shall not go into more detail at this stage but later, it may become necessary to say a little more about Joy's little physical peculiarities.

Adding interest to her brightly coloured clothes and clunky black walking boots (with smart bits of chrome on the laces) all of which proudly set her apart from her dowdy, and mostly overweight, neighbours, Mrs S has a novel and intriguing hairstyle. Her naturally grey hair is evidently very long and she patiently erects it every morning into a remarkable structure resembling a soldier's busby in shape, but not in colour, for Joy's busby is dyed bright orange.

The busby thing has a life of its own. As she walks, it wobbles about in time with the movement of its owner's legs, threatening to collapse and envelop her face, leaving her looking like some alien plant life setting out on its evolutionary road into the animal world.

As to the rest, her face is small with an unfortunate curl of her lips which gives the impression she is constantly sneering at everyone, and perhaps she is. Her nose is not her best feature so, in kindness, nothing more should be said about it.

It is quite difficult to settle on the Siptac's eye colour as, like her husband, she rarely looks directly at anyone, preferring to stare into the nearest hedge, as if shrubbery is far more interesting than anything else in the world. Her voice is surprisingly penetrating and sounds as if she has a peg on her nose.

Busy, busy, busy all the time is the lady Siptac's motto. Unfortunately for them, much of this busyness entails being busy about other people's private business. And that makes her unpopular in the village; but this is Coldstow and she is not unusual in being disliked.

We have started with the Siptacs, male and female but, later, we shall have to examine the credentials of everyone who is anyone in Coldstow. – You have been warned, so don't complain about this later. Now's the time to stop reading and go back to the TV if you are squeamish about naughty doings.

* * *

Sad to say, not a few of the villagers keep little secrets they would prefer not to have generally known. Of course most of these are quite trivial but, like everyone else in this world, the residents all like to present a perfect face to others and to lord it just a little over their neighbours. Unwise, but that's what humans do, if given the chance.

Having their private lives poked into is never very welcome to any of the villagers as there is always some juicy fact, or fabricated fiction, that may pop out and, once something juicy has popped out, there is no way of popping it back in.

Of course, Ms Siptac sees nothing wrong about her prying habits. Being nosey and spiteful is in her nature (in fact it is all her nature) but she justifies everything she does on the basis she is Doing the Right Thing.

And there is nothing she likes better than to sit in her own eyrie by an upstairs landing window, camera and binoculars at hand, watching her neighbours about their activities and looking up rules in any rule book she can get her hands on, whether it's something about animal protection or the local council's manual on rubbish collection or the maximum permitted height of a garden shed. All very laudable perhaps but not if you are on the receiving end.

If there is a purpose behind this perpetual troublemaking, it is simply this:

Joy Siptac is ever seeking power, power to control Coldstow and its three public institutions of Church, Trade and Leisure and power to manage its entire population into serfdom.

In this, Joy is not unique. Even little Coldstow has several such. Wherever there is a group of people who may be governed, someone will appear and govern them, and when the Siptacs arrived in the village, all of its established facilities were, naturally, already under the control of someone or other.

So a war for power broke out between village newcomers and the existing management; a war that was to be fought with no quarter offered, or asked, and one that would be watched and enjoyed from the sidelines by much of Coldstow's population.

* * *

Looking out again from his bedroom window and pondering on

the Siptacs' characters, he wondered if that habit of nose pokery had gone too far in their previous neighbourhood, hence, their move to Coldstow. Perhaps some sinner had made continued life there a little too uncomfortable for them.

After closing the blind to exclude the source of his unpleasing thoughts, he walked across the room and downstairs to face another boring Coldstow day. Nothing changed for the better in this place and he hated the tedious routine.

As ever, his dog, Freddie, was waiting for him by the kitchen door. As ever he collected her on his way outside and, as ever, stood on the gravelled yard, silently awaiting the major evacuation. This start to the day was always teeth grinding. By the time it was done with, he had generally lost such good temper as his night's sleep gave him and he would be lucky to recover it before lunch.

It always went the same way. Freddie would wander about sniffing delicious old urine stains on the stones. If it had rained and there weren't any smells, the sniffing just took longer; a lot longer. After some minutes she generally squatted and peed.

On a really good day she did the main thing first and he would feel he could set out on their walk, leaving the pee to be done at the roadside. But this was rare. Most days it was the other way around. A pee, then her aimless wandering about would continue, back and forth, sniffing at each turn and disgustingly licking her lips at the thought of all that smelly piddle. If this lasted more than fifteen minutes he would throw down the small catch-it-if-you-can shovel, take off her lead and put her back in the kitchen accompanied by a few unprintable words. It wasn't any use skipping the evacuation and just walking off with a full Freddie. That meant a series of piles dropped outside some troublemaker's gateway and a major road cleansing job. Poo bags just didn't answer.

He was late that morning; it was nine am and ten minutes into the Procedure when he heard voices next door. Normally this would have had him silently returning to the kitchen and a cup of cheering tea but the Big Event was about to happen, so he stood his ground and couldn't help hearing the row developing on the other side of his garden wall.

It was part embarrassing, part amusing and wholly unusual to hear a bit of Coldstow trouble being aired right out in the open. Evidently there was someone else at next door's gate and she wasn't happy.

"Hey, you."

"Talking to me?" - from Mrs S.

"Who else? What's your husband up to with his binoculars, peering at me in my garden?"

"What rubbish, Mr Siptac doesn't have any binoculars. If he did he wouldn't know which end to look through. It was probably me; I was looking at goldcrests, not you. But you do have odd breasts. I should keep them covered up if I were you."

"You should be ashamed of yourself, saying such things; it's disgraceful if a woman can't be topless in her own garden without peeping Siptacs ogling through her hedge. I've seen you before, peering and peeping at other people. You're sick. It's time something was done about you."

Apparently Harold Siptac appeared on the scene at that point for the man suddenly stuck his silly oar into this promising engagement:

"What's the problem? Can I help? Did I hear you wanted your binoculars, Mrs S?"

His voice sounded odd; perhaps slightly slurred. Surely not at this early hour? - But one could hope.

"No you bloody well can't and I don't. Go back in the house you dozy old fool. – Have another drink."

Whoops. Not perhaps the nicest way to treat your own family when they're trying to help, but Mrs S really isn't very nice, and the reference to drink was unwise in the circumstances and, of course, jumped on immediately by her at the gate.

"So, that's it, is it? Your loony husband, if that's what he really is, gets drunk by nine in the morning and doesn't know when to keep his mouth shut. I'd like to know what he's going to say next for my amusement."

"You can go to hell. I'll report you to the Council for building that shed in your back garden if I have any more out of you. You don't have planning for it – I checked. On second thoughts, I'll report you anyway. We can't have people like you breaking the law and getting away with it"

This was developing nicely. He wondered what else was going to come out, but for the moment there wasn't going to be any more as the other woman signed off with a simple

"Sod off."

Forgetting poor Freddie's walk, he wandered with her back into the house, for once abandoning the daily porridge and treating himself to a full cooked breakfast. Unexpectedly it was going to be a good day, whatever else it might have to offer later. Suddenly he liked one of his neighbours.

Chapter 2

A little spite goes a long way.

The obscure West Country village of Coldstow lies on a narrow and winding minor road that connects the main highway north out of the small town of Larkston with, well, not very much really, apart from a maze of more minor roads where a stranger lacking satnav might easily become lost and remain so until next Doomsday.

There are no connecting lanes, no junctions and, apart from gateways and the village car park, no passing places for several miles. The village is a ribbon of thirty or so buildings placed singly and in groups separated by occasional stretches of high banks and agricultural hedges.

These hedges close in on the road as the year advances. By June, even the most determined tourists stay safely away until the annual autumn hedge cutting clears a wider way and lets in some welcome daylight. – That is if Andy Westleigh, the unreliable local hedge cutter, can be bothered to do his job and his aging machinery doesn't break down.

The place is surrounded by miles of hilly farmland and woods. Very attractive for a passing visitor to look at, but inaccessible and uninteresting to tourists who prefer coasts and moors where they can do the outdoor things that tourists like to do. Besides, there is little or no fun to be had in Coldstow itself; the place is too busy with its own unpleasing affairs to spare any time for entertaining strangers.

This isn't an area for pretty thatched cottages and ancient, low ceilinged inns, where nothing has been built since the year 1660. But there are a few farm buildings which are very old indeed. Most of these awkward structures were converted into unsatisfactory homes years ago by some lumpish builder under the eye of a completely insensitive planning authority. In the process they lost what little character they may once have had, but they do retain the doubtful benefit of being cool in summer to set against their small windows, dark, chilled rooms and year-round damp.

The associated farmhouse to which these barns once belonged lost its ancient charm at the same time the barns were "developed" and we have the same anonymous builder to thank for that. The house has been re-roofed with something grey, but isn't slate, and the walls have been re-rendered in curious decorative swoops and whirls that bear no relation to the work of any plasterer from the past.

We may as well look at some more of the local architecture while we are here. Best to get it over with. Let's start with the best building and let the rest come as they will.

Coldstow's small Victorian church is appealingly simple and all the more welcoming because of it. The stonework is smart and well executed with neatly cut sandstone quoins at each corner and every opening. The steeply pitched slate roof is faultless and the generous entrance porch, complete with its wide timber seats, is inviting. The surrounding graveyard is comfortingly full of local names and looks nice in the summer after its fortnightly mow.

Simplicity is repeated inside the building, but here it's always church-cold and, apart from looking at an ancient and rather boring font, casual summer day visitors find nothing to keep them there and return to the welcoming sunlight that streams through the entrance doorway. There, if they are stuck for something to do, they may read the church notice board with its sad list of occasional, and rare, church services and a faded notice with a misleading list of the mobile library's visiting days.

The itinerant vicar has little to do with this church and no interest or concern at all in the village residents, but she may have some trivial role to play later in this narrative.

Incongruously, the church is quite a lot smaller than its Georgian rectory, suggesting that the Church of England lost much of its concern for Coldstow's spiritual welfare some time during the reign of William IV. Naturally the rectory was sold many years ago; it has since lost its nice outbuildings and a couple of small fields which gave it some balance and is now owned by someone resident in the Far East, but no one knows either his name or what he looks like.

The ecclesiastical authorities appear to have progressively lost all remaining interest in St Mary's through the intervening decades. Twenty years back the village at last lost its very own vicar and was obliged to share one with another parish. Now it must share with three other parishes and its congregation has effectively vanished.

The only other public buildings are a corrugated iron clad convenience store and sub-post office run for "the Community" by two elderly ladies (who detest customers for the mess they make); a fair sized public house, run by Dave and Stan (who detest customers for the mess they make) and a village hall which is managed jointly by the shopkeepers and their enemies, the publicans.

So much for Coldstow's facilities – more than many villages but nothing to write home about.

Apart from the old farm, Coldstow's houses are built in the various styles of the last two hundred years. All have been extended or "updated" from time to time. The result is an unsatisfactory and ill-assorted jumble of poor materials, bad workmanship and varied states of decay.

Our new friends, the Siptacs, live in their fairly modern two storey property (the one that once had a nice garden, but we mustn't keep on about that). They keep it maintained in a state of ugly, cold blooded perfection and the paved garden is now entirely soulless. Mrs S makes sure it is all kept that way by her other half and Mr S appears quite happy to do what is wanted as this enables him to stay out of the way and, so far as possible with the wife that he has, to enjoy a quiet life.

We left this cheery couple enjoying their little victory over the sunbathing lady. That was Sally Redfern who lives alone in the largest (and best) of the converted barns. She is dark haired, not quite slim and always dresses well (except when sunbathing in private). Her age is uncertain, but she is one of those rare women who is very attractive without quite being beautiful. Sally works as a freelance technical writer which pays very well indeed, but Coldstow does not even know that much about her. This ignorance conveniently allows the gossips complete freedom to manufacture a history for her, which they have done with no goodwill whatever.

Mrs Redfern hasn't lived in Coldstow more than a few years and she really isn't bedding in at all. She doesn't even know this yet; so she has a long way to go and probably won't make it. Sadly, the village is likely to beat her; it's a tough place. - Far worse than any town.

What Sally hasn't realised is that newcomers to the village must learn to be secretive and coldly, falsely, friendly toward their various neighbours. This is a very effective and amusing way of setting people up to be insulted and hurt.

Once these basics are learnt, newbies may hope to become part of the establishment. This is not the same as acceptance. No one who hasn't been born in Coldstow, or the local hospital, is ever accepted by those who have that advantage. But it's the nearest best thing. Sally could never be part of the establishment, but Joy Siptac was there almost as soon as she arrived.

* * *

Returning to her barn after that little contretemps with her neighbour, Sally poured herself a fat gin and tonic in equal proportions and no ice. She gulped this one standing and immediately made another for more leisurely, and seated, consumption.

She wandered out to the front patio and the inviting swinging garden seat. Going over that angry conversation again and again, she thought of all the clever things she ought to have said if only she'd been prepared. It was too late now; she could hardly go back to the Siptac person across the road and request a replay. Time had moved on and, for the present, her vigorous V sign in that general direction had to suffice.

Unfortunately just at that moment Joy walked past and caught the full venom of it.

Sally glared angrily at the sky.

"Things going well as usual. It had to be her, didn't it? Thanks a lot."

So, of course, "*things*" didn't stop there.

∗ ∗ ∗

That autumn was a real Indian summer. Yet another fine sunny morning saw Gerry Allen getting ready to leave for work. By nature Gerry is a naturally easy going and cheerful man. Unusually for a Coldstow resident he rarely has any spiteful thoughts and, being loved by his worldly-wise wife, he has been largely protected by her from the nastier realities of human nature; that is to say the Siptacs of the village and their like.

On his way to the back of the house and his rather nice car, he heard the slam of the letterbox in his front door and turned back to see what had arrived. – Being one of the world's innocents he still hadn't learned to fear mail, whether posted or electronic, but that was about to change.

It was far too early for Coldstow's normal postal delivery, which commonly arrives sometime between three and four o'clock in the afternoon, certainly not at a convenient hour of the morning. But, being Gerry, he gave no thought to the unusual arrival time of the large, flat, white envelope on his doormat.

He bent to pick it up. It bore no name, just the first line of his address: "*Titheleigh*". Turning it over he wondered if it was for him or his wife. Having no further guide, he slid his finger under the flap and carefully tore the envelope open.

Inside there were just three photographs, no note to accompany them and explain. The prints were large, bright, shiny, colour photos of a woman half seated, half lying, in a lounger against a white background. She was wearing jeans and nothing else whatsoever. He peered more closely. It looked like…

"What have you got there Gerry?"

His wife was standing behind him and already looking over his shoulder. He turned to her, wondering vaguely if she could explain this remarkable circumstance.

But one glance at her face warned him that here was trouble, and trouble on a scale previously unknown in their peaceful marriage.

"I don't know, these came through the door, there isn't any letter with them."

"What's written on the back then?"

He turned the pictures over one by one; the middle one of the three bore in confidently large print:

'To Gerry; a memento of a wonderful time.'

He stood there in his small hallway, speechless, unable to understand what was happening to his protected and comfortable world. Mentally floundering, his brain tried, and failed, to cope with it all.

"Give me those you bloody little cheat."

And she was gone, gone to sit in her kitchen and cry, gone to get ready for a battle and then a war, gone to find a new life even.

* * *

One of the most dependable sources of income for the average small town solicitor is the neighbour dispute.

The thing is, once they start, these little money spinners can't be stopped. Rather they escalate and develop a life of their own. Mr X has a bad day and takes it out on Mr Y, his neighbour, for using his lawnmower on a Sunday. Mr Y retaliates by bending the aerial on Mr X's car. Within a year they are pouring petrol through each other's letterboxes and the lawyers are onto another winner.

A day or so, and a couple of angrily sleepless nights, after the Siptac encounter, Sally Redfern was sitting in her kitchen, trying, and failing, to concentrate on a modest crossword that ought to have given her no trouble at all. She had a horrid feeling that she was in for a lot more trouble and more sleepless nights – as if she needed them. The Siptac wasn't going to let this one go; the woman was spiteful and dangerous.

Sally stood up – being upright helped her to think – and pondered on what to do. Go away for a holiday perhaps…

She wasn't allowed any further time to develop that idea.

Someone had knocked sharply on her front door. Expecting trouble and feeling slightly ill, she lacked the courage to open the door and, instead, quietly made her way upstairs where she could look out of her landing window onto the lane and see what, or who, was there.

There was a woman; but it wasn't Joy Siptac. Looking from above it was hard to identify her visitor but whoever it was, she was on a mission. The next knock was much louder, quite violent. That was too much. Without further thought, she abandoned all pretence that she was away for the day and thrust open the window:

"Whoever you are, you can stop trying to break down my door and learn some manners."

She hadn't meant to speak; it had been wrenched out of her by the violence being done to her house. Another war was on.

The unidentified woman looked up; red-faced and obviously angry, it took Sally a moment or so to recognise another of the village newcomers and someone she had thought was a friend, or as near a friend as Coldstow will ever allow.

"I'll come down."

"Yes, you bloody well will. Quickly too or I'm going to make a scene on your doorstep."

There didn't seem to be much she could say in reply, unless she wanted the whole village to be involved in this. Probably most of it was already listening in, mouths open, notebooks in hand.

Opening the door, she stood aside to allow her sometime friend to enter, or more accurately to barge into and past her to engage battle on her enemy's home ground. Plainly this wasn't going to be an occasion for putting the kettle on; more likely this visit marked the end of those past happy occasions.

"Sorry I spoke like that; didn't realise it was you. What can I do for you?"

"You can stop making advances to my husband, that's what you can do and while you're about it you can leave the village and take your nasty habits with you. You're a slut; we don't want people like you living here."

When you meet an acquaintance, you don't expect to be struck in the face. For Sally, this was worse than being slapped. She had no real friends and few acquaintances in Coldstow; she certainly couldn't afford to lose those she did have. – What was this about? Could she find some way to calm things down?

As she was about to find out, the short answer to the last question was: no, she could not.

"Don't pretend I don't know what's been going on. I'm not a fool."

That was enough for Sally Redfern. Burning her boats, she took up the challenge:

"You are indeed a fool Jenny. I've done nothing with your husband and if I wanted an affair with someone, I wouldn't choose Gerry for any money. He's a stupid bore with bad breath. You suit each other perfectly."

"Flattery will get you nowhere. I Caught Gerry with these. Look at them and deny it's you if you dare."

Trembling from a mixture of white hot anger and fear of what the envelope held, she forced herself to appear calm and slowly, deliberately, opened it.

There were the three photographs of herself lounging topless against that plain white background.

Unable to understand any of it, she just stood there silent and open-mouthed. She barely heard what her visitor was saying and hardly cared; the pictures were all she could think about. They were certainly her but who took them and when?

Having had her loudmouthed say, her one-time friend walked out without another word. Sally dropped into a chair and stared blankly at the half open front door.

A sound of laughter came from somewhere nearby. The voice was all too familiar.

Chapter 3

Suicide, accident or murder?

Coldstow's inappropriately named "Happy Fireside" pub isn't quite as old as it tries to make out. Yes, the building is ancient (hence the head banging timber beams in the, low ceilinged public and saloon bars and the slightly higher steel joists in the adjoining Dyninge Roome) but this used to be another farmhouse until a retiree from somewhere in the Midlands bought the building as a derelict shell and forced it, protesting, into its role as a Real Ale Country Pub.

The place had no character as a farmhouse and, after all the new owner's efforts and money spent, it still had no character and remained so under the management of a string of subsequent hopeful landlords who successively broke their hearts and zeroed their bank balances trying to make the business pay.

There were two insuperable problems: first, almost the only source of trade was Coldstow itself. Too few people living in the village and most of them either poverty stricken or too mean (or both), meant the income from bar and restaurant didn't even cover running costs.

Secondly, the narrow, overgrown lane and the pub's total lack of any positive ratings, promised no welcome to tourists and very few made the effort to discover the delights of the Happy Fireside and its short menu. Any that did were unlikely to return. The food wasn't worth it.

Landlords Dave and Stan were the latest in that long line of sad failures, but they hadn't given up yet. The locals who had gleefully reckoned their bankruptcy was just eighteen months away, were now running a sweepstake on the exact date.

Half beaten by now, the couple had cut down their opening hours and stopped doing evening meals two days a week. When Stan had one of his heads, they simply didn't open at all. Like a bus company that cuts services to balance the books, this slimming-down approach was unwise and self defeating.

Many people couldn't remember what days and what hours the Happy Fireside was open, so they simply avoided the place and drove a little further to the Jack's as Good as his Master pub on the main road. There the food was mostly reheated, prepacked stuff from a commercial catering company but it wasn't any worse and at least the place was always open when you expected a pub to be.

Oh, yes – and, most of the time, Jack's was also comfortably warm. Besides, the very, very friendly barmaid at Jack's was younger than Dave and better looking than Stan.

* * *

He was sitting alone with his usual pint of Old Amber by the cold fireplace in one of the Happy Fireside's uncomfortable armchairs. He felt slightly sorry for her and wondered if he ought to buy her a drink. Better not; it was likely to be taken the wrong way. Coldstow didn't look for the better side in anybody. But he caught her eye and raised a friendly hand just to prove the whole of Coldstow wasn't unkind, only most of it.

Some women look good on a bar stool; others don't. Whatever she sat on, Sally might have been modelling for an expensive furniture catalogue. It's all about natural grace and that's rare.

It was the day of her spat with Jenny. Sally was perched on her stool, entertaining an early evening gin and tonic and trying to remember the name of the woman at the far end of the bar. Of course, it was the pub's cook; but why wasn't she in the kitchen? Possibly one of her days off, although she didn't think so.

The cook was evidently several drinks ahead of our Sally and it wasn't yet seven o'clock. Either she'd started at opening time or, more likely, primed herself at home before leaving.

She obviously wasn't looking for a quiet evening out.

Jo Downe, for that is the name she uses, is the one-time Happy Fireside chef (well, cook really, but she's quite competent with plain food). Having been told by a cowardly text from Dave that morning that the Happy Fireside couldn't afford her services any more, she had spent the day working herself up into a fit state to cause a heap of trouble for her ex-employers. And here she was, all ready for that enjoyable task.

One mustn't be unkind about appearances. You never know if that unshaven man has just lost his cat or the lady with lipstick on her chin is having a worrying time with her corns. So we have to be careful about drawing attention to little oddities.

But descriptions are necessary and Jo Downe did stand out from the crowd, provided the crowd wasn't too tall. Then aged about forty, she was short and not thin. She had worn her hair long since she was a teenager; such gay abandoned hair styles are fine for young people but there comes a time… Well you have the picture, very long slightly greying hair isn't always agreeable, particularly if it hasn't been washed for a day or so. And it doesn't help in the task of cooking.

Jo's make-up was always generous but she had gone overboard for the occasion of her war with the pub. Apparently concerned that she might have missed a bit, some areas had clearly had a double coating. The only undecorated item was her short and, just today, rather red and shiny, nose.

In common with so many of us, Jo Downe didn't dress in styles to suit her proportions. Stretch jeans aren't for everyone, especially the style which has too little material from waist to crotch; the sort that have to be hitched back into place with every few strides, until their wearer at last gives up the hopeless task and lets it all go. And it's a puzzle to know why some people buy their clothing a size or two smaller than it should be; a lady's upperworks ought not to be that close to falling out, Jo, and that bulging bright green T shirt doesn't go with denim.

But Jo was having a bad time and must be forgiven one of her occasional lapses into the binge drinking which provided rich material for the spiteful local gossips. In fairness, on her better days she could, and did, look quite attractive.

A large brass bell with a very white cord hangs over the Happy Fireside bar. Stan rings it very gently (and just once) when it's time to close and send the happy customers reeling home along their leafy lane.

Now fully ready for her fight, Jo seized the rope and rang the bell as it had never been rung before, in fact she almost swung on it as she gave it a good thirty seconds work out.

Stan's anxious face peered briefly into the bar; recognised the visitor, deduced her probable intentions and disappeared, all well within three seconds.

The sound of a door quietly closing somewhere at the back of the kitchen brought the ex-cook's temperature to melting point and she duly melted. Denied her prey, Jo scanned the room and fastened on poor Sally. *If it isn't your day then it just isn't.*

"You know what that Dave thing's been up to?"

Our bystander sank a little further into his broken armchair, desperately hoping to stay unnoticed and wishing he had stayed home that evening. The Siptac episode was enough excitement for the day and he didn't want a ringside seat for more revelations, however entertaining.

"No, Jo, I don't and I don't want to know. The day's been bad enough already."

If he could have done so, he would have said: *"Sally, that's not going to stop what's coming. Bow your head and stay quiet."* But it was already too late. The brief opportunity to gulp the rest of her drink and escape unscathed had gone.

"I'll tell you and everyone else 'ere… and in the whole bloody village."

She waved vaguely around the room, pirouetting ungracefully with the effort, then clutching at her favourite bell rope to keep upright and, incidentally, ringing another peal to summon the dead.

At this point the outer door opened and there were the Siptacs. They didn't normally drink at the Happy Fireside but after getting caught in charge of a tipsy husband, Mrs S had decided, if he was going to drink, it had better be done in the pub where she could exercise proper control.

Whatever her faults, and there are plenty, Joy Siptac doesn't lack sharp wits. She had summed up the state of affairs in the Happy Fireside's bar even before the door closed behind her. And she sensed the opportunity for a bit more malicious troublemaking. When she last met Sally, temper had got the better of her and her voice had showed it. Under perfect control now her nasal speech was almost purring:

"Good evening everyone – and especially you, dear Sally. I see you're wearing a bra this evening – so wise. Not drinking too much I hope; you must try to cut down dear, it's not good for your temper."

But Sally wasn't going to be drawn so easily. She said nothing but very deliberately drank the rest of her gin then stared fixedly and obviously at Mr Siptac's forehead which now bore a sticking plaster; it hadn't been there earlier in the week.

"My husband had the bad luck to walk into our shed door."

The explanation was broadcast to the room in general.

A burst of laughter came from Sally but it was Jo Downe who kept the ball rolling:

"No you're wrong there, Siptac, old thing. You don't have a shed, so the old goof couldn't have walked into its door. No shed, no door, no walkies into it. Simple logic."

It hadn't taken long to get under Joy's skin.

"You're drunk Mrs Downe, or whatever you call yourself; and you're the wrong side of the bar. You're the cook here, so off you go and do your cooking. That is if there's anyone left in the village that you haven't poisoned. And it's time you had a visit from the food hygiene people. Come to think of it, I might give them a call."

" – you, too."

Having lurked for half an hour somewhere "out at the back",

Dave and Stan had decided to face whatever the bar might throw at them – they just couldn't afford to lose any more business. Pub bars without anyone behind them to take customers' orders don't keep the bank manager happy.

Dave's last meeting with the bank (on his own, as Stan had a migraine that day) had not been as amicable as either he or the manager would have wished. Indeed, it had been the manager's own insistent suggestion on that day that Dave and Stan should sack their cook and save some wages by microwaving the pub's meals themselves.

From his seat by the cold fireside, he had a unique view across the bar and into the private area behind. A door at the rear opened and mine hosts appeared. He watched as Stan and Dave stood there for a while, largely unseen and evidently hesitant. Suddenly Dave, apparently pushed from behind, stumbled forward into the business part of the pub.

His arrival was greeted with derisory cheers.

Stan who apparently remembered something he had forgotten to do, turned back and left his partner to play the star role alone. That piece of cowardice wasn't going to be forgotten.

"Evening all. What can I get you?"

Bravely said, he thought. But the voice had been a touch too high pitched and Dave's face, which was normally a childlike pink, was an awful grey. He wondered if the man was really ill.

Joy walked over to the bar:

"I'll have a tonic water and my husband will have half a pint of your cheapest beer."

That brought another loud laugh from Sally Redfern,

"Wow, The last of the great spenders! Careful your hubby doesn't get too drunk to keep himself under control tonight."

For once, Joy couldn't think of a smart reply and she sensed danger, so she simply ignored this little attack. There would be opportunities to get back later.

As someone who had arrived at the pub's bar with a great mission, Jo Downe had become surprisingly forgetful of it. But it would return to her once she cleared up a question that was bothering her.

"Wot's up with the shitpac then? Does he get randy after a brandy? I'd like to see that; the old fool looks too soppy for that sort of thing."

Joy was on the back foot now; the evening wasn't going in the right direction at all, but she wasn't going to slink away, leaving her enemies to enjoy their victory.

"I think we shall sit down and enjoy our drinks over here, Harold. The publican will serve us at our table, when he can be bothered to do so."

Oh dear, he thought, why must you do this, Joy? There's another irretrievable enemy made in an instant.

But Dave was too immersed in worries about what might be coming from Jo to have noted anything said by Joy Siptac. He was one of those people who know no hate. He just wanted a quiet life but it wasn't his lot. Stan was a coward and Dave had to deal with all the problems life threw at them, but just now he had no idea how to handle things.

Perhaps reminded by Joy's reference to her lost job, Jo Downe suddenly remembered why she was there.

"Oy, you. Got sumfing to say to you."

"Oh hello Jo. I didn't see you there. What will you have. It's on the house."

"That's nice, didn't see me – aren't I big enough. Want me to stand on a chair or sumfing? Wot I want, you streak of nothing, is my ** job back."

Turning round to the room in general, she set about putting everyone in the picture; and then some.

He could write the script for what was coming. The only hope was that Jo Downe would fall asleep in the middle of it. Well, no-one else was going to help. He got up and walked to the bar.

"I'll have another pint please, Dave. Have one yourself and what are you drinking Jo?"

Dave looked at him gratefully, drew the beer and, without looking at Jo who seemed a bit stuck for words just then, poured her a generous neat whiskey from a bottle under the bar.

The interruption had taken some sting out of the situation, but not enough. Drink in hand, Jo turned back to address the room:

"Wot you don't know is I got the push this morning. The old heave-ho, the sack… Where was I?"

"Getting the boot Jo", said some helpful person in her audience.

"Did you? That's funny, I did as well, seems to be happening to everyone. And do you know how? Well I'll tell you. By ** text, that's how. From this Dave thing here. No, I mean this 'ere Dave thing. I've been cheffing 'ere for years and no complaints; well not mostly. And I get shacked by text – two hours' notice; just don't come back cos were going bust. And thish Dave thing couldn't say it to my face. Wot d'you think about that? And I've 'ad to make meals with a load of rubbish they've bought in from some crap supplier and told to keep my mouth shut; 'ome made pies, my backside.

And that Shtanley object wot's been watering the beer… Where was I?"

"Watering the beer Jo." said another helpful voice.

But Jo had lost the plot. After swallowing the last of her drink, she collapsed very gently and slowly into a surprisingly small bundle that lay still and pathetic on the hard floor.

No one said anything for some time; even Joy Siptac had just enough grace left in her cold heart to know that was a time to stay silent.

He stood and walked across to the little bundle. Jo was quite unconscious; deeper than any normal sleep. He picked her up and carried her out to his car, followed by Sally who held the door open as he placed Jo on the back seat.

"Do you need someone to come with you? You don't have to do everything alone, you know."

Rare kindness – he hadn't had much of that in the last seven years. He certainly hadn't expected it here; irrationally he felt slightly tearful.

He had a mental picture of what the rest of that night might hold; farm mud, darkness, Jo being sick perhaps. No, it wasn't the way he wanted to get to know Sally Redfern; he wasn't yet sure he wanted to know her at all.

"That's kind of you, but I'm ok. I'll just hand Jo over to Chris; it's no big deal."

She turned and walked away without another word.

* * *

Downes is one of several farms that border Coldstow. The half mile long, concreted track from the village lane takes you to the small farmhouse and a batch of stone buildings that were built long before tractors and Ministry regulations changed agriculture into what it is today. None of the buildings remained particularly useful. Here a piggery with no pigs, there a byre with no cows and a cart shed or two just not quite large enough to accommodate young Christopher Downe's four new and vast modern tractors. But, human nature prevailing, all the buildings are full of something, mostly items that will never be used again - we all have difficulty throwing things out.

The structures where the real work is done are a hundred yards beyond the house; vast crinkly tin sheds, some full of milking cows which never go outside to graze, fodder stores, machinery buildings and sheds with vast bins full of whatever farmers have bins for. The place is a factory where work continues day and night. Lights are always on, milk lorries come and go and various machines run about with cattle feed and take away the resulting product nearly as much in the night time as during the day. The village hates the place but several local people work at Downes and most of them draw some benefit from the place one way or another, so they keep their feelings largely unsaid.

This is a big grassland farm with huge fields (the hedges were taken out years ago under some Ministry grant before the same power decided to hand out taxpayers' funds for having them reinstated) but Downes still boasts two or three areas of old (but not ancient) woodland to remind everyone what countryside once looked like. And, of course, there are grants for woodland management too.

In some places Downes land runs right up to Coldstow gardens and there are, as one might expect, seasonal mutterings about overspray and smells according to what's being spread on the land from time to time.

You might think that young Christopher Downe would have more than enough dung to meet his needs but apparently not, because he buys in additional quantities of fertiliser which comes from waste eggs. The smell is indescribable but Chris doesn't notice it any more, so he doesn't care.

The greatest public annoyance is the state of the lane. It's bad at ploughing times and worse with muck spreading. In one way or another, there really isn't much of the year when some busy agricultural activity isn't going on and fouling the road. There is, therefore, little love lost between farm and village but there are individual exceptions and one of those is the friendly relationship between Chris and his partner's rescuer.

* * *

He drove slowly and very gently along the access track, wondering for the thousandth time why he allowed himself to get involved in this wretched village and its people. Just finding Christopher was likely to be a problem. He might be anywhere in his kingdom and it was too dark to go wandering beyond the main yards.

Downes farmhouse is dwarfed by the factory buildings. Successive members of the family have lived there for generations and apparently none of them had seen any need to make it larger or, much better, to knock down the wretched little place and build something that matched the scale of the land which belonged to it.

In common with his forbears, Christopher saw nothing inadequate about his home. If there was money available to spend, it would go to buying machinery or more land. That was Downes policy. This wasn't the only farm that he owned.

He left the car and walked across the well lit yard. As ever, the house was unlocked, but it was empty. He called out for Chris, shouting for help, that Jo was in his car, that she was ill. There was no response.

"Here we go", he thought, and set off towards the factory, hoping to meet either one of his workers or, better still, Chris himself.

He had no luck at the first shed. The huge building was brilliantly illuminated and full of cows, and their peaceable sounds, and their sweet smell, but not one human being. That seemed wrong, as if such a crowded and busy place ought always to contain at least a few people. This was too sci-fi for comfort.

Working his way around patches of darkness and puddles of farm filth, and still shouting, he reached the next building: another cattle shed but this time no cattle and, again, empty of people.

This was ridiculous; where was everybody?

The welcome noise of some machine starting up brought him out into the yard and running toward the loader before it could disappear again. The driver saw him, stopped and turned off the engine. In the poor artificial light, he had half expected this would be Chris himself; but the man wasn't the size of his massive friend.

"Hi, I'm looking for Chris – Mr Downe. Do you know where I can find him?"

The driver didn't know; he hadn't seen his employer that day. Could he help?

"I've got Mr Downe's wife in my car; she isn't very well and I don't want just to leave her alone in the empty house."

The driver was a human being: "I'll come across to the house with you; I can sit with Jo until Chris comes back."

"Thanks, that's really good of you. I was beginning to wonder if there was anyone left on the whole farm."

Neither of them spoke as they walked to his car.

"She's in the back."

He was thinking of Sally as the man helped him. He was grateful but, for a moment, wished it was her standing there and holding the door so close to him. Angrily, he put the thought behind him; stay away from people! Learn your lessons!

The small bundle on the back seat hadn't moved since he placed her there and it made no sound as he lifted her out and the two of them carried Jo into her home.

Death is easier to cope with if you have some expectation of it. There had been no forewarning of this. Jo hadn't been a close friend but he had liked her for her good cheer and rare basic honesty. He had thought to protect her that evening, and now this. Vulnerable and in his care, he had failed her completely.

* * *

He got home just after four that morning. The local policeman had the case in hand (or not, according to how you viewed his abilities). The doctor had made her brief examination – nothing useful from her yet – and poor little Jo was taken away to be – well, he didn't want to think about that. Chris Downe, who had appeared some time during this depressing performance, was taken away, lost and silent, for questioning by the police

There was no question of sleep now. He made some tea and sat in one of his kitchen's hard chairs trying to think about something, anything, pleasant. He couldn't do it. His garden, the woodland, Freddie, lost old friends, his work; his mind refused to fix on any of them, always defiantly returning to that evening. So he gave in and let his thoughts run wherever they wished to go.

In time, he dozed and later slipped into sleep, still in that awkward chair. Perhaps the physical discomfort contributed to his uncomfortable dreams.

It's said that dreams have their purposes and one of them is to sort and store memories of the day's events. So it was for him that night: memories of the day were to return and trouble his sleep over the next few months; he wasn't alone in that.

* * *

The Happy Fireside bar remained silent for several minutes after he left, his earlier presence marked poignantly by the untasted pint left standing on the bar. Insensitive Joy Siptac was first to speak and, of course, she had to be spiteful.

"Well, that's a bundle of news, I'm sure. It just shows what sort of people live around here. Watering the drinks and selling rubbish under the name of good home made food. It's disgraceful. I shall take it up with Trading Standards and the hygiene people. Hopefully they'll do something this time. I wonder what we pay our Council Tax for. It's almost too much having to look after everyone's interests for them. All the phone calls and the travelling over to Town Hall; the hours I spend with my binoculars – and not a word of thanks since I came here."

"You're a saint Mrs S. You do your duty. No one could check up on people like you do."

Joy looked suspiciously at her other half; was there something hidden there? She had wondered recently whether Harold was really quite as simple as he seemed.

"Well, yes I suppose I am. Now finish up your watery beer Harold and we can leave these sorry people to think about their crimes; let us hope they see the error of their ways before long. I've just got time to leave a note for those idiots in the shop about their new sign. No planning consent, wouldn't you know it?"

"Leaving so soon Joy?"

Sally wasn't going to miss the opportunity.

"I'll come with you; they'll have to be told that they're idiots. Can't let them go on without knowing; not fair on them. We can add that to your note and put it in through the shop letterbox. – Good cleansing start to their day tomorrow."

For the second time that day, Joy Siptac could think of nothing to say. She felt she was slipping and that worried her.

With insulting perfection, Sally held the door open.

"On you go; happy meddling."

There was nothing for it but for the Siptacs to leave. Joy silent, white with anger and orange hair wobbling dangerously; he on the other hand smiling sweetly at nothing in particular and calling back over his shoulder:

"Thanks for the beer, Dave; very nice as always."

"Yes", thought Joy, *"There is something up with him, but I'll soon stop it, whatever it is."*

So the bar was left to the victor. Not that Sally felt she had anything to celebrate. The day had lost her a good friend and she had hated being a spectator at the Jo Downe episode.

Poor Sally hadn't been well treated by anyone that day, except her rather offhand neighbour. She hadn't marked him as a warm human being but in fact he'd been rather touchingly kind both to Jo and to Dave. In many ways he seemed almost the opposite of Robb. Strange that she could be strongly attracted to both men.

* * *

It was late and near closing time before the Happy Fireside played out its last scene that evening.

Sally was staring at her empty glass. Was that the third or the fourth? Well, it certainly wasn't the fifth unless you counted the afternoon and that was a long time back.

Dave had disappeared. She looked up at the little rope hanging from the lovingly polished bell. Did she have the courage to follow Jo's earlier lead? And just as she reached out to it, the entrance door opened to disclose Christopher Downe; wealthy young landowner, farmer and partner of Jo.

Sensing a sale, Dave materialised from "out the back" where he and Stan had been having a little set to; something to do with Stan's earlier lapse of courage. Oh yes - and beer watering.

"Good evening Christopher. Your usual?"

Actually Chris Downe had only visited the Happy Fireside a few times in the last year, but Dave had a good memory and he did try to make the customers feel at home. He just wasn't suited to the role of jolly publican.

Chris ignored the offer: "Looking for Jo. Anyone seen her this evening?"

Dave wasn't sure how to answer that one. The wretched woman seemed to be infesting his life that day and he didn't want any more of her just then. Perhaps Chris didn't know about the famous sacking by text. So, being Dave, he said nothing at all. It was left to Sally to answer.

"Yes Mr Downe, she was in earlier but she didn't feel well, so someone drove her home."

Sally was choosing her words wißth care; she wasn't about to say anything more than she had to. If any cats were going to be allowed out of any bags, someone else could do the job.

"Oh! Well, I haven't been back to the house yet; I expect she's there. In that case, I'll just have that quick beer. It's been a long, hard day."

And Sally, feeling the same need, but for different reasons, added to the pub's takings for the day by the price of a double gin and just enough tonic to help the spirit on its way.

Perhaps all those happy little cocktails were helping her to think or maybe it was the energetic but brief encounter with dear Joy that had got her brain cells going. Whatever the cause, her mind was working overtime. Something was odd, even wrong. She couldn't work out exactly what, but she would keep working on it.

Chapter 4

As old empires crumble, new emperors arise.

Coldstow likes to gossip; in the pub or the local shop, Garden Club meetings, small family groups, around a table in the farmer's shop café on the main road, at a convenient gatepost, in fact anywhere where people can stop and gab. It's almost as fast as emails and much more fun.

Electronic communication is great for many purposes, but good gossip has to be word of mouth; how else could all those little extra half-truth tittle-tattles be created and then sent on their spiteful ways? And it's liberating; electronic data has a disquieting habit of getting stored and copied and an equally worrying trait of proving indestructible. But words spoken into receptive ears dissolve and disappear into the air almost as soon as they come into being. Like little may-flies; a brief life, and a merry one, and nothing left behind to trace their origin.

Local news had been very sparse before the death of poor little Jo Downe and Coldstow's malevolent tongues eagerly embraced the opportunities it offered. Especially since there was a spicy rumour that the examining doctor wasn't now quite as sure of the cause of death as she had been at first. Heart failure, yes, but apparently there were barbiturates present in quantities not easily explained and Doctor Ledger had missed this. The coroner had a few acid comments to make before recording an open verdict and the gossips made the most of that.

But rumours fade if there's nothing to nourish them and eventually the tattlers found new subjects to feed their spite. So, eventually, Jo's departure wasn't talked about any more, except by her few friends who missed her - and cared.

The local police, well, let's be accurate, Police Constable James Mabbtree, investigated the circumstances, filled in the necessary forms and, leaving the file in the hands of his superiors, moved on to other matters. PC Mabbtree wasn't very keen on murders, or, indeed, anything else that took him out of his comfort zone, or away from his greenhouse, which amounts to the same thing.

Without any further evidence, and believing this was probably a case of death by misadventure, the police decided they had nothing to work on, so nothing more was done.

Was Jo's death murder or accident? If murder, there was no obvious suspect and no known motive. So far as Coldstow knew, there was no wealth at issue; she had only a little inherited money of her own, a car, not much more.

Yet he wasn't satisfied and neither was Sally Redfern but, as they didn't know one another particularly well, it was some time before they spoke together about Jo's death.

We must leave them both to think while we look at some other little problems that were engaging this cosy little village just at that time. Perhaps there are connections to be discovered here or maybe there are not.

* * *

Sisters Louise and Rene Crabbe had managed the village "convenience" store since it opened some eight years ago; indeed they managed, or effectively controlled, just about all the facilities in Coldstow, save for the public house - and they had their eyes on that.

By this time, spinster Louise, the retired headmistress of a local primary school, had become slightly loopy. In her life, she had little to do with men, save for a brief romance, at the age of thirty, when she gave her, now broken, heart to a young priest who proved to be more interested in her financial assets than her physical ones.

Childless Rene, a little younger at sixty five years, managed her husband and his struggling carpentry business, until the poor man died, exhausted and broken by both business and wife. She then reverted to using her maiden name and the title Miss.

The two old ladies are similar in appearance. Both are painfully thin and not as tall as their slenderness would at first suggest. They both have their father's short nose and their mother's prim lips, which rarely smile. Neither of them has ever used make-up and they certainly won't start now. Louise's grey hair is plaited and fixed in a bun on top of her head; Rene's grey bun is screwed or nailed or otherwise fixed just above the back of her neck. This variation of bun location is really the only safe way to determine which Crabbe you are dealing with.

Their voices are similar, powerful, firm, uncompromising. Just as you might expect from a headmistress used to overpowering noisy pupils on the far side of the school playground and from a woman who has had to do constant battle with the numerous complaining creditors and customers of her husband's failing business. But, of the two, it is business manager Rene who is leader; headmistress Louise is content to yield decision making to her sister and more so now that she is showing signs of a little mental deterioration.

As to dress, since the sisters share the use of their long dresses and decorative beads, it is unsafe to presume these are any guide to their identities.

Just as one might expect of two people who manage large parts of Coldstow's public assets, the sisters live in the centre of things, close to the village hall and their shop. The Crabbe's modest straw thatched cottage has the convenience of low cilled windows that overlook elements of their empire and the car park that serves them. Accordingly, they miss nothing; it is almost impossible for a pedestrian to move anywhere about the village without either Rene or Louise noting it, and informing the other.

Crabby House, as unkind locals call it, is a one-time farm cottage with a couple of awkward looking extensions originally built to provide for a growing family at one end of the old building, and to garage Mr Crabbe's car at the other. Internally their home has stayed unchanged since their parents died some twenty years ago, and it wasn't modern then. The décor throughout is tired cream paintwork which should have been stripped and renewed years before. In common with half the homes in Coldstow, it is for ever dark and either cool or very cold. And there are serious damp problems, but neither Rene nor Louise notices these things any more, if they ever did.

Against one of its outside walls, the kitchen at Crabby House contains a great square sink next to a short length of wooden worktop over four cupboards. On the other external wall an aged Rayburn woodburning range burns for twelve months of the year and supplies the ladies with hot water in very small quantities. Perhaps it is a little indiscrete to mention this, but the kitchen must double as a bathroom when wanted as there is no plumbing upstairs. The sisters have devised an economical system for their weekly baths, but we need not go into that. Suffice to mention that their tin bath is comfortably large.

Apart from the kitchen, there is a large traditional pantry and a "snug" with a coal fire where Rene sits to the right and Louise to the left, each on their own Windsor chairs – the only items in the place that have real value, although the sisters do not know it.

Nothing can be said of the upstairs accommodation as, apart from our two ladies, no one still living has been invited to visit there.

The Crabbe family has held sway over the village ever since, well, since a long time back, when they owned most of the land around and about, including what is now Coldstow's large car park and the areas occupied by the "convenience store" and the village hall. This land is still owned by the sisters who receive a modest, but welcome, income by way of an index linked ground rent paid to them by the local council every half year.

It has never been quite clear if the Crabbes actually own the shop and the village hall buildings but they behave as if they do and no one has ever had the inclination, or courage, to say different. It was, therefore, a matter of course that, once built, both shop and hall would become part of the Crabbe family empire and managed by Rene and Louise.

Coldstow's inappropriately named convenience store was created when the nice little village shop and post office closed ten years ago. It then became a pretty, thatched cottage which sold very readily to some people from the Midlands. They and their rather noisy friends dutifully stay in it for a fortnight every July and a week at Christmas, leaving it closed, sad and empty for the rest of the year.

With a rare show of community spirit, the villagers (well, a few of them) banded together to raise enough Lottery cash and restore a redundant corrugated tin chapel into useable state. Some additional Lottery funding met the cost of fitting it out as a shop, adding a post office counter and creating a store room at the rear.

The problem with converting old buildings to new uses is that the finished articles suffer from the inevitable compromises made on the way.

Externally Coldstow's ugly dull green community store has just one window to light its sales area and an awkward entrance door that opens the wrong way out onto a narrow stretch of pavement.

Unfortunately the building has a low roof and the path by its entrance is a little higher than it should be. As a result the head of any daydreaming customer who is above five feet tall is liable to give the overhanging gutter a sound wallop. On the good side, the gutter is made of plastic and nine out of every ten head bangers are merely bruised. The remaining ten percent are permitted to receive, free of charge, some sticking plaster to stem the flow of blood that would otherwise soil the shop floor, or perhaps even the food on display.

Indeed, the only convenient thing about the place is an over-large car park lying to one side and at the rear. The community store shares this facility with the adjacent community hall which was also constructed with the benefit of another obscure Lottery fund.

Internally the store is painted white, although it's getting a bit knocked about and faded now and would benefit from some love and attention.

The sub-Post Office part is very small but cheerfully decorated with lots of slightly offensive official notices, just as you find in a doctor's surgery waiting room, but less physically intimate. And the Post Office area has two card racks. The first contains postcards with photographs of the local area and a few that are a little naughtier. It isn't clear how these naughty cards got past the censorship of the shop management but there they are, and they have put some rare smiles on the faces of several villagers (both male and female) since they were put on display.

The second rack has a mix of the useless sort of cards that are pre-printed *"For my dear second cousin on the occasion of her fortieth birthday"*. Not one of them is *"Left blank for your own message"* and not one of the cards on this rack has been sold this year.

It isn't easy for customers to see between all the notices and card racks and through the post office protective grill to the shop person in the recesses behind. Very often this is because there isn't anybody there to see. In that event, there is a small button on the counter that operates a loud buzzer to summon attention. Use of this buzzer is not welcomed by the staff and they tell any offending customers so in plain English.

At first sight, the store itself appears to contain very little useful stock. The apparent emptiness of its shelving is emphasised by the lonely presence here and there of odd grocery items. On one level a packet of plain biscuits sits at a safe distance from two tins of sardines and a bag or so of sugar, then a few tins of soup and various unfamiliar brands of tea and instant coffee.

Lower down, bags of dog and cat food share space with some school exercise books next to a couple of locally made cherry genoas (don't be tempted - they revert to cake mix in the mouth). Surprisingly, at the rear of the shop the shelves at all levels are fully loaded with alcohol for sale in all its many forms; more sales are made here than the rest of the shop in total.

A net of turnips, two half hundred weight sacks of muddy potatoes (locally grown, no unnecessary food miles here) and some sad, wilting carrots all stand about on the floor adding their smells to the other not quite pleasant odours that permeate the place.

There is in fact lots more on sale here, edible and not, but all so spread about in the over-large tin shed that much of it fails to catch a visitor's attention. As a result a good deal of the food is now past its due date for eating, but the ladies who manage both their store and its customers, never throw anything out. They prefer to buy the stale stuff for themselves, at a suitable discount, and, so far, neither of them has died of food poisoning.

Apart from part timers behind the counter, the Crabbes are assisted in running their shop and post office by long suffering Jenny Allen who deals with the book keeping, orders supplies and soothes both the angry customers and the angry suppliers after their various confrontations with the sisters.

Such fallings out are commonplace as the shop is run strictly according to an array of arbitrary rules governing everything from customers' cleanliness to where they may stand. It isn't easy for local people to remember and obey all these Crabbe Regulations and impossible for strangers to know them at all but the sisters allow no transgression to pass without public rebuke.

* * *

Coldstow's village hall is a large single storey building, typical of the numerous such structures that have appeared pretty much everywhere courtesy of Lottery money. It is clad in timber which has now weathered from bright orange to an acceptable silvery tone. The flat roof substantially oversails the walls, giving the place some proportion and much needed style. There are plenty of large windows on the south and east sides and the entrance way is one vast area of double glazing so that the hall's interior is bright and welcoming. Unusually for Coldstow, it is also warm.

Internally the hall still retains a faint smell of newness; it is well lit and the main ceiling is as high as one might need for a game of badminton. The walls are painted in a pleasant shade of white with some avian name like Swan Feather or Dove Cream. The architect earned his fee by boldly specifying bright blue stacking chairs and similarly coloured internal doors that serve the small kitchen and other necessary facilities.

Although the sisters exercised complete control of their shop, it had not been possible for them to attain a similar power of dictatorship over the hall. Some nit-picking rules attached to Lottery money had required the establishment of a committee to manage the place and the best that the Crabbes had been able to achieve was a shared dictatorship.

One Sunday evening in each month the Village Hall Committee meets in the hall to discuss and settle the various sorts of matters that come up wherever there is a village hall to be managed.

On the occasion of September's meeting, the attendees were, as usual, the Misses Crabbe, Dave and Stan from the pub (Stan for once being free of his usual Sunday migraine) and long suffering Jenny Allen, present for note taking and tea making.

Unusually two more villagers came to the meeting.

Mr and Mrs Siptac had turned up unannounced and gained entry after a preliminary skirmish outside the entrance door in which the Crabbe sisters were defeated in their joint attempt to keep the gate crashers out.

As always, Joy Siptac had done her research with care. The Village Hall Management Constitution did indeed contain an obscure clause allowing for any Coldstow Council Tax paying resident to attend Committee Meetings and the Crabbes found they hadn't a leg to stand on. The Siptacs duly sat down, Joy at the head of the table and her Harold on her left side. As these were the same two seat positions that the Crabbes always occupied, there was another little disagreement. And the business of the evening hadn't even started.

"That's my chair Mrs Siptac. Please move further down the table so that the Committee may carry out its business in orderly fashion."

"I don't see anything about who sits in what chair in the Hall Constitution Miss Crabbe. You do seem to be hopelessly ignorant of rules that you surely ought to know if you are to continue as a

Committee member."

Rene could feel her face glowing and, indeed it was now a brilliant red - she really would have looked quite attractive with the use of a little blusher; but as we have noted, it's too late now.

"I don't know what you mean about 'if I am to continue'..."

"I should have thought it was plain enough. It's high time you and your sister accepted that you have your failing hands too full in trying to cope with the shop without mismanaging the village hall too."

"I am quite capable of mismanaging shop, hall and anything else that needs my abilities, thank you and I don't see what my incompetence has to do with you."

And of course Rene realised as soon as she had said it that she had walked into a trap of her own making.

"Well, at least we are all in agreement about your incompetence. I trust we can move forward now without more argument. At great personal cost of my time, I have come here this evening to put the hall management on a proper footing. And from what I've seen of this Committee, it's not before time."

Rene could hardly speak. This was all so outrageous, so completely unexpected. What was the woman going to do next? And with that question there came the chilling thought that this Siptac person had already won a series of battles that evening and neither she nor her sister had been able to make even the smallest dent in her armour. How was this awful evening going to end?

Dave and Stan had stayed silent throughout this happy little exchange. Neither of them had any liking for the domineering sisters; neither would have been particularly concerned to be free of their own Village Hall Committee duties. In fact they were quite enjoying their ringside view of Joy's attack.

Driven by some impish desire to keep the pot boiling away, Dave asked the question half the room wanted answered:

"So, what are you leading up to Joy?"

"I'm not leading up to anything. But I know my duty and I've been looking at the Hall Constitution. I've got a copy of it here; I shall read it to you as it's plain that none of you have ever done so.

How you can be running things without knowing the law, is a mystery to me and to Harold here:

'Rule 22(i) Appointment of Committee:

A Committee member shall be appointed at any meeting of the Committee provided the new member is resident in the village and is proposed for the appointment by another resident.

The appointment shall not require any vote of approval by the Committee.

Upon appointment of the new member, the longest serving member of the existing Committee shall be deemed to have resigned.'

That is clear enough, I think. I am pleased to tell the present Committee members that I am willing to serve as a new member. Say your piece Harold; come on, speak up."

Whether he had any thought of his own on this matter or not, Mr Siptac knew his duty and he had been well schooled.

"I propose Mrs Joy Elise Siptac to become a new Committee member of the village hall. Oh, and I'm told to say as well, that I want to be a Committee member too."

Joy glared at him. He could make a mess of anything.

"And, for my part, I propose Harold Siptac as a new Committee member. That means there are now two new members and the two longest serving (if I may use that word) members are automatically removed. Miss Crabbe and Miss Crabbe are now mere observers and I must ask them to sit at the far end of the room and of course, remain silent throughout the remainder of the Committee's proceedings. I shall be the Chair and Mr Siptac will become Treasurer of the Hall Fund. No doubt Mr Wood and Mr d'Arteur will find something useful to do in due course, although I don't know what that might be; the village hall doesn't have any beer for them to water down. And now I'm sure we all need a cup of tea. So off you go Mrs Allen and, just on this one occasion, I think you may have one yourself."

Successfully resisting the temptation to smack the Siptac's head for her, Jenny went out to the hall's small kitchen to cool down and make tea for the largely dislikeable group seething away in the main hall.

She looked at the tray of filled mugs and wondered which would be Joy's. If only she could be sure. Well, the woman had all the good fortune that horrid people seem to have, and spitting in her tea was really a bit too childish.

But she wasn't going to let things go without doing something to make herself feel better about it. Best to wait; a time would come.

Jenny re-entered with her tray just as the furious Crabbe sisters left, one red faced, the other the colour and shading of a blotchy aubergine. They said nothing to Jenny's sympathetic *"Good Night"* and probably neither saw nor noticed her. Setting the tray on the table in front of Stan, Jenny walked out of the hall without a further word. The Siptacs could minute their own meetings.

* * *

Back at their own cottage, Rene and Louise indulged in a verbal contest to see which of them could speak the loudest about the evening's disasters, what they thought about Joy Siptac and what they ought to have said or done but they hadn't thought of at the time.

Eventually they calmed down enough to speak at conversational level.

"I'd like to kill her. Who does she think she is? God? If there's any justice in this world of sinners, she wouldn't live through the night.

What are you thinking about Rene? – I know that look, you're planning something. Are we going to kill her?"

Rene said nothing for a while and Louise made them a much needed pot of tea, knowing her sister wouldn't be drawn until she was quite ready.

"I don't think killing is enough Louise. Everyone has to

die; her death would just be what's coming to all of us. - No, it needs a different approach. She has to be made miserable, really miserable."

"How are we going to do that?"

"I don't know yet. I'll think about it for a while. Remember the old saying 'Revenge is a Dish etc.'"

And there matters rested for a time. Joy and Harold got on with managing the village hall and, incidentally everything and everyone connected with it, and the villagers got on with the happy task of nurturing their hatred.

Chapter 5

Challenges, newcomers and hopefuls.

Coldstow's residents include quite a few people who are a little cranky and some, perhaps more, who are extremely so. It's in the soil.

The extremists can't stop themselves thrusting their pottiness onto the rest of the village and to do this, they need to gain a power base. That of course is the nature of such people. Most of the more traditionally minded residents find this vaguely amusing and happily view the fanatics as comical light relief; others are indifferent; a few, however, are inclined to become annoyed.

The Repplington-Smythes (he a Repplington and she a Smith) were newcomers who lived in a converted farm building, smaller than a small barn but a good deal larger than a small henhouse. The Old Pig Barn squats between the entrance to the old vicarage and young Mr and Mrs Collinge's newly renovated cottage. Externally it is an ugly building; inside it is unwelcoming, gloomy and ever cold; but the developer had found it hard to sell and it was cheap to buy.

These double barrelled Smythes like to present themselves as eco warriors, determined always to take a hard line on every issue that affects the planet, and quite a few that don't. They are offended by wealth and dislike anyone they suspect of having more money than they do.

Mr Repplington-Smythe (Sam to his friends, in the days when he had some) is about sixty years old but looks a little younger. He appears to worship his slightly younger partner, but appearances can be designed to deceive. She, in turn, openly despises him.

At the age of fifty-five, Sam was invited to retire (or be dismissed according to his choice) from his labours for the pensions department of some local council in the Home Counties. Having chosen the former and less stressful option, the couple promptly moved to the affordable countryside. They told their eco-friends their departure was "to escape to a cleaner life." But you can't stop people reading their local newspapers and their neighbours were as pleased to see them leave as the council's Head of Pensions.

Since arriving in Coldstow, Sam had taken up the tasks of gardener, decorator and nosey parker's assistant. All full time jobs in their own right but he seemed quite willing to work himself into an early grave if it gratified his dear Susan.

Sam is a tall man and soldierly in his bearing. Although he has never had any connection with our armed forces, he is quite happy to let people think that he probably has a distinguished service record and, after all, it is up to people to think what they wish. His occasional passing references to the Middle East don't contain any complete untruths.

Having worn a grey three piece suit to the office for all his working life, Sam is incapable of dressing to match the countryside he now lives in. At his most casual, he wears neat white overalls to cover – well, whatever he has on underneath, and a smart blue cap which serves to keeps his bald head completely free of paint, and spiders. Such clothing doesn't fool the locals; working people in Coldstow are vouched for by the stains on their overalls, the cracks in their skin and bright red flat cap lines across their foreheads.

The life of a country yeoman has, however, brought some colour to Sam's cheeks and a light tan to the visible remainder of him. At first sight he is not unattractive but a closer view dispels the hope that the redness of his nose is caused by sunshine. Neither his teeth nor his breath are pleasing, but the neat, grey, soldierly moustache is very smart and matches the narrow band of short hair that runs around the back of his head from ear to ear.

In short, Sam is careful of his appearance and happy to think that women are attracted to him. Well, there is no harm in thinking, unless it leads you into awkward situations. There have been occasions when … Well we need not go into that because his Susan has always done what was required to set him back on the right track whenever she decided it was necessary.

When she isn't at home, Susan Repplington-Smythe is generally off in her small, but polluting, motor car to attend some committee meeting with like-minded eco-people, all busying themselves with the unwelcome management of other people's lives. If she isn't doing this, she may be found standing silent, camouflaged and stock still in gateways or bits of woodland, peering through binoculars at something or other.

Whether the subject of her study is wildlife or the local farmer's breaches of Sub-paragraph 1(b), Rule 51, Schedule 3 of some obscure Act of Parliament, we shall never be sure, as on such occasions she affects not to see anyone who passes by and, of course, if you don't see someone, you do not have to speak to them.

Like her partner, Susan is tall. In her sensible non-leather shoes she is perhaps just a couple of centimetres shorter than Sam.

Believing, if not hoping, that All Men Have Designs on Her, she is as completely unattractive as she can make herself and Nature has given her all the help she can in that direction.

Years of laying into and criticising everyone except her fellow eco-heroes have left her small mouth wearing a permanent *"I've just swallowed a caterpillar"* look. As no one has ever seen her teeth in public, we can know nothing about them but they are probably very white as she tells anyone who will listen to her that she lives a very clean eco-correct life. And of course that must be true or she wouldn't say it.

The countryside sun has thoroughly dried Susan's unprotected cheeks and nose which enjoy no kindly attention from their owner, apart from nightly scrubbing with vegetable oil based soap. They are now so cracked and peeled, white and red; that sensitive people would cringe and turn away at the painful sight, if there were any sensitive people in Coldstow village to do the cringing.

For perfume the lady depends on the faint odour of the good leeks and red onions from Sam's garden. Her knotted hair, whilst always clean, is far too long for her age and totally unmanaged.

Susan's style is eco-traditional: long skirted dresses, plastic (certainly not leather) belts, curious collections of wooden bead necklaces and brightly coloured rings. Not quite the fashion of the sixties era which she admires so much, but she thinks it is, and that's what matters.

She has never forgiven Sam for his malfeasances at the Pensions Department, whatever they were. When you have spent your adult life (and maybe more) looking down your nose at almost everyone else; it's very hard to find the roles suddenly reversed. Susan hadn't planned on ever leaving their small suburban house and her downtrodden neighbours; it had taken her half a lifetime to subdue them and all that effort was wasted in an instant by Sam's disgrace.

One might think that there are similarities between the Siptacs and the Repplington-Smythes. Both like to poke their noses in where they can and as far as they can. Both couples have little sensitivity or humanity; both are latecomers to Coldstow.

But there is no warm relationship here. The Siptacs despise the Repplingtons for their poverty and Joy Siptac is almost sure there is some delicious unpleasantness in Susan's household which she will winkle out some day. In fact Joy is already nearly there.

And, for their part, Sam and Susan hate the Siptacs for their large fossil fuel guzzling car (which they secretly wish they could afford themselves), their well heated house (how nice to be warm) and the vast amount of groceries ostentatiously delivered there every few days. These are more than the Repplington-Smythes could ever eat and better than they can afford.

But the strongest source of animosity lies between Susan and Joy; both are power seekers and both know that there are battles to be fought in the future and a long term war to be won or lost. A village cannot have two ruling queens.

So there was far more of ill-will than friendship and their mutual dislike was about to come out into the open and get worse.

– More fees on his horizon for the local solicitor perhaps.

* * *

Fiona Abbot, the new vicar of Sideleigh, was e-mailing her uncle, a kindly old bishop with tolerant views and a great fondness for his nieces.

'Hi Uncle Bish.

Hope you're well.
Well, like wow, so now I'm a vicar – can't thank you enough for that.
Bishy dear, you know you asked if I'd look over the parishes round here and let you know what's going on in Deadsville. Well, not a lot.
The old vicar who runs the next three parishes (that's Spattersleigh, Ewer and Coldstow) is a really nice old guy and I love him already but I'm really afraid for his health. He hasn't been taking any services for weeks and everyone else (including little me!) is having to stand in for him.
I was thinking as I'm here and Spattersleigh and so on are sort of next door, why don't I take over the whole business - only for a while of course.
I really don't mind all that extra work, it's just good to be helping others out.
If you like the idea, can you organise it at your end? Don't mention my name, I'm not after any praise. As you know, I never do.

Lol,

Your Filly'

* * *

The new vicar of Coldstow (well, stand-in vicar, but these arrangements do have a way of becoming fixed) made her appearance a few weeks after the Bishop had learned of old Reverend Wyke's little problems and very kindly placed him into retirement, where he died two months later, mourned by his loving parishioners and his small family of two sons and an adored (and adoring) granddaughter.

It had taken Fiona a while to get round to this, the smallest, and therefore least important, of her three new parishes. She was very busy just now with all sorts of busy things to do and her vicaring jobs had to take their turn.

The regular Coldstow congregation was now very small, consisting of the two churchwardens from Ewer parish, the man who cut the churchyard grass and the Crabbes. But on this day, with the arrival of their new vicar, the little church enjoyed the very satisfactory attendance of a dozen villagers and a couple of strangers.

The rev Fiona had brought with her, not just a case with her vestments and communion paraphernalia but also a very youthful and good looking assistant curate. They were clearly old friends.

There is nothing very interesting to an outsider about a simple communion service and nothing very interesting happened during this one.

But Coldstow people are quick to observe details which many might miss, especially if they sense trouble, a new source for resentment or a delightful scandal to gossip about, or even create. And any one of these three delicious pleasures was liable to bring about the other two.

And Coldstow duly latched onto the young curate and fabricated some nonsense about a relationship with their new vicar. This wasn't completely unexpected, as some unkind gossip had already passed around Fiona's several parishes. So her three new congregations were primed in advance.

Reverend Abbot is a modern and worldly wise cleric. She has no hang-ups about the human race and knows it for the faulty thing it is. Faults however can be turned to one's advantage especially if one has no conscience.

It's said that, if you want celebrity, all publicity is good, no matter what it is. Fiona had learned this early on in her first career as a journalist, noting that the clean living politician gets nowhere beyond running some very minor ministry but the out and out rogue whose behaviour is frequently "exposed" in TV documentaries and the national press is a likely bet for prime minister a little further down the line. So, having judged to perfection the mood of her several rural congregations, she proceeded to upset them further.

There appeared notices on all her church notice boards reducing the numbers of services and altering the times of the rest to awkward and unfamiliar hours. A few weeks later regular services at Spattersleigh and Ewer ceased altogether.

Avoiding any criticism of laziness, Fiona appeared at any and every event that might be expected to have some media coverage. Speaking out against the past and present misconduct of the Church, she spread her net wide, from lectures at Mother's Meetings in village halls to ranting from her portable lectern at steam fairs. And, wherever she went, there was her pet curate, handing out leaflets, smiling and looking very pretty, and young.

And it wasn't long before Fiona became an attraction in her own right. People were as likely to attend local cricket matches and farm auctions to hear, and see, her public performances as they were to watch the play, or purchase a few acres of grassland.

Her sad congregations had no idea what was happening either to their churches or their way of life. It's one thing to fail in your duty to attend a church service but quite another to find that your church has plainly turned its back on you. So, the Church of England found itself receiving an increasing flow of mail, posted and e-, complaining about Fiona Abbot and her outrageous doings (or her failings, however the writer might choose to look at the matter).

One way or another, the majority of these complaints came home to roost in the Bishop's in-tray. Being fond of his niece, he wasn't inclined to accept that his protegee had done anything very wrong. So long as she had her faith, as far as he was concerned, a little youthful criticism of the clerical establishment wasn't likely to cause any real harm, even though he was very much part of it himself. But complaints leave their mark, even on kindly old bishops.

So, nothing was done to mend fences, the damage continued, and Fiona found ever more subjects for loud complaint, mostly directed at people who weren't likely to fight back and mostly aimed at pleasing people who were looking for trouble.

* * *

A week had gone by since the Crabbes were sent into the outer darkness. The Siptacs had blossomed into their public role of village hall management.

So far, only a few things had changed. Joy had altered the timetable of the bridge club meetings so that it was now obliged to convene at four o'clock on Wednesday afternoons and to terminate activities by six thirty. This was of course to save on lighting costs and had nothing to do with the fact that she played whist and detested the supercilious bridge lot.

On the other hand, whist was moved from an awkward four thirty start to the more convenient time of seven in the evening. And the badminton club found their pastime was no longer catered for at all. The new Hall Committee learned from a well-wisher, who had made enquiries at Town Hall, that the hall did not have the necessary safety equipment to accommodate such violent games. Happily Joy didn't play any games (well, not physical ones) so she was spared any personal disappointment.

Having got control of the hall and twisted her knife into a number of people she disliked, Mrs Siptac went silent for a while. But she wasn't idle; far from it.

* * *

'Grand Meeting of Fiona's parishes
Saturday 8th October
Coldstow Village Hall

Hi, everyone. For anyone that doesn't know, I'm your new vicar — and not just yours. I'm in charge of pretty much every little church around here now.

Just want to tell you:

There's going to be a fun meeting in the little hall at Coldstow next Saturday. I'll start with an opening speech, then it's the turn of the kiddies and their mums to have fun decorating the hall and the church to welcome a GUEST SPEAKER!!! No names yet, you'll all have to be patient but I can promise you a BIG SURPRISE.

Then, it's more fun with WAKE UP VILLAGES AND SMELL THE COFFEE; It's time to throw out those oldies who think they know how to run things.

Just bring your own refreshments – you can't expect your little worn out church to pay for everything you know.

And don't worry! I'm not going to sell God to you; this has nothing to do with boring religion; there won't be a dog collar in sight I can promise you.

See you Saturday!

Rev Filly'

It was a fine sunny morning, just enough breeze to make the colourful Autumn day alive and to be glad of it.

But such pleasant things had no effect on Joy Siptac who was walking to the village store, planning to buy nothing and to amuse herself by baiting the Crabbe sisters in their own lair. – She meant to take over the shop at some time and she might as well begin the process.

With her head full of delightfully spiteful plans, she hardly saw the Church notice board. Unsurprisingly, few people ever looked, as it rarely had anything new to say, and nothing of much interest to a non-churchgoer.

But something caught her attention; a large white sheet of paper written on in bold magic marker orange and decorated around its margins with swirly curves in more bright colours. It hadn't been there yesterday.

Joy read the notice and, unbelieving, read it again, very slowly.

"What does this revfilly thing think it's up to? She doesn't own the hall; hasn't any right to have meetings without my consent.

I'll soon stop this nonsense. Fun meeting, guest speaker, kiddies decorating - cheek!"

A thought came to her accompanied by a slightly sick feeling of apprehension. She walked over to the village hall. And there was an identical white page. It was fixed firmly over the last notice that Harold had put up to tell all the untrustworthy villagers that the hall kitchen was closed until further notice because someone had been pilfering sugar.

Entirely forgetting her plan to give the Crabbes another going over, Joy turned and hurried back home to think and plan. This vicar thing needed a sharp lesson and it would have to be given before the coming Saturday.

* * *

Unknown to Joy, Susan Repplington-Smythe had also been making her way to Coldstow's shop that same morning. Being a little behind her enemy, Susan had slowed for no better reason than a desire to see and not be seen. She didn't expect anything interesting.

But the Siptac, normally the spy, not the spied upon, behaved in the most interesting fashion. It was like watching a poorly acted charade; first she stopped, quite suddenly, in front of the Church notice board; she seemed to find it very interesting but perhaps not pleasing. She then walked on to the hall and apparently read another notice there.

It seemed odd that she would be surprised by anything at the hall – after all, she ran the place; surely no one would trespass on the Siptac's home ground; would they?

Joy's sharp turn to retrace her route home took Susan by surprise. Having nowhere to hide before she was seen, she stood still and waited:

"Good morning, Mrs Siptac.

Anything interesting on the hall notice board is there? - I saw you reading it."

To her delight, Joy passed by, grim-faced and without a word. Susan hurried across to the Church and read the offending poster, then its companion by the village hall.

The physical result was exactly the same as with Joy. Susan dropped all thought of shopping, turned and hurried back home where she could digest her news and plan how best to use it.

Entering her kitchen and finding the house free of husbands, Susan made tea for herself and sat down to think. For perhaps the first time since she arrived in this wretched place, she felt uplifted, almost happy. She opened a tin of biscuits; there was something here to celebrate, although she wasn't yet sure what it was.

The vicar's notice had been a shock for the Siptac and, despite her lack of imagination, Susan could see why; it was a gross trespass on the woman's little realm. It was going to be hard for her to deal with it without upsetting a vicar, of all people; and others in the village (indeed almost all of them) would be delighted to see that long Siptac nose out of joint.

Susan thought for a while, trying to imagine what Joy would do but she got nowhere; the woman was very clever, manipulative and devious. No one could read that mind.

But, as she was about to give up on finding anything useful in her little package of knowledge, Susan thought perhaps she was thinking from the wrong end. The proper question was not: what will Joy do? But what did this information have to offer for herself?

And immediately she wondered if she could use the notice board trick herself. Could she get control of part of Coldstow, - recover some of what she had lost out of her old life?

The village hall was a lost cause now. The pub held no attraction for her. There remained the badminton, whist and bridge clubs, the Garden Club and the Church.

Excluding whist, the only games that Susan played were the same sort that Joy played; she just didn't play them as cleverly. That left gardening and church. She would sleep on it.

* * *

And all the while that the warring parties of Coldstow were fighting their little power battles, Jo's few genuine friends continued their efforts to uncover the truth about her death.

It appeared that no investigation whatever was being made by the local police and it distressed him that his closest friend was suspected of Jo's murder. He had to clear that shadow for both their sakes. Lack of obvious motive isn't proof of innocence; that had to be achieved by another route.

Although he thought Mabbtree was lazy, and possibly corrupt, he had to speak to the man – any information would be welcome; he had got very little so far.

Constable Mabbtree, wearing his uniform (short only of jacket and helmet), was digging over part of his vegetable patch, taking advantage of another warm day to do a job much more important than his patrol duty in Larkston.

"Morning James. Looks like hard work; fancy a beer?"

The Constable made no reply but accepted the offered can. He plugged away at his one-sided conversation, talking about vegetables, praising the man's success at the Coldstow summer show and asking garden advice he didn't need. Eventually he broke down the barrier. Constable Mabbtree couldn't resist the temptation to brag to an amateur, and at last he got the opportunity he needed and asked his question:

"I was wondering the other day if the investigation into Jo Downe's death is closed now. – It's just that I made a few notes at the time and if I can safely throw them out now."

"I don't see there was any call for you to be making notes about it. If you've got any information about Mrs Downe, it's your duty to tell the police and any evidence should be handed in to me."

"Oh, I see. Well of course I don't have any evidence so there's nothing to hand over to you and any information I had to give is in the statement I made at the time; I've nothing to add to that. Goodbye James. Enjoy your day off."

He sauntered away. At least he had learned that Mabbtree was netting any evidence before his superiors got hold of it. And he was cheating on his job; he hadn't donned his uniform for a day's leave; he was meant to be out doing whatever it is that policemen do and that wasn't done in his back garden.

If the man was dishonest in his job, he was untrustworthy in all ways, and why was he apparently suppressing any new evidence about Jo?

Chapter 6

New challenger for an old empire.

The Church Committee ran Coldstow's nice little church. Even small buildings need repair from time to time and there was always plenty to do, all of it needing work and money. The place had to be cleaned and the grass cut (an awkward job in a graveyard) and there was an everlasting list of repairs.

So, there was a lot to be done and a lot more work behind the scenes to find the necessary funds.

There were five people on the Committee; our old friend Sally, the publicans and St Mary's two churchwardens – Maurice D'Arteur and Rene Crabbe. These two never spoke to one another if they could help it on account of an occasion when Rene had welcomed what she thought was a little flirtation from Maurice, only to discover it was nothing of the sort.

Stan and Dave had joined everything when they bought into the Happy Fireside. It had seemed a good idea – get to know the natives, make friends, gain customers. But it hadn't worked. Coldstow ate people like them and spat them out. Now they regretted being involved in anything, the church included.

Rene Crabbe was a Committee member partly because she had always been a churchgoer and partly because she believed in keeping other people under proper control; you never know what will happen if you don't keep a close eye on things.

And Sally had simply been pressured into the job by her own conscience and a vague hope that she might meet a few kindly people. After all, it was a Christian church. She was of course correct, but this was Coldstow and the kindlier Christian teachings hadn't yet reached the place; probably they never will.

Cranky Maurice had been a churchwarden since the death of his father rendered the office vacant for him. Morose by nature, he rarely spoke at these meetings; his only contribution lay in making the rest of the Committee uncomfortable by his Grim Reaper like silent presence and his rare, but searing, caustic comments.

The Committee met regularly twice a year, once in November to discuss Christmas activities and in April, to organise the Church Fete. It also convened at other times to discuss any matters that needed attention, money, the recurring bat problem, money, the various vicars' misconducts, money ……

The practical work was done by four or five volunteers who ran stalls, made cakes, held coffee mornings, polished pews for a non-existent congregation and broke their hearts in hopelessly worshipping the dear old vicar, but not the new.

Jo's would-be rescuer on that sad night in the Happy Fireside was one of the few who did any physical work. He had never intended to be involved but no one else offered to cut the grass on the first occasion when the Committee decided it must be done. So he found himself doing it, spending a hot summer day mowing around the numerous mounds – just that once.

Of course it hadn't been once; the Committee just assumed he would cut the grass as often as they wanted thereafter, and at no cost to anyone but himself. He could count the number of thanks he got on his thumbs, and two to spare.

He hadn't minded the work; churchyards are very peaceful places and a lot of nature can be found in them. He liked that. What irked him was Rene's dominant attitude.

"The church grass is growing far too long again; you ought to have cut it last week. Please see to it before the weekend; I'd remind you the fete's on Sunday. And please take your cuttings away. They're unsightly. And please keep your mower somewhere else; it's dangerous for the smaller children."

The members were having an irregular meeting one evening which, for once, did not include the subject of money. It had come about following the appearance of a sheet of paper on the church notice board:

**'Church Committee
Urgent Meeting
There will be a meeting of the Committee at 6.00 pm on Thursday 13th October in the Church to resolve various serious problems.'**

The notice was unsigned and no one on the Committee knew, or admitted they knew, anything about it.

So the members called a meeting for six pm on the coming Thursday. They weren't going to risk not being present and they feared the obscure reference to "problems".

Unusually, the full Committee attended, together with the various unpaid volunteers and a few intrigued residents who had no interest whatever in the church but sensed some delicious revelation was on the way, bringing a fresh fund of trouble for the gossips to enjoy.

Between 5.45 and 6.20 pm the members sat silent and increasingly nervous in various pews while the rest of the crowd, some sixteen in number, sat, stood or wandered about and grew increasingly impatient for a bit of worthwhile excitement.

At 6.21, having judged the time to perfection, Mr and Mrs Repplington-Smythe entered, or, more accurately, she made an entrance and Sam trailed in some way behind.

Susan sailed up the aisle and, without any hesitation clambered into the pulpit. The whole thing was perfectly done; her purpose achieved completely. There was just one problem. Having very carefully prepared and written her little speech, Susan had forgotten to bring it with her. Now, that's an error Mrs Siptac would not have made.

"I'm very gratified to see so many of you here. I hardly expected the entire Committee to bother to turn up; such a rare event. I have called this meeting because I discovered some worrying facts about the mismanagement of our poor church's affairs. Naturally it was my immediate duty to bring these matters to the attention of the Committee and to the residents in general…"

Here Rene Crabbe interrupted:

"Impertinence! You don't have any right to call meetings. Only I can do that. And you don't attend Church or take part in any church business. Never have done so. Get down from that pulpit at once and leave now. If you have anything to complain about, which you surely do not, you can put it in writing to the Bishop."

There were noises of approval from the rest of the Committee and from a few Repplington-Smythe haters in the audience. But just as many wanted to hear more and said so.

"Everyone has the right to be in our church, Miss Crabbe, even poor me. I'm surprised that someone who claims to be a Christian, and a churchwarden at that, doesn't know that much. Of course, if everyone here wants me to leave without hearing what I have to tell you, they are free to say so and I'll go."

Sensing another public defeat on its way, Miss Crabbe muttered something that sounded very un-Miss-Crabbe-like. The rest of her Committee stayed silent and looking rather shrunken, or perhaps they had just slipped down a little more deeply into their respective pews.

The remainder of those present made it quite clear they wanted to hear any juicy news that might be going.

"Well, it's so nice to feel welcome."

"No one said you're welcome," said some nameless person in the general crowd. "Just get on with it; don't push your luck."

There was general laughter. Sensing that not pushing her luck might be good advice, Susan did get on with it, but she had recognised the clothes peg voice; time enough for revenge later.

"Tucked safely away in your little village, none of you know this but I'm very well known in powerful circles for my tireless work in saving life on this planet from extinction. In fact I expect very soon to be receiving an award recognising my contribution to global warming."

She was conscious that there was something not quite right about the way this sentence had come out. A few giggles from the floor, and something said about farting, told her it might be wise to get on to the detail.

Unfortunately, having got caught up in worrying about what she had already said, she failed to take enough care with what she was about to say. From that moment onward she was like a walker always looking over her shoulder at what she had just trodden in and so repeating her little accidents.

"Everyone has to do their bit, even little villagers like you. But, sorry to say, I'm very disappointed in some of you.

Here, in our church, we sit among an area of natural plant and wild life in the form of the old graveyard."

Again, she felt things weren't coming out as they should. A little devil in her mind was asking her why she had said sit when, apart from the Committee, almost everyone, herself included, was standing and she hadn't meant to suggest that wild life looked like a graveyard.

She soldiered on.

"But what are the Committee doing? I'll tell you…"

Another troublemaker butted in.

"We can see what the Committee are doing. They're sitting there listening to your twaddle."

She ignored this rudeness.

"Your precious Committee is cutting the grass and destroying the habitat for all the birds and animals and, er, things that need to live in it."

She hadn't meant to suggest that the whole Committee had been roaring around the graveyard each with their own motor mower. And why couldn't she think of the word "plants". Why, oh why, had she left her written script at home?

Poor Susan started to flag; the energy in her was being replaced by a sort of tired acceptance that this was just another rotten day in her life; and it had started with such high hopes.

"Anyway, the point is, churchyards ought to be left uncut and the Church Committee isn't being green as it ought to be."

The first heckler was in for another round, "they look pink to us; aren't all committees pink?"

Ignore it, ignore it.

"I've had a meeting with the Wildlife and Countryside Officer at the District Council about it and she agrees: the grass ought not to be mown by the Committee. And I've been appointed, well it hasn't quite been confirmed yet, to keep watch on things in this village and tell the Council if the Committee doesn't do things that are green."

She had lost it completely. God knows what this gang of yokels was going to make of that.

As she got down from her perch, Susan looked for her Sam. For once she really needed him but the speech had been too much to bear; he hadn't even stayed for the final paragraph.

She left the church, alone, to the accompaniment of a delighted cheer. There was no ill-will in this. The crowd had been delighted by the entertainment and, incongruously, she was loved for it.

* * *

Susan Repplington-Smythe was sitting at a late and unsatisfying breakfast on the morning after her eco-speech in church. She had suffered a sleepless night, and, unusually, tearing into her husband, as if every horrid and unfair event that had happened that evening was his sole fault, hadn't made her feel any better. And Sam wasn't around just then to receive another barrage.

In fact, naughty Sam wasn't even in the village. Having had quite enough chastisement that morning he had walked over to Jack's. There, and not for the first time, he found comfort in chatting happily with the very friendly young barmaid, in having perhaps just one gin and tonic too many for wisdom and in wondering if he could find some way out of his loveless marriage.

In short, Susan's future wasn't looking good at all. Her failed take-over attempt, intended to be the start of a new empire to replace what she had lost from the past, was misfortune enough. Now her husband was making a little world all of his own that foretold an end to her unhappy marriage, but perhaps that was no bad thing for either of them.

* * *

The benefit of that cheerful cocktail, gin and tonic, is also one of its drawbacks. Enjoy a couple, or maybe three, and troubles lose their edge, perhaps they disappear altogether, at least for a time. But you can't have a cake and eat it. If the mind is going to switch off after a second drink in the bar, it won't be much good at remembering what happened in the pub after the third. Less still if you have had a preliminary drink or two at home.

Sally Redfern was struggling to recollect that evening in the Happy Fireside, when he carried Jo out to his car. Something was wrong and it would keep troubling her until she worked out what it was.

Having nothing much to work on, she wrote down what she could remember of the whole episode, starting with a list of everyone at the Happy Fireside that evening and when they arrived. She wasn't quite sure about that one, so she turned to consider which of them might have had a reason to kill Jo. Sally didn't know anyone in Coldstow very well; they might all, or none of them, have had some motive. There were at least three on the scene that evening; Joy Siptac, exchanging words with Jo, and Stan and Dave, both worried by Jo's revelations about cheating their customers.

None of that seemed to be anywhere near to a motive for murder. Of course, there was always the husband, or partner, just because husbands and partners are well known killers but Chris Downe hadn't arrived until much later.

So, if it was murder, how was it done? Answer: evidently poison, there was no apparent violence.

Who had an opportunity? It had to be someone close enough to the bar to spike Jo's drink, and here Sally floundered, almost giving up. For it presupposed a murderer came to the Happy Fireside to kill Jo on the mere chance she might be there that evening. Who carries poison about with them in case their intended victim might happen along?

But this was an exercise to clear her mind of a niggling problem, so she went on with it.

People who came up to the bar at about the right time included the Siptacs, Jo's rescuer – Sally didn't want to believe he was a killer and shied away from including him in her list, so she didn't, two strangers who ordered bar snacks and the local policeman. She could think of no one else; her brain was getting bored and obstructive; perhaps that was all the suspects.

But she had forgotten two people who hadn't got onto her list at all: Jo herself, and the pub waitress who took the bar snacks order. Of course it was ridiculous to include Jo but was it? She might have killed herself by some accident.

Sally felt her analysis had got her nowhere; there was no obvious murderer and no obvious crime. Her thinking was full of "ifs" and "maybes". Perhaps her teasing mind had misled her and there was nothing suspicious after all; but she still didn't think so.

She needed to talk to someone with a brain, someone she could trust; there was only one.

Chapter 7

Strife in a clerical world.

The Misses Crabbe were sitting in their damp and gloomy kitchen, drinking out of date tea from the shop and licking their wounds. Losing control of the hall was bad enough but to see Joy Siptac throwing her weight about, and glorying every day in running the place, was too much to bear.

And on top of that, Susan Repplington-Smythe had challenged Rene's Church Committee and given its foundations a good shaking. That episode had done nothing to enhance village respect for it, although it was still intact (just).

"Are we going to kill her too?"

"Don't be silly Louise, that's the third you've put up for execution in so many days; we can't kill everyone we don't like, and it would have to be one at a time, not altogether."

The sisters sat quiet for a time, one plotting, the other dreaming of a Siptac and Repplington-Smythe free world where Coldstow had become an orderly, well-managed village and everyone recognised the benevolent reign of two much loved and selfless old ladies.

"And what about the vicar's notices? We can't have the village lot wandering about painting and scribbling on the church. Who's going to get it off afterwards?"

"I'll speak to her about it. She can't want the place spoiled; it's her job to look after it. I expect she's just not thinking straight; it's a hard job looking after four parishes"

No time like now, thought Rene, going out to the shop to make a call.

She wasn't able to speak with the rev Filly but her pretty young curate made an appointment for her to see his (or her) superior at 3.00 pm that afternoon. – And please be prompt, dear Fiona's workload was heavy and her time precious.

For some reason Rene didn't feel that things were going very well. The vicarage was Fiona's home ground; there had been rumours that the place had fallen away from what one normally expected of a clerical establishment. Rene felt she didn't want to know about that; it would probably distress her and she didn't need any more unpleasantness in her life just now (as if anyone ever does want it).

And she hadn't liked the reference to time being precious. Rene's time was precious too. But she couldn't turn back now.

She wasn't going to be early and kept sitting about, that would be too demeaning, so she arrived at one minute to three. - Prompt as required but suggestive of being just as busy herself.

But poor Miss Crabbe was left to stew on a hard chair in the vicarage hallway for thirty five minutes during which no one apologised for keeping her waiting and indeed no one appeared at all. She could however hear voices and laughter coming from the big reception room nearby and sounds indicative of drink being drunk and food being eaten.

The beautiful old vicarage was very familiar to Rene Crabbe. She and her sister had been here frequently over the years, enjoying the hospitality and friendship of people all now dead and mostly forgotten. Tennis and croquet parties, reading groups, vicarage teas, church fetes and private dinners. Old times! The place was full of memories, even its familiar old smell was pleasing.

But there pleasantness ended. There were changes, wanton spoiling that disgusted her.

The walls in the old hallway had been repainted from a soft white to a violent blue. The work had been done so incredibly badly, it might have been a deliberate affront. The fine mahogany joinery was smeared with blue paint in numerous places. The lighting had been "modernised" with bright "daylight" bulbs that emphasised the harsh colour of the paintwork and highlighted its defects. The lovely old, polished parquet floor was covered in cheap blue carpet tiles that had lifted in places. A long, rough trestle table against one wall was covered in pamphlets and, a concession presumably to humanity, a small glass vase of bright yellow chrysanthemums; it seemed impossible that the mind at the back of all this vandalism could be responsible for that bit of cheer.

All the lovely old hall furniture that Rene knew so well had disappeared. She didn't care to think of what might have happened to it.

With nothing better to do, she turned to the table's literature. There was a good deal of it but it had nothing relevant to familiar church matters. Most of the leaflets were political, supporting obscure groups in foreign countries. Some attacked the church itself.

Rene could bear no more. She turned away, collected her coat and walked out.

* * *

Getting out of her car on her return to Coldstow, Rene spotted the vicar's assistant leaving the church. For want of any better way of shedding the day's irritations Rene glared rudely at the young curate. But, of all the reactions she might have expected, or hoped for, her spite was rewarded with a kindly smile. She went indoors, embarrassed by her own behaviour.

"How did you get on with the vicar – is she going to stop people scribbling on the church?"

"I didn't see her. I don't want to talk about it. It's all sick; I can't bear what's happening to us."

"Are we going to kill her too, then?"

"Probably. – I'm going to bed."

But Rene did not go to her bed. Leaving by the back door she walked to the end of her garden and locked herself into the small outhouse where she could think and plan without interruption from her sister. Over the years this had become the one place where she could find the necessary peace.

Some time later she emerged from her sanctum and, instead of returning to the house and Louise, she left her garden by the small gate in the wall that gave directly onto the village car park.

* * *

Joy Siptac sat in her smart modern grey kitchen, drinking tea and thinking about the Revfilly. In this she was unknowingly doing what several others would do that same day, including the Crabbes and Susan Repplington-Smythe. Perhaps it was catching.

Although she spent the rest of that day thinking hard, unusually, Joy's devious mind hadn't come up with a solution to Revfilly's notices but, just as she was going to bed that night, she had the beginning of an idea and by morning it had grown into a Plan.

"Harold, I need you to do something for me. I want you to make a call to the vicarage at Sideleigh. Speak to the curate; if you can't get him (or her, whichever it is), then hang up and try again later. No, I do not want you to speak to the Filly thing …"

And so Harold dutifully made his call and, after a couple of tries, he did indeed speak to the pretty curate and he got exactly what his wife wanted.

We have already met the Rev Fiona and know her to have been very deeply committed to the things she was very deeply committed to, most especially her own career. These laudable qualities kept her very busy, almost too busy to attend to the spiritual needs of her several parishes.

And Joy Siptac, quite correctly as it turned out, felt she could rely on those calls on Fiona's time to keep the reverend away from unimportant little Coldstow until the following Saturday.

"Hi. Is that the Western Press newspaper office? … It is? Good. I'm Miss Crabbe, secretary to the several church parishes around Spattersleigh. You'll know all about our vicar, Fiona Abbot. Oh, you've come across her before – always news worthy isn't she? The thing is, we've got a huge public meeting planned for Saturday at

Coldstow. It's to give an opportunity for non-Christians to speak out about anything they want and our vicar's keen to have it all properly reported.

…No, I don't mean she's after more publicity. But she works so hard, she deserves all she gets.

…You will be there? Good."

Joy put her phone back in her pocket and smiled to herself. Two birds, one stone.

And there were one or two other calls to be made but not by a "parish secretary".

Late that dark evening, Harold slipped down to the Church and removed both Fiona's notices. On the village hall board he put up another. At first glance it looked no different from the one it replaced.

'Grand Meeting of Fiona's parishes
Saturday 8th October
Coldstow Village Hall

Hi, everyone. For anyone that doesn't know, I'm your new vicar – and not just yours. I'm in charge of pretty much every little church around here now.

Just want to tell you:

There's going to be a fun meeting in the little hall at Coldstow next Saturday. I'll start with an opening speech, then it's the turn of the kiddies and their mums to have fun decorating the hall and the church to welcome a GUEST SPEAKER!!! No names yet, you'll all have to be patient but I can promise you a BIG SURPRISE.

Then, it's more fun with WAKE UP VILLAGES AND SMELL THE COFFEE; It's time to throw out those oldies who think they know how to run things.

Just bring your own refreshments – you can't expect your little worn out church to pay for everything you know and Coldstow's too mean to give anything to anyone.

And don't worry! I'm not going to sell God to you; I don't believe in any of that stuff myself. There won't be a dog collar in sight I can promise you.

See you Saturday!

Rev Filly'.

* * *

Saturday did not "Dawn Bright and Clear". Apparently whoever may have been in charge of Coldstow's weather on that day decided there had been quite enough continuous sunshine for the year and switched over to the more usual South West wind and fitful drizzle with occasional sunny periods. Coldstow doesn't mind this, it's comfortingly normal. - A sad sort of day for sad events.

Susan was recovering from the embarrassment of her little setback at the Church Committee meeting. Feeling a need to be among people again, she left her cottage, intending to set out for the village hall and Filly's entertainments. She hadn't got into the lane before spotting the Siptacs.

Anything and everything about her enemy interested, even excited, her. She felt the sort of thrill that a fox must experience on first sight of a rabbit. Automatically she ducked back out of sight beside her porch and waited.

Joy and Harold went by and walked slowly toward the centre of activity. There was that about their apparently deliberate disinterest that aroused delicious suspicion in Susan. She followed them, ducking quite unnecessarily into every available hiding place in the most ridiculous fashion and clutching her phone, camera ready, as if she were acting out the part of a spy in a spoof movie.

The hall car park was busy, but not with cheerful village mums and children expecting to decorate the church. Indeed, the crowd seemed humourless and rather ill-tempered.

He was there to show a 'Police Presence' but PC Mabbtree wasn't feeling very sympathetic with the Rev Filly. He, too, had read the troublesome notice; this was all the vicar's doing and, as ever, other people (that is, himself) were likely to suffer for the meddling wrongs of others.

Joy watched the scene for ten minutes or so. Yes, it had all gone very smoothly, and now here was the Revfilly to manage the happy throng.

If Fiona had expected a group of friendly villagers ripe for being lectured and cannon fodder for her next career step then she must have wondered what on earth had gone wrong; she was used to being outrageous but not openly hated by an entire gathering. There was no welcome here, quite the opposite; several people were openly heckling her. But outwardly she showed no emotion and Joy had to admire the woman's strength of character.

"There's the vicar that doesn't believe in God. Fiona the liar."

"Coldstow doesn't want you, we'll show you just how mean we can be…"

And so on. The crowd were actually jostling their own vicar, pushing her, making her stumble. She looked around for any friendly face, any possible source of help. There was none, even her little curate had disappeared.

Joy's attention was taken for a moment by the delightful sight of Rene and Louise being given a hard time by PC Mabbtree who had just learned from a Western News reporter that his paper had been told of probable trouble that day by someone called Crabbe. It could not have worked out better but, when Joy turned to look again at how the vicar was faring, Fiona had disappeared.

"I don't think we need stay here, Harold. We shall go and have an early lunch at your Jack's as Good as his Master public house. I'm sure you will meet some old friends there and perhaps one not so old."

"I don't feel up to lunch dear. I'm for going home and perhaps a bit of cheese on toast."

"Nonsense – my treat."

Susan watched them leave, then walked back to The Old Pig Barn and a cup of refreshing tea. For some unaccountable reason she felt much better.

It was lunchtime when the pair reached Jack's. To Harold's surprise a table had already been booked for them. Even after all the years of spite and trickery, there were still times when his wife's scheming made him feel totally powerless; there was never any chance of outwitting her. She was just too far ahead of everyone else.

And Joy continued to ride her luck.

"Is that your special young friend I've heard so much about, Harold dear?"

"I don't know what you mean Mrs Siptac. I have been here occasionally, but I don't remember seeing her before."

And Joy's luck had run out for that day for the graceful, dark haired woman who came over to serve them wasn't Harold's friend and he really hadn't seen this one before. But she, too, was very attractive. Wistful thoughts of being Mrs Siptac free fleeted through his mind - again.

* * *

"Come away with me, my dear. This day isn't a good one for any of us."

She obediently took her aunt's hand. They walked together across the busy car park, through the angry crowd and set off along the lane out of the village. They spoke no words but each held the other's hand very tightly.

After some twenty minutes her aunt spoke once more.

"That's enough, dearest loving child. It's all over now."

She made just one sound - a pathetic screaming sob and fell silent again.

They turned, held one another very close for a silent minute and retraced their steps to the murder scene.

"Now it's for you to do your part. God will guide you, my special one, as he always has since you were born. We are in your hands as you are in His. Whatever happens, you bear no blame."

Chapter 8

Sad times.

Whether Fiona had found the crowd too threatening and discretely left the village or for some other reason, she wasn't seen after the heckling incident and, without their vicar as focus for the anger of many and the interest of a few reporters and casual sightseers, much of the gathering melted away.

One corner of the large car park that serves both the Siptacs' village hall and their enemies' shop is taken up by a variety of steel containers. Some, now almost lost to sight in a vigorous growth of brambles and wild shrubbery, have been there for years, their purpose and ownership forgotten. The enclosed containers are locked, but two or three council owned skips are emptied every month or so.

As it happened, a waste disposal truck arrived to change one of these containers just as Constable Mabbtree was feeling that he might at last go home to enjoy a quiet lunch and a little televised football. Sadly for him, that hope wouldn't be fulfilled.

The truck dropped off its empty skip and reversed to take a full one; the driver left his cab and walked around to a pile of insulation that had slipped to the ground, but he didn't pick it up.

The body was lying as if laid out with care and partly covered by the fallen material; this might have been deliberate but, if so, it was poorly done concealment.

Her killer could hardly have expected that a rusty skip, part overgrown by brambles, would be moved so soon. Otherwise, she might have remained undiscovered for longer, but it was a very short time since the vicar was seen in public by her unadoring parishioners. The time of death was easy to fix.

After the usual rigmarole: taping off the scene, the ambulance, more police people, the doctor, the taking of numerous photographs and evidence collection, the female (as opposed to that other heartless police word "male"), was gently lifted from her temporary resting place and set face upward on a stretcher.

She looked surprisingly small in her handsome dark cloak. His police interview over, he had walked across to the scene and looked sadly at poor Fiona Abbot, vicar of several parishes, activist, friend of the pretty curate and, from time to time, either atheist or agnostic. And, incidentally, the focus of loathing from not a few people who, rightly or wrongly, had detested her in life and now may have regretted their improper feelings and thoughts. If hatred of a cleric isn't a crime of especially large magnitude, just at that moment he felt that it ought to be.

A short distance away, the pretty curate was kneeling on the tarmac, crying. He wanted to help but could find nothing to say and dared not reach out a probably unwelcome hand; in this, as ever, his judgement was quite correct.

* * *

The Detective Chief Inspector in charge wasn't pleased to find that PC Mabbtree had apparently allowed quite a few of the potential witnesses in the crowd to drift away without even taking their names. But there were still some dozen or more people present who could be held in the Siptacs' village hall pending interview. And there was one late addition to boost the numbers.

Joe ("the Red") Barlow is (or hopes to become) a well-known activist in any number of highly contentious political areas. Unable to make up his mind which of these several fields offered the fastest route to stardom, he had diluted the exercise of his talents a little too much by pursuing every course at once. But he continued to work at it; hopefully he will get where he deserves to be eventually, although, at the age of forty five, time isn't on his side any more.

The Larkston taxi stopped in the road beside Coldstow's closed off carpark and out popped Red Barlow, all ready to make his invited speech.

He had expected some welcome, at least from his friend Filly. But, instead of her, there was a gathering of police (he had no difficulty identifying plain clothes detectives), a dozen police vehicles and a village hall that appeared to contain a number of prisoners.

Being quick to recognise the familiar signs of Big Trouble, he was getting back into the taxi, and wondering how he was going to pay a fare he hadn't budgeted for, when the not-so-friendly hand of PC Mabbtree grabbed his shoulder.

"Don't know what you're doing here Barlow but you can explain that to the Chief Inspector."

And so Mr Barlow found his way into the hall where he could share standing room with all the other hungry and thirsty unfortunates that Sergeant Susan Ibrahim had placed there.

∗ ∗ ∗

Doctor Ledger had made her brief report: Fiona had (probably) died one to two hours before her examination; death was (probably) caused by the obvious wound to her neck (probably) made by some very sharp and narrow instrument. - Following Jo's death, the doctor wasn't going to make another mistaken statement at the scene of a crime if she could help it. – Keep it vague, Doctor; hedge your bets.

The ambulance went away to, well, wherever ambulances with corpses go, and the police continued with their interviews.

Having spoken to all the potential witnesses and cleared away those who seemed least significant, DCI Cardler started again on the Crabbe sisters. Rene fielded all his questions, leaving Louise to look as thoroughly frightened as a guilty old lady might look; and the Chief Inspector deliberately stared hard at Louise throughout.

"Why did you telephone the Western Press newspaper?"

"We didn't telephone anyone. Well, certainly not the press. Why would we do that?"

"We know you rang the press. You told them there was a meeting at Coldstow and they ought to have a reporter here. You gave your name and told them you're the parish secretary. I'll ask you again: why did you call the newspaper and how did you know there'd be something to report on?"

"I've answered you: I didn't call the paper; we didn't know anyone was going to be murdered – how could we? This is all ridiculous, if we'd known about a crime, I wouldn't call a paper. I should have told the police, although having seen your lot, I can see it wouldn't have been any use.You're being stupid; it's obvious, even if there was a phone call, and we've only got your word for that, Chief Inspector, the caller must have pretended to be me. Find him, or her, and you've got your murderer. Now let us go. You've no right to be abusing elderly ladies. Do we look like killers?"

"As to that, I've met killers who looked a lot more innocent than your trembling sister. I'm not done with you yet. Both of you stay in the village until I say different."

But just as they were walking away, Rene had a delicious thought and turned back:

"If you really want to know facts, instead of making up a tale to suit yourselves, you ought to interview the Siptacs. They've been acting oddly about the Vicar's meeting (well, especially oddly - those two are always odd)."

"Who are these Sitcaps? And what odd thing have they been up to that we ought to know about? – Don't be secretive Miss Crabbe or I'll put you back in the hall and you can wait there for another interview."

"Their name's Siptac - Joy and Harold. They manage, or more accurately, mismanage, the village hall. I saw him in the dark taking down the Vicar's notices and putting another up on the hall notice board, although it didn't look much different. They were both lurking about around the edge of things this morning and then they disappeared. I shouldn't be surprised if she murdered the vicar; she hates everyone."

"Where are they now?"

"How should I know? Probably on a plane to somewhere while you lot waste time interrogating old ladies."

In the continued absence of all Siptacs, and with no more information to be had from Rene and Louise, the officers started to work through the rest of Coldstow's population. It wasn't long before they lighted on Susan Repplington-Smythe.

Susan had plenty to say – and, as it was almost entirely anti-Siptac, attention turned back to Joy and Harold who, at that moment were lunching at Jack's, unaware they had become wanted criminals in their absence.

So, enquiries were made, the inevitable helpful witness popped up in the form of Dave from the Coldstow pub and the Siptacs were located. And, of course, none of these misfortunes would have happened if Joy had not been quite so unpleasant to quite so many people.

* * *

We have seen before how quickly news (especially the unpleasant sort) speeds through Coldstow. The fact of Fiona's murder naturally broke records; it had reached all her parishes and every obscure outlying farm before late afternoon. This wasn't the first murder in recent years but it was the most exciting and important. The vicar had been a national celebrity and the local population looked forward with relish to reading about it, and about themselves, in next day's national press.

News that passes word from mouth to ear, and so onward, is rarely reliable and the rumoured causes of death were, of course, various and largely wrong. But some onlookers had the dubious fortune to see poor Fiona's throat when the body was turned over, and before it had been respectfully covered. For them, there was no question how she had died.

* * *

It was Joy Siptac's misfortune that she couldn't help being superior and rude. It hadn't taken Detective Chief Inspector Cardler long to lose what little patience he had left by the time his constables brought her back to the village hall.

So Joy, but not Harold, who had been kept at the hall by way of splitting up the two of them, found herself at the police station in Elcester where she was left to cool off in an interview room for an hour.

"What were your feelings about the reverend Fiona Abbot? And, before, you answer, I warn you we've been told you were furious about some notice she put up at the church."

"I wasn't furious. I never am. If you misinterpret things, I shan't answer your foolish questions. Do I look like a murderer?

And it wasn't the church notice that annoyed me. It was at the village hall. I run the hall and I won't have people riding roughshod over me."

"I'll take that as an admission you disliked the vicar."

"Take it any way you want; I can't be responsible for your failing to understand the English language. Where do we get our police from? - The University of Ignorance? Did you get your degree in stupidity or do you retake it next year?"

"Being rude isn't going to help you, Joy. Why did you take down the vicar's notices?"

"I didn't. That was Harold. And I'm Ms Siptac to you."

"Why, Joy, did you telephone the Western News and pretend to be Miss Crabbe."

Joy stayed silent. For once she was frightened. The police seemed to have far more information than she could have imagined. What else did they know that still had to come out? She could only guess where all this was going and the possibilities were more in number, and far more serious, than she dared to think about.

* * *

Feeling the need for a change, he had gone to Jack's on the evening of Fiona's death. At least the bar staff were pleasanter company than Dave and Stan and he needed some cheer just now.

The Happy Fireside would have done better to employ one of the nice girls at Jack's; the increase in trade would have more than covered the cost. Too late now.

Lost in his habit of thinking about other people's problems, he hadn't noticed the woman now standing beside him at the bar. She had a nice, warm voice.

"Well, what are you thinking about? Today's horrid events or something nicer?"

Coldstow people just didn't talk to one another unless it was family or troublemaking gossip. Perhaps Sally hadn't been there long enough to be destroyed yet. Taken by surprise, he almost took too long to reply; she seemed about to turn away.

"Well, not today's happenings, not just at that moment. In fact I was wondering why Dave never thought to employ a cheerful barmaid; it might have been the difference between profit and failure."

"I couldn't agree more. Drinkers don't want long faces to look at; most people go to pubs because home isn't much fun. Well, I do. Though I suppose it's mainly a break for you and Freddie on your walks together."

He looked at her, surprised, and pleased, that she knew even that much about him. He wondered what had happened to her energetic boyfriend and for the moment decided he didn't care.

"Not today it isn't. I needed to see welcoming faces and get away from all the backbiting gossips. There'll be plenty of that in our local this evening – I can't bear any more of it."

They stayed silent for a while. For some reason this comforted both of them. They each had more they wanted to say, to share doubts and suspicions that they were finding ever harder to keep to themselves.

Both started to speak at the same time and laughed.

He tried again:

"I wanted to talk with you about Jo. Have you got time? It might take a while."

And that was how they came to share their first meal and a companionable evening together.

"I assumed you'd want to discuss what happened today, not poor little Jo. Don't worry, I won't pass anything on; I've got doubts myself but they're probably just me not thinking straight."

"I don't think it was suicide, Sally; that makes no sense. You saw how Jo behaved. She wasn't suicidal; angry, yes but she didn't want to die; she wanted revenge. I suppose it might have been natural causes but the inquest didn't say so. That stupid doctor nearly missed the barbiturates. And if it wasn't suicide or an accident, it was another murder. If it was murder, why and who? And now there's another thing: two murders in a small village in such a short time. Is there a connection? So what's been troubling *you* about it?"

Sally thought for a while. He seemed genuine. He had been kind to Jo that evening, although she had wondered… No, don't go there, she must start trusting people in this difficult world or she would go under.

She spoke slowly, choosing her words; trying to recall exactly what she had seen and why it had bothered her. It wasn't long ago but, after Fiona, Jo's death seemed to belong to another world.

"I think it has to do with what happened after you took Jo home. Mr Downe came into the bar. He was in a state; I don't think it was acting. He always seemed a very placid type and that night I thought he wasn't his usual self at all, but then I don't know him, and you do. The thing is, he came in looking for Jo and I couldn't understand that. If she wasn't at home by that time, how come Chris didn't meet you taking her back there in your car. He surely wouldn't have passed by without asking if you'd seen her. The only explanation is that he walked the long way from his farm to the pub and that makes no sense either. If he was anxious to find Jo, he wouldn't have dawdled through muddy woods in the dark. I assume you didn't see him when you were there?"

"I didn't know about any of that. Chris turned up at the farm a long time after I got there, but I couldn't say exactly when. I was kept there late, dealing with police and answering questions;

I wasn't taking in anything else. I'm afraid my old friend, Chris, is a murder suspect – spiking Jo's whiskey and leaving her to die. If he did, I wonder where he went afterwards and why."

"I've no idea; perhaps somewhere that he thought gave him an alibi, although I can't quite see what use that could have been. One reason for him being away might simply be that he couldn't bear to see it all happen. – Don't forget he probably didn't know Jo was going to the pub to have it out with Dave. It would have been a shock for Chris that she wasn't at home when he went back and looked for her - if he did."

"That might explain his state when he arrived at the pub."

They both fell silent again. Each thinking over the implications of this exchange; he feeling deeply sorry that it was his friend they were discussing; she in turn feeling sorry for him.

"Well if Chris killed Jo, the murders surely can't be linked. I can't see Chris having any reason to kill Fiona. He was one person she hadn't got to. He isn't a churchgoer – chapel if anything, I think. And I didn't see him there today; it's not like poison, you can't stab someone from a distance. Sorry, I ought not to have mentioned that."

Sally sat silent and shocked; she hadn't known how the vicar died. Changing the subject, she talked with him about Freddie, who obligingly said hello for the third time, and they each ordered a final gin and tonic before driving the short distance home in their separate cars, taking their separate and common thoughts with them.

* * *

Extract from Friday's edition of the Western Press newspaper beneath a photograph of a weary looking and dishevelled man, now lacking his trade mark orange wig:

'On Wednesday of this week Joseph "the Red" Barlow was found guilty at Elcester County Court on charges of theft from two residents while being held for questioning at Coldstow village hall in connection with the murder of Fiona Abbot, vicar of Sideleigh and its three subsidiary parishes. Mr Barlow was ordered to perform fifty hours community service, to pay a fine of £100 and to make payment to his victims in the amounts of the sums stolen by him.

It is understood that the Establishment Attack Party has withdrawn its support for Mr Barlow's election campaign. Neither the EAP nor Mr Barlow were available for comment.'

So ended Mr Barlow's political career. Let us hope that he finds some other upward route.

Chapter 9

Another empire changes hands.

Coldstow's Garden Club, or "CGC", as it is generally called, was formed some twenty years back by cranky fifty year old Maurice D'Arteur. By the time we are talking about, having seen a lot more of people and their stupidity, Maurice was an even crankier seventy year old with no time for anyone. But he was still President of the CGC.

The club members hated him. It wasn't just his attitude to them; Coldstow is so full of hatred that his rudeness went largely unnoticed. The great problem with their leader and founder was that he had become an absolute dictator with weird ideas that were becoming embarrassingly weirder.

Maurice lived, alone by then, at the end of a terrace of three ex-council houses a few miles from Coldstow itself. Being the club's founder, one might expect him to have had a good display of flowers but none of these houses retains any front garden whatever. Two are gravelled over, the third is paved - badly.

The need for these hard-standings is plain. Cedric had two cars in his life and he still had them, although he hadn't driven for many years, and the cars showed it. The middle house was evidently owned by a family with children of about that age when they need plenty of vehicles to tinker with. And the owner of the far end house operated a thriving mobile hot dog business of which no more need be said.

Maurice's proper garden is a long, narrow strip of land running away parallel to the highway and hidden from public view by a tall leylandii hedge. The area is entered by a wicket gate from the place where the old cars live. Immediately the visitor is in another world. This is a large garden but so packed with plants, especially shrubs and trees, that the visitor struggles to assess its size. There's no doubt that Maurice had green fingers – everything is growing enthusiastically, too much so.

It's a common mistake to fill a garden with vigorous plants. It comes from a natural desire for instant effect, and ignoring those warning labels at the garden centre:

'Ten year height approx. 10m. Spread approx. 2m.'

Ten years really isn't long in gardening terms. So must Maurice have repeatedly made this mistake. His plants had taken over and three quarters of the garden now lay in deep shade.

But there is nothing bonkers about having an overgrown garden. Plenty of people are stuck with one. Our Maurice had developed peculiar hang-ups all his own.

He had lived in the same house since childhood. Whether he ever had a father to know is uncertain, but he and his mother stayed together for sixty years, until the old lady died some time back. Never sociable, shy and now alone, Maurice wasn't always thinking straight and it was much to his credit that he formed Coldstow Garden Club. It must have taken a lot of courage, because there is nothing that Coldstow enjoys more than snubbing kindness. But while his club thrived, Maurice's mental state did not.

On the last occasion of the garden's opening to CGC members, some twenty or so trees had been fiercely, cruelly bent down to the ground and tied there by long lengths of brightly coloured, patterned material. Bizarrely, a couple of handbags hung in the foliage.

Maurice has a temper but anyone would want to know and, as he seemed in a good mood, some brave gardener asked:

"Why are your trees tied down and what are you using to do it, Maurice?"

It was a good day. The reply wasn't *"Mind your own damned business"* but a serious answer to a serious enquiry:

"I'm training trees to be weeping varieties. I tie the branches down and keep pulling them a bit more each week. I use Mum's old dresses and that keeps the birds away as well."

Three club members looked at each other with raised eyebrows, one put a forefinger to her head and twiddled it about. Others simply stood and silently aired their mouths. Two new members, who hadn't yet done any gardening of their own, took careful notes.

* * *

Over a drink or two at the Happy Fireside that evening, a few CGC members met to discuss the afternoon's entertainment.

The mutineers included the Crabbe sisters (who, except on rare and special occasions only drank alcohol at home or when someone else was buying), Sally and her new friend (the man who cuts the church grass and maybe doesn't any more), the Repplington-Smythes and gentleman Gerry Allen on his own (his wife having refused to sit in the same room as her former best friend).

And there, too, were Mr Siptac (Joy unwilling to face a world she couldn't dominate just now), Dave and Stan who actually liked gardening, or at least visiting gardens, which is almost the same thing, and Chris Downe, the CGC treasurer, who happens to be more interested in gardening than you might expect of a twenty eight year old farmer.

Susan had got over her disastrous Church Committee experience and was back on her hunt for power but Gerry Allen was first to speak:

"He can't possibly stay on as President. He's lost the plot altogether, and that's not a pun. This is serious, if we have him as speaker next time the local clubs meet, we'll be laughed at more than him."

Sally disliked what they were doing:

"The problem is: how do you get rid of the guy who started the club. It seems unfair on him. And you'll have to decide who's going to do the assassination and take his place. I don't like it."

Louise butted in:

"Does that mean we're going to kill him? How are we going to do it?"

Alarmed, Rene stamped on this before any more came out:

"Don't be ridiculous Louise, people don't get killed just for being a nuisance."

"But I thought…"

"Well, don't think. This isn't one of our jokes."

Sally and her friend looked at the Crabbes as if they had suddenly changed from old ladies into a pair of pythons. They exchanged slightly open-mouthed and wide-eyed looks as of *"What have we got here?"* But the meeting moved on and perhaps no one else noticed the sisters' little conversation or, if they had, chose to keep their thoughts to themselves.

Sensing a great breakthrough and the best piece of luck since she had come to this horrid village, Susan wanted to push matters on, and do it quickly. She hadn't even heard what the Crabbes said.

"Of course I haven't lived here very long but I'm a keen gardener and I'm very good at it. As you all know Sam and I are very keen on being green."

That didn't sound right but she hurried on, determined this wasn't going to be another session of continual blunders.

"I've managed lots of clubs and societies. I know you're all very busy people and, of course, I am too, but I'll offer to take up the position."

Careful about your choice of words, Susan, people are beginning to grin.

"I mean if Maurice, bless his ancient heart, leaves then I'm ready for duty."

And so it happened; fully intending to remove the woman from office once Maurice had been disposed of, the meeting voted to sack their President and appoint Susan Repplington-Smythe in his place. The man who cuts the church grass didn't vote; he had always liked Maurice. Sally abstained because she liked her grass cutter - a feeling that was growing stronger and more possessive by the day, and she wasn't resisting it.

It was left to Susan to inform Maurice officially.

She went home with the couple's only torch, walking on air as Sam stumbled behind in darkness, muttering:

"Very good gardener indeed. She hasn't had anything to do with the garden since we came here, apart from eating my vegetables and farting."

When they arrived home, Sam went straight to his little shed, turned the dartboard around and threw three darts with great accuracy into the mouth of the woman whose photograph was pinned to the back of the board. Then he switched out the light and returned to the house which he absolutely refused to call home.

It didn't take very long for selfish Susan to secure her position as President of Coldstow Garden Club. Having heard on the village news network about how Jo was sacked, she sent a brutal text to poor, unaware Maurice:

'Hi Maurice. Just to let you know that the Garden Club has elected me to be its new President now that you're too old for the job. Of course we're all glad to see you go so that you can have a nice rest. And the members think it best that you don't come to any more meetings because you have a habit of upsetting people. LOL Susan Repplington-Smythe.'

"That should do it nicely. He won't come back from that." thought Susan.

But it wasn't going to end there.

* * *

A few days after Susan had got herself into the top job, a small number of CGC members met at Jack's. They incorrectly felt they could discuss matters there without tripping over Siptacs and Repplington-Smythes; and they had a private matter to settle.

On this occasion the only people who attended (and the only ones who knew about the meeting) were our old friends the Crabbe sisters, Gerry Allen, Sally and Chris Downe. To the Crabbes' annoyance, the last two had learned of the meeting at the last moment from Gerry and, being themselves, they came to see fair play.

Sally wasn't happy:

"I don't like this secret meeting business. It's underhand and probably against the club constitution. It ought at least to have been notified to all the members. And Susan should have been told."

Rene wasn't going to allow any backsliding:

"We agreed at the last meeting, the Repplington-Smythe woman would only be President for long enough to get Maurice out of our hair. Whatever she is, she isn't a gardener and she's no use to the club. I don't mind if she stays on as a member, although I'd rather she didn't. We've got to be rid of her. She's a liability. Remember she can hardly say a sentence without putting her foot in it. Half the rabble at the last Church Committee meeting were openly laughing at her. It was the same at the Garden Club meeting. The woman can't say anything that isn't full of innuendo."

"That may be so, but it doesn't give us the right to be dishonourable and as I recall, the rabble, as you call our fellow villagers, actually cheered Susan when she left. At least she makes people laugh, which I have to say, you don't."

"There's no need to be rude Mrs Redfern. I don't want to make people laugh; I daresay I could if I wished to."

"Well, go on, make us all laugh. I could do with cheering up."

The meeting was starting to fall apart. Rene Crabbe felt things weren't going well; the few members present seemed to favour Sally, not her. It was unfair; they had agreed to remove the Repplington-Smythe woman and Rene, rather meanly, looked forward to it. Events at the church meeting, when Susan had got all the attention, still rankled with her. This was supposed to be Rene's revenge and it was slipping away.

"I'm not trying to make you laugh; I don't know what sort of thing you find funny. And I don't want to know. I suppose going about topless is your idea of a good joke; it's not mine."

That's the trouble with a small village; you just can't keep anything secret. The room went silent; Gerry went red and Sally turned to steel.

"If I wish to be topless, I shall be. Come to think of it, why not now?"

She stood up and began to remove her coat.

It was too much for poor Gerry; Sally's assets had got him in trouble once already – perhaps to the extent of losing his marriage. – And he loved his wife dearly.

"Enough! Sally, please sit down. We're here to deal with a simple Garden Club matter, not to fall out between ourselves for all time. Let's get on with it and take a vote – please!!"

Sally sat down. For the rest of the evening she refused to look at Rene and Rene returned the compliment.

"I, Rene Crabbe, being a member and secretary of Coldstow Garden Club propose that Mrs Repplington-Smythe be removed from the office of President of the club forthwith and that this meeting then proposes some other member to take on that office. All in favour hold up their hands."

Then:

"All against the motion to remove the Repplington-Smythe woman, raise your hands."

Rene and Louise voted for the motion; Sally and Gerry voted against and, not wanting to upset anyone by taking sides, poor Chris Downe abstained and so got himself disliked by everyone for the rest of the evening.

Rene coloured bright red. She could barely speak.

"The vote is tied. Under the club's regulations, that means the motion isn't carried. The Smith woman stays as president. And you lot haven't heard the last of this."

Rene swept out of the pub closely followed by Louise who could be heard quite clearly saying:

"Are we going to kill all of them now, Rene?"

"Oh, shut up."

* * *

Susan hadn't attended the meeting to oust her, mainly because she knew nothing of it until a day or so after it happened.

If she had been removed, no doubt Rene would have found a neat way of leaking the meeting and its outcome in a way that would have caused Susan the maximum distress. But there were others who could do this delightful job and gain just as much pleasure by hurting the Crabbes instead. That's Coldstow all over.

You can't hold a meeting in a public house bar and expect it to stay secret. The Jack's as Good as His Master is quite a busy place. The two bars are large and overlook one another. Some of the regulars, male and female, like to go there after work to have a quiet drink, relax after the day's toil and enjoy the friendly company of the staff. Whenever he could escape his home life, Harold Siptac was one of these happy early evening drinkers. Had it been possible, he would have been there every evening, and perhaps at lunch times too.

The secret Garden Club meeting was held on one of those rare days when Harold had been able to spend the whole afternoon, and on into the early evening, chatting happily with his warm-hearted barmaid, Cheri (that's the one that Joy hadn't yet met).

He had seen the Garden Club Committee in their meeting without being noticed by any of them. This may have been down to the fact that he was hidden behind a convenient pillar at one end of the public bar. This was his usual parking place for the good reason that he could see whilst not being seen and, if necessary, escape via the back door that led out to the men's facilities and on to the pub car park. From there he might reach home with nothing other than his breath to suggest that he hadn't been busy in his little shed at the end of the garden.

Intrigued by anything that might help a little malicious gossip to grow and flourish, Harold moved closer to the little group and was greatly helped in his eavesdropping by a steady rise in the sound of their voices. What began as whispered secrecy had become quite public, at least between Miss Crabbe and Sally Redfern.

There came the motion by Rene Crabbe to remove Susan from her position as president – and Harold hadn't even known she held the office. There followed two showings of hands and then there were the Crabbe sisters, striding off as angry as could be and threatening the others. Threatening them even with death!

This was a real news scoop. Far better than the usual sort of tattle. The Repplington-Smythe woman had somehow got the top job in the Garden Club. Now, the members were falling out over removing her and Susan evidently didn't even know about the meeting.

His first thought was to tell Joy; it would impress her, and she would know just how to use this little windfall to its maximum benefit.

But he immediately realised there was no way of telling Joy about a meeting in Jack's without admitting he had been there. Then came a further thought; there was nothing in this for him if Joy took over, she would use it all purely for herself, as she always did, and he was really quite tired of his spiteful wife. Why should he do her another thankless good turn?

So, Harold decided to say nothing to his wife and wait for an opportunity to have some fun of his own.

* * *

Happy in her new presidential post and unaware that she had almost lost it immediately, Susan was sitting in her cold kitchen at the Old Pig Barn and wondering how best to move forward with her career development. This started her thinking about the battles she would have to fight on the way.

One thing was clear, her number one enemy was the Siptac and this reminded her of Joy's behaviour on the day of Fiona's death. There had been something very odd there. After turning it over in her mind for some ten minutes or so, she thought:

"I know, what it is. - She knew something was going to happen; it was as if she planned it and watched to see it was going as she wanted it to. So why did she leave when she did and take her Harold with her away from all the action?"

She thought for some further time.

"Yes, I have it. - Once she was sure her plan was working, she needed to be away from there. Wanted an alibi maybe? No, that's not quite it. - She didn't want to see something that was going to happen. Bit of both I think."

Susan got up, feeling pleased with herself, and made a cup of tea to help her thoughts along.

She could get no further that day. Perhaps more information might come her way if she waited. The thought that she might be about to uncover some really nasty truths (or half-truths - it didn't matter which) about the Siptac made her want to skip around the garden like a twelve year old.

But it was a fine sunny day and there were bound to be eyes that watched and mouths to report on such eccentric activities so she just imagined herself skipping - as she had skipped in her youth, before Sam.

Beware Susan, the Siptacs really aren't nice people and jealousy is a strong emotion – perhaps the strongest of all.

* * *

Susan wasn't the only villager to remark the Siptacs' odd behaviour on the vicar's final day among her flock.

They met again at Jack's, almost, but not quite, by chance. By silent consent they both sat at a table in the pub's neat garden.

The October sun was amazingly warm - a true Indian summer and a great rarity in Coldstow, where it rains most of the time and, when not actually doing so, it's just a temporary relief while the weather gathers its strength for the next series of downpours.

The trees were holding their leaves well that year. There was plenty of colour to delight the eye of anyone that bothered to look. There were even some cheerful flowers still showing in the sort of pots and baskets that nice pubs have about the place to keep their outdoor customers happy and encourage them to stay on for perhaps just one more cider, or a coffee, even lunch.

He bought her a drink, now without any fear it might offend or be misread, and they sat silent for a time, two troubled people drawing comfort from the easy companionship of an undemanding friend.

Of their personal woes, they said nothing. But both of them had been thinking about their last meeting, the discussion about Jo and whether Fiona's murder was connected with it.

He gently broke the silence:

"I don't believe Chris had anything to do with Jo's death. I've known him quite a long time; he's been a good friend and he isn't the sort. Although I'm not sure I'd recognise that anyone is. In many ways Chris is the classic innocent abroad. But it can't have been suicide either. You saw her that evening. She wasn't suicidal, she was angry. The two just don't go together. They're mutually exclusive. And who takes poison to kill themselves, then leaves home to go to the pub? It's a nonsense."

"So, unless it was an accident or some odd medical condition, it was another murder?"

"Mm. I suppose so, Sally. I can't see it was an accident. How can it be accidental to take barbiturate tablets? She wasn't a child and certainly not stupid. I liked her for her intelligence. – And her directness."

He grinned at the memory of Jo's directness with Dave and the Siptacs on that evening.

She thought for a while.

"Did the useless doctor say anything about Jo having something wrong with her health?"

"Not that I know of; she always seemed quite fit."

"I do know that GP. I might get something out of her before she runs off to hide behind patient confidentiality. Well there are a few things to look into. I'll speak with the doctor; you can dig around to find what your friend Chris Downe was doing that day. Now what about Fiona?"

"What about her?"

"You know what I'm saying, dear heart: what are we going to do about her murder? I dislike Joy Siptac like poison but I'm sure she didn't stab anyone's throat. She's far too sneaky; a cold planner, not a hot-blooded risk taker and whoever did for the vicar, it can't have been carefully planned."

"How do you work that out?"

"Think, Sherlock. You kill someone in broad daylight with loads of people about and nowhere to hide the body except a busy car park – anyone could do better than that with a bit of thought."

He sat silent again. Yes, she was right. It was a crazy way to get rid of someone. Either the murderer was a fool or just didn't care about being found out. His heart thumped – he had suddenly realised she called him dear heart.

He wasn't to know that, having been barren of warm friendship for all too long, Sally had been struggling to keep those words, or something very similar, from escaping her ever since they sat down together. Now they were out and she couldn't just grab them and put the flighty things back where they came from. Perhaps she didn't want to.

He liked being her dear heart but, wanting not to offend her and wary as ever, pretended he hadn't heard that nice phrase. Tread carefully, it was the safer course. Not for the first time, he recalled that day at Limbury and two people in a parked car. Was she still involved with him?

"If it wasn't Siptac (and I agree it isn't her style), who else in the village? And how can we investigate? Why should we?"

Sally wasn't quite sure if she had any good answer. Perhaps she just wanted to develop their friendship. And why not? She had come here to escape her troubles; hoping for a happier life. Pity she chose the frozen wastes of Coldstow but she wasn't the first to make that mistake.

Well, face up to it; if she was going to suffer another cold-shouldering, best to find out now and go no further down that familiar rocky road to tears.

"Of course, if you don't want to join my new investigators club, you don't have to. I just thought you'd want to see the right person caught. And you know you're fond of the Siptacs really, you're just not admitting it."

He grinned, thinking of all that spite. There was something about doing good for the wretched woman that appealed to him. True Christianity – thankless giving.

And if it helped this new friendship develop – well he liked the idea more than he dared admit. But take care! – too much past pain; he didn't want any more.

"I don't care about the Siptacs; well not much anyway. But you're right of course, We can't have our vicar being murdered as if it was as unimportant as another council road closure. Right now I can't see what we have to go on but that doesn't mean there's nothing. I suppose the one thing we have is time. Let's both think about it and see what we come up with. Meanwhile we're concentrating on Jo. Ok by you?"

"Fine by me."

They spoke no more about murders during lunch and, afterwards, went their different ways. Five minutes later he was back at their table to collect Freddie. For the first time ever, he had forgotten her.

* * *

The death of old Maurice, churchwarden, gardener and well-known grouch, was just another event to lubricate the inventive minds of the Coldstow gossips. Found some days after his demise in his cottage, a few miles outside the village, he had used some unpleasant gardening implement to bring life to a close. In his hand was a letter apparently sent to him some weeks earlier but here was no suicide note:

'Sideleigh Vicarage

Dear Mr D'Arteur,

It is my duty to advise you that your services as churchwarden at St Mary's, Coldstow will no longer be required after the end of the current month. The church will be closing its doors then and I anticipate it will be put up for sale and redevelopment later in the year.

I understand that you are far beyond the age when the Church could expect to receive any useful service from you and no doubt you will spend the rest of your days in easy retirement.

Yours sincerely,

Fiona Abbot

Vicar of Sideleigh, Ewer, Spattersleigh and Coldstow parishes'

Another message, sent to him by text, was found on his phone. We do not need to look, as we already know its content – it was written by Susan Smythe and had nothing to do with church matters.

Whether Maurice believed his vicar had a power to dismiss him we shall never know. Strangely, the intention to dispose of St Mary's would have been news to the church authorities had they been told of it, neither would Fiona have recognised the content of her apparent letter which was carelessly dated the day after she died.

Some spiteful tricks go too far, especially if they are cleverly designed to kill; but that's Coldstow; the place recognises no boundaries.

Chapter 10

Relationships wax and wane.

To most who know her, there is nothing to like about Joy Siptac, but no one could honestly say there is nothing to respect in her.

The woman has grit.

Detective Chief Inspector Cardler had been hard on her but it had got him nowhere. Joy gave as good as she got, fearlessly obstructive, rude and attacking as much as defending throughout her interrogations. At the end of it all both of them felt exhausted. It was a drawn game, but the police weren't satisfied and said so before Joy was sent home and told to stay in the village.

One might have thought her recent experience would have dulled her desire for troublemaking, at least for a day or two. Not so; she was straight back to being her usual, undelightful self.

She hadn't forgotten meeting Susan on the morning when the Vicar's notices appeared. It wasn't long before Joy worked out what had happened that day; well, as near as made no difference. - Susan had watched her reading both notices and seen Joy's reaction to them; afterwards she had read them herself and knew at once that Joy wouldn't let the vicar get away with trespassing so far into village hall territory.

Having reasoned that far, Susan may not have guessed quite what Joy would do but she could be sure it would be both spiteful and clever.

So far, so clear. The question was *"How would Susan make use of her little piece of secret gold?"*

Perhaps, Joy thought, she had made no immediate plan and,

being far less intelligent than her enemy, she might never have thought of one. But when the Vicar's death was discovered and Coldstow was all over policemen, then what an opportunity for Susan to strike! All she had to do was tell the DCI that Joy had been angry with the Vicar, that she and Harold had been lurking around the edge of the gathering on the day of Fiona's murder and simply point out that they had disappeared.

So Joy had the whole picture: why she was suddenly suspected of involvement in murder, how she came to be held and interrogated and who she had to blame for it all.

Yes, she thought, the Smith woman needed a lesson.

"Mr Siptac; I have a job for you to do and try not to make your usual mess of it…"

And Mr Siptac did what his good wife asked of him and he didn't make too big a mess of it.

* * *

By good fortune (or evil chance, according to one's point of view) Joy Siptac's sister (another waspish piece of trouble) lived in Epptree, a small town in the jurisdictional area of a certain district council in a county on the East Coast. – You would hardly think that Coldstow might be affected by goings on so far away; it is indeed a small world.

And the sister was very happy to do what was asked of her; after all one must always look after one's family. Having an approximate date and a name to go on in her local reference library, finding the right edition of the Eastern Press newspaper took her little more than an hour.

It would have taken even less time if the name had not been changed, but there was no doubt she had the right person. Subject to a little aging, the photo emailed by Joy was he.

* * *

There is no copyright in obvious ideas. The sort which no one else thinks of until you do, then:

"Oh, that's obvious. There's nothing new in it. I'm sure that must have been done before."

Or, simply:

"I knew that all along; doesn't everybody with a brain?"

But a simple idea (like misusing your local public notice board to some selfish ends for example) can stand obvious, but unrealised, for years until one bright spark lights upon the concept. And then any number of possibilities come to mind and others, having perhaps less original minds, climb on board, too.

Joy Siptac had no hesitation in re-using her old ideas. If it worked before, do it again, never mind the possible criticism of unoriginality. On the day after receiving her sister's email, the Church notice board, but not that of the village hall, bore a new (and large) sheet of paper with a nice photo of a local resident and a not so nice little news article, originally published by a small local newspaper based some long distance away.

The article wasn't complete. Somewhere near its half way point, someone had curtailed it with a neat series of dots, adding

'Further Information to Follow.'

The notice was entitled:

'Shy but famous local Coldstow resident hides his fame from friends and colleagues'

By noon that day, there was hardly anyone in poor Fiona's several parishes who hadn't either read about the activities of Sam Repplington (otherwise Samuel Repplington-Smythe) or heard a highlighted version from someone who had.

And that included Susan.

* * *

There is nothing quite so unnerving as to meet your good friend one morning with the expectation of a smile and a kindly greeting only to get a silent look that says '*Why aren't you dead yet?*'

"Good morning dear. I hope you slept well. Tea and toast or something more substantial today?"

"Go to bloody hell."

Now Sam isn't the brightest light in Coldstow but he does know his Susan, and it's never a good idea to enquire overmuch when there's something horrid just over the horizon. But he just couldn't help himself:

"What's wrong dear? Has someone upset you? Can I help?"

"Yes, you can take your tea and toast and go to bloody hell, like I just told you and, on your way, enjoy the village notice board."

Sam really didn't want to see whatever was waiting for him on that troublesome board, any more than he wanted to go to hell, but he did need to get out of that house and, of course, curiosity is a very strong human failing. None of us is immune; we just have to know the worst, even though it's going to hurt.

The interesting news about their famous neighbour had already spread around the village and there was no one left at the church notice board when Sam reached it. But there were enough curtain peepers to see his arrival on scene and record the event, some by memory alone, others electronically. Coldstow really isn't a very nice place; it's something to do with the clay soil.

Sam read his little personal history all alone, not with a sinking heart, for his heart had already reached somewhere below the soles of his neatly polished brown boots before he had left home, but now with rising anger at whoever had done this dreadful thing.

He felt the need for a drink as never before. It was too early for the Happy Fireside to be open and too close to this awful scene. But Jack's was open by the time he reached that welcome haven, and the nice friendly barmaid was on duty.

This wasn't just home from home; it was better than any home he had lived in since his marriage and the nice barmaid was everything that his Susan was not.

"Morning Sam. Usual?"

"No, I'll have a neat gin – a double."

"Don't be too upset Sam. Lots of people dip their fingers in the honeypot. You just got caught."

She turned away to the optics. When she turned back with Sam's glass in hand, he had gone.

* * *

Some years before, in a rare, and very brief, period of public spirit and available Lottery money, the residents of Coldstow village and neighbouring Ewer had joined together to install a nice little oak bench beside the main road over to Larkston. The verge at that point is wide, the bench well set back from the highway and the views wonderful, but the bench is too far from the village for an easy walk and there is nowhere nearby for tourists to park their cars.

For some time after it was put in place, the grass around the bench had been kept neatly trimmed and the hedge behind carefully cut back. But the seat was unused, and the villagers lost interest. As a result, Sam was almost concealed by long grasses and those various nameless seed laden plants that like to send their offspring out into the wider vegetable world via people's socks and trousers.

But that wonderful view from the bench outward remains.

This part of England is not rated by its local authority masters as an area of outstanding natural beauty (or AONB as soulless people insist on calling fine countryside) but it _is_ outstandingly beautiful. The road at this point has climbed for some miles to reach a local high point and then run on for another mile or so along a ridge which marks the watershed between two river valleys. To the east one may see as far as the moors. In winter these are often covered in snow. In other seasons they show a wide range of soft pastel colours. Lit in patches of bright sunshine that emphasised the hills' dark hollows, the moors were brown-green and purple on the day Sam rested there.

From the moorland hills back to Sam's road, the land rolls gently up and down. Steeper areas are mostly covered by woodland; the foliage changing to rich autumn colours just then, with occasional formal areas of dull green Forestry Commission spruce. Elsewhere the level land is covered in irregularly shaped, and mostly small, fields bounded by wandering dark green hedges. A few of these are cultivated arable but the vast majority of the land is used year in, year out for grazing sheep and cattle. This is a major milk producing area; the sheep seem to come and go but the Friesian, or one of its close relations, is ever present in numbers.

The land to the west was hidden from Sam's bench behind a field hedge, tall, unkempt and over-ready for its brutal biennial cut. But if he could have looked beyond it, Sam would have had a view very similar to the one before him, save that the far hills are replaced by very distant glimpses of a grey-blue sea under a wide sky.

Such peaceful places as that bench and such views as it offers (for anyone willing to look) can only calm a tortured mind. Having sat there for a quarter of an hour in the autumn sunshine with a gentle wind blowing around him as a reminder that he was out in the real world and among living things, Sam recovered some of his natural inner peace.

After all, he thought, Susan will get over it and, if she doesn't, I've lost nothing much. She doesn't love me; never has. And I don't much care what the village says about me. They're mostly pretty horrid and half of them are doing something illegal themselves when they get the chance. And, if Susan wants a divorce, that's fine by me. I'll find someone else, someone nice who thinks I'm worth something.

Here Sam went off into a little daydream (twenty minutes of it actually) in which he imagined… Well, we shouldn't peer too closely into people's private longings. Suffice to say that in his dream, he had jettisoned the now not-so-nice young barmaid in favour of someone else who was rather older and not so much very pretty, as very warm and sexy.

It got rapidly colder, as waning autumn days will do. He

wished he was home with a hot meal in the offing – even one of Susan's eco-meals would have been welcome – but Sam had walked a long way in his bewildered state and both warmth and food were miles off.

He had hardly noticed how far he walked after he left Jack's. But he was conscious of it now; the prospect of another five mile journey on foot was hard to face. Sam wasn't as fit as one might expect of a man who lived a properly eco life.

He stood and straightened his stiff joints. A few drops of rain falling from an apparently sunny sky made him look upward and behind him. Clouds to the west were a violent, unrelieved purple-grey. He set out down the road, sidestepping onto the verge to avoid occasional traffic. The few drops became many, then a continuous steady cold rain that ran off Sam's bald head, down his neck and onward to wherever it might cause the greatest discomfort. His polished brown boots lost their shine, turned a darker shade and filled with water that squirted back over his ankles at each step.

The traffic increased, as it always seems to with heavy rain, and it became more difficult to cope with; at times the verge disappeared and Sam had nowhere to go out of danger. Drivers of several cars and a couple of vast white vans flashed lights or sounded horns at him.

He became ever more distressed; the journey seemed endless as if he was lifting and putting down his feet but getting nowhere. He didn't know the road well; at every turn he expected to reach familiar ground and see Jack's welcoming lights, but instead, there were just more bland hedges stretching away with the road running between them up to yet another horrid bend.

A car horn sounded behind him. Suddenly angry at the whole horrible world, without looking he gave the driver a vigorous V sign.

The car passed him, slowed and stopped. Sam's heart sank; now what?

'Angry driver punches local man and leaves him for dead on the Larkston main road'.

But it wasn't an angry driver; it wasn't even upset by his rude gesture.

The passenger window silently slid down as he came up beside it.

"Get in Sam; you shouldn't be wandering about in the rain on this busy road. What do you think you're up to?"

Sally Redfern had been doing a little investigative digging during a trip to the local town. She was feeling pleased with her day's work as she drove back to Coldstow and looking forward to sharing it with her fellow PI, when Sam appeared on the road in front of her. Knowing how the poor saturated walker must feel, the rude sign didn't bother her at all. She might have done the same herself in the circumstances.

Her nice luxurious car was warm and it smelled of her subtle perfume. Sam was torn between feeling cheated by his lot – Susan, poverty, the meanness of his life - and longing to be a part, a very large part, of this wonderful feminine world. How women differed! If only…

He caught up with his racing thoughts just in time and forced himself into normality, or at least, a show of it.

"It's very nice of you to pick me up; I'd been out for a long walk, like I do every day; got caught by the weather though. Of course I don't mind at all but Susan worries if I get wet."

Sally said nothing. She hadn't known that Mr Repplington-Smythe went walking at all. And the couple didn't seem to have the sort of relationship where his wife worried much about him. But then she really didn't know either of them well.

He had to raise the subject and know what she thought:

"I suppose you've seen the notice today at the village hall? The notice that's supposed to be about me."

No, Sally explained she had been away since the early morning. She didn't ask what the notice said. She really wasn't interested and her mind was on other things; how she was going to get her car dried out after she disposed of her saturated passenger and whether there was any possibility of a quiet dinner out with the other half of the investigating team.

"A pack of lies. You mustn't believe any of it. Susan's very angry. It's that Siptac woman of course, causing trouble just because the police are after her and she wants to get the spotlight onto someone else."

"Well, I'm sorry Susan's upset; I expect she'll get over it though. These things always blow over and Mrs Siptac can be a bit hotheaded at times. She's probably very nice if you can get to know her."

In common with the entire rest of the village, and then some, Sam had heard of the topless sunbathing episode and wondered how Sally could be so nice about the wretched woman. It didn't occur to him that this was upbringing – you don't show your feelings to strangers.

"You're too generous; we all know what a hard time she gave you over being topless."

And foolish Sam just couldn't stop himself from looking at the relevant part of Sally's anatomy for one long moment. Sally said nothing more on the remainder of the short journey and Sam had no idea that he offended.

"Bye, Sally" – it was the first time he had used her name – "If you're in the bar this evening I'll buy you a drink and maybe we can have dinner some time – very soon."

"Goodbye Mr Repplington-Smythe. I shan't be going out this evening."

Sam went back to his wife's lair, feeling cheered by his time with Sally and quite ready to stand his ground when the attack started.

Sally garaged her car, leaving it with all doors wide open and not just to dry the passenger seat.

* * *

That same evening she met her investigating partner at Jack's.

"I went over to my family lawyers in Winchester today. I had to see young Mr Leslie Clarke, he's the son of Alfred Clarke - Bilberry and Clarke, solicitors. I've known him for ever. He's always called young Mr Clarke but he's in his sixties now. A nice man and a good friend. His firm acts for the Siptac family – don't ask me how I know, I just do. It goes back to a boundary row between our old neighbours and Harold's parents.

Anyway, after we'd finished our business, we chatted for a while and I brought the subject round to Coldstow and its odder residents. Like all lawyers he doesn't give much away but he likes a little gossip. Apparently someone from the village (he wasn't telling me who, but I bet it was a Siptac) had asked one of Leslie's partners to find out where some new neighbour came from. Bilberrys rather cleverly got what was wanted just by using public sources – partly Land Registry, I suppose, but there was more to it than just that. Now you don't ask a solicitor to do that sort of digging unless you're being underhand. You simply lean over the garden fence with a friendly cup of tea and say 'So where did you live before you came here?' I can't see how it ties in with either Jo or the vicar, but it's a sneaky act and I bet there's something big to discover behind it."

"Mm. Well done Sally but, like you, I don't see a link with either of our murderees. It's very interesting but for the time being we'll have to put it in the box marked 'Wanted on Voyage'. Are we dining this evening?"

"Of course Sherlock, and it's my turn to pay, as we agreed. You must know that I've turned down a good offer to grace you with my highly valued presence tonight."

"Who's that? Tell me so I can punch his nose."

"Shan't! – Not if you're going to make a scene. But, as you're not, it's Samuel Repplington-Smythe."

"You mean the famous pensions fraudster, talked about from Coldstow to, well, wherever gossips cease to exist?"

"I didn't know about that; perhaps that's what he was babbling about in the car this afternoon. Is there a notice up in the village about it?"

"Of course! I'd forgotten that you hadn't seen it. We'll have a look on the way home, and you can scribble graffiti on it. I've got a nice pen for you to borrow, but you have to promise to give it back. Now, I don't know what all this two timing with naughty Samuel is about, but it's got to stop or I'll leave you to do your PI work with your other suitor and good luck with that one. – Understood?"

He couldn't have said anything to please her more.

"Understood, my dearest."

Again, she hadn't meant to say that. Once more, the words had slipped out as if they refused to stay bottled up inside her, but she couldn't have said anything that would have touched him more closely or made him happier.

That problem she had with bottling up words when he was close to her, was becoming acute - and it was going to get worse with unforeseeable and painful consequences for them both.

Sam heard nothing of their conversation, but pictures beat a thousand words for what they tell. Unable to bear watching any more, he got up stiffly from his stool at the other bar and quietly left.

* * *

Susan had spent much of the day of Sam's fraud exposure tearing herself apart in her small and gloomy kitchen at The Old Pig Barn. Her first reaction to Joy's notice had been to attack Sam but, largely because he had disappeared out of sight, she turned to the source of this outrage and, after indulging in murderous thoughts of her own and imagining the woman dying a variety of excruciating deaths while she watched and gloated, she started to plan revenge.

* * *

Being with Sally for even that brief journey of luxury had given back to poor deluded Sam some of his confidence in his power over women.

So, after parting from Sally, he had gone back to his home expecting to find his Susan there, hopefully a little less angry than when he had left and, also hopefully, maybe even prepared to cook some dinner.

But Susan hadn't been there, either to attack or welcome him. And the place had that very settled silence of a house that contained no life and hadn't done so for some time. Sam got no response to his call and a brief look into each of the few sparsely furnished rooms confirmed Susan was out.

He felt afraid. Not for any clear reason, but she had been wild in her anger that morning, hot tempestuous anger and now the opposite – cold, unreadable silence. Was he afraid for her, or for what she might have done? His mind wanted to start imagining things and he dared not allow that.

For the second time that day, Sam walked out of his home and eventually found himself at Jack's where he took up his usual corner of the public bar and tried not to hear what his one-time favourite barmaid might be saying about him to the other customers. In fact she said nothing unkindly but, when you are upset, it is sometimes hard to think good of other people.

And the day had still not finished with poor Sam, for, as he sipped his ale and looked around him for some friendly face, there in the dining area he saw his nice new friend, Sally.

But the gorgeous Sally wasn't alone (and hadn't she said she wasn't going out that evening?). She was so obviously happy - and who was that bastard with her?

Sam felt sick; everything that was happening to him seemed designed by some horrid power to tear away every source of comfort in his hard world.

* * *

When he reached home, Sam poured himself a rare glass of whiskey. This was greatly daring as Susan kept a close eye on the level in the bottle which was only there for the sort of important visitors that liked to drink spirits at daytime. And it really wasn't practical to add any more water to the bottle; he had already gone too far with that one.

He wandered into the cold sitting room, which doubled as entrance hall, and sat down into his faded armchair to think over his woes just as he had sat on the old oak bench earlier that day. He slipped into sleep carrying his waking thoughts seamlessly into dreams in which Joy Siptac and the two barmaids at Jack's were fighting with Sally Redfern for the honour of taking him out to dinner and whatever further delights might follow.

But those pleasing dreams were broken and lost irrecoverably by a gust of cold air and a deal of noise as Susan entered the house. Hurriedly, and unsuccessfully, trying to hide the glass under his chair that was too low to accommodate it, Sam struggled to tear his mind away from its nice dreams and bring it to bear on the miserable reality of the present.

"Hallo dear. Have you had a nice day out? Where did you go?"

It was a brave effort in the circumstances, and it ought to have failed completely. The day being what it had been, Susan should have turned on him with a snarl and carried on from where she left off that morning. But she did not. It would be too much to describe her as friendly, but at least that bitter tongue was absent and, if it was only away for an hour or so, getting itself sharpened ready for another round later on, Sam was oh so grateful to have his wife back home and being her best self at that moment.

"I've been to Elcester. I had some business to do. It doesn't concern you."

And then, amazingly:

"I'll make us some supper while you finish your drink."

He didn't understand how she could have changed so completely in such a short time, but Sam never had looked into his wife's mind and he could not have guessed that she had spent an hour that morning slowly accepting that his past wrongdoings were history for the two of them. He had done nothing new to create this state of affairs. The blame for that lay squarely elsewhere, and it was up to Susan to deal with their little difficulties, as she had always done.

* * *

**'Bilberry & Clarke
SOLICITORS
16 Eastern Gate, Winchester SO23**

Ms S Redfern

*The Old Granary
Coldstow
Nr Larkston*

My dear Sally,

It was such a pleasure to see you yesterday. I enjoyed our little talk, as I always do.

I was very sorry to hear about the breakdown in your relationship with Peter. As I mentioned, the news had already reached me some time ago from another source. Your visit was not, therefore, entirely unexpected.

Of course I shall be more than happy to act for you, and I fully understand your desire to bring the matter to a close with the least possible distress for all concerned. Knowing Peter almost as well as I know you, my dear, I am sure he will want to cooperate with us to the same end. I have written to his lawyer today. Please leave everything in my hands for the next ten days or so; I trust we shall have some positive news by that time.

Sally, you did not say if you have a particular reason for wanting a divorce at this time. Whatever the reason may be, and whoever he is, I wish you good luck and a far happier life in the future.

Your friend as ever,

Leslie.

Leslie Clarke, Partner'

Chapter 11

More strife.

Harold Siptac was growing worried.

Through all their married years, he had been Joy's faithful servant in her spiteful journey through life. He had supported her secretive operations against enemies, neighbours, even (and at times, especially) friends and he had done it all without question.

But the vicar's murder carried him beyond all past boundaries. It wasn't that Harold suspected his wife of the killing. If questioned on the subject he would have said truthfully that she was probably capable of it, if there had been a good enough reason, but he could see no motive, so the question didn't arise.

What worried him was the involvement of police and the Chief Inspector's questioning. He and Joy had such a long history of nasty little activities, he felt some of it was bound to come out eventually and, once it did, where would it stop? The authorities had limitless resources for research, once they had reason to go looking.

And, unlike his wife, Harold had a certain respect for, or more accurately, a fear of, their fellow villagers. She had upset most of them at one time or another, and there were plenty who wanted revenge. He raised his fears with Joy when she returned from her inquisition:

"I'm bothered Mrs Siptac. This Fiona murder's going to mean a lot more digging by that Chief Inspector. If some of the things you've had done come out, we'll both be in big trouble. It's time we stopped interfering; at least for a while. You can't control what people say to the police. You can see that from the way the Smith woman sicked them onto you."

But Joy wasn't interested.

"I don't know what you mean Harold. I haven't done anything. If you've been up to something I don't know about, that's your affair. And I'm not going to stop being a good citizen just because your policeman can't do his job – just think, fancy suspecting little me in this business! I gave him the answers he deserved and sent him packing. I'll do the same next time if necessary. And I've found out that Chief Inspector whatsit hasn't always been a good little boy himself. So he needs to watch out and I told him that too."

"Really Joy, you're too cool about this. You can't go threatening policemen. They don't like it and I still think we should take a step back and let other people take the strain. Half the village might have knocked Fiona off her perch; let them explain themselves like you did."

"Now there *is* a thought Mr S. We can start by spreading a bit of gossip here and there. The Crabbe weirdos need a wake up call for a start."

Harold stayed silent; there was no use in saying any more to this irritating woman. Not for the first, or the last, time, he wished he had met and married someone else. Someone like… well, he didn't dare go there; it was too painful.

But Harold couldn't keep to himself his little piece of background knowledge about Susan Repplington-Smythe and the presidential appointment that she had almost lost. Speaking rather like a child saying *"I know something you don't know"*, he started again:

"Joy, dear. I have a bit of news you may find useful, I mean interesting."

He waited but Joy refused to take the bait and he was forced to continue, giving all and getting nothing back from her as always:

"Your friend, Susan, was made president of the Garden Club the other day. They wanted to get rid of the old bloke who founded it. Funny thing is, as soon as she got the job and old Maurice was thrown out, they wanted to give her the boot as well. But they couldn't get enough people to vote for it and now she's in there for ever if she wants it, well for eighteen months at least."

"I don't know what you think that has to do with me Mr Siptac. I haven't any interest in your foolish Garden Club, unless it's done something illegal. Has it?"

But Harold knew his wife all too well. She had been very interested indeed in his news; she just wasn't going to gratify him by admitting it.

"You know of course that the Crabbes pretty much run that club and they were the ones trying to remove Susan. They looked pretty miffed at the meeting."

"What meeting? Were you there? Where was it and why didn't I know about it?"

Harold had quite forgotten the risk of telling his wife about the meeting but it was out now.

"It was in the pub yesterday. I overheard it."

Joy looked at him suspiciously but this wasn't the moment to put Harold through her wringer. That could wait for another time.

"Well, you took your time about telling me. But I suppose I can still do what's needed."

"Not more, Joy, for heaven's sake. The Crabbes and the Repplington Smythe woman aren't soft touches. I beg you; please leave it, at least for now."

But Joy took not the least notice of her husband's pleas.

* * *

'To Mrs Repplington Smythe

President of the Garden Club
The Old Pig Barn,
Coldstow.

Dear Mrs R-Smythe.

I hope I'm not bringing bad news that you don't already know but I can't just stand by and leave you in ignorance of what Some People have been up to at the Coldstow Garden Club.

The Club Committee, or some of them anyway, had a meeting – in a local public house of all places, where anyone could overhear what they were up to. I don't want to get anyone into trouble so I mustn't say where, or exactly when but it was only a day or so ago and it wasn't at the place where we all know they water down their beer.

These people, certainly no friends of yours, wanted to oust you from your rightful place as President and they put this disgraceful business to a vote right in the middle of the public bar for everyone to watch.

You probably won't be surprised which two of the Committee (a pair of sisters who shall be nameless) were the instigators. But not everyone fully agreed to the motion so it didn't get passed. But I'm sorry to tell you the rest of the people taking part didn't seem very keen to keep you either.

I do so hope this is of real help to you and I wish you all the very best in your future dealings with the Coldstow garden lot and that you are able to bring its reprehensible committee under control.

Your ever Loyal Well-wisher.'

As the Loyal Well-wisher said again when the letter was sent on its way *"Two birds with one stone."*

* * *

The Crabbe sisters, Rene and Louise, were enjoying a rather stale toast and old egg breakfast courtesy of the superfluous stock in their village store when the letter arrived, along with a few bills and a couple of begging charity letters. Rene opened it and sat for some while open-mouthed.

"What's up Rene? Something unusual?"

"It's a letter that seems to have come to the wrong people by mistake. And what a mistake!"

But a moment later, having turned the envelope over to see what more it might tell her, Rene realised this was a copy of a letter and it had been very plainly sent to "The Misses Crabbe" at their correctly given address. Shocked, worried and angry, she wondered what was going on now. The world seemed to be going mad.

Rene passed the letter across to her sister. Louise read it in her turn and went white, then red, then purple.

"I'll tell you what this is; it's troublemaking by that Siptac thing or even, possibly, a devious plot by the Smith woman if she has the brains for it. We'll have to find out and kill whoever's responsible".

"No, Louise, we shan't kill them. Anyway, not yet, but we shall get to the bottom of this. The first thing to do is find out who was in the pub that evening and which of them would have been capable of this."

Louise thought carefully, trying to recall that evening and the faces she had seen. Her recollection was quite good, but it is often hard to remember things that seemed unimportant at the time.

"Sally-with-the-bra was there, and farmer Downe, and the gorgeous Gerald. And a few people from out of the village. I don't think anyone else was in the bar where we were all sitting. We can forget the outsiders and I can't see it was any of the other three Committee members. They're not the type and I don't think any of them cared that much about the Smith woman to want to help her. Not that this letter would do her any good."

"I suppose she has received it?"

"Must have done surely. We'll know as soon as we next see her. If looks can kill, we'll be the dead ones, not her."

Any doubt whether Susan had seen her letter vanished later that morning when Rene came out of her little Post Office cubicle and met that lady face to face across the shop counter.

Susan hadn't come with an intention to buy anything and when she left, Rene was as angry with her visitor as Rene was with her.

Two birds; one stone.

* * *

The problem of how to deal with the Siptacs of this world is that they are not merely evil, they are also very clever and forward thinking.

Whilst the Crabbes and the Repplington-Smythes, not to mention numerous other seething sufferers at the Siptac's hands, were forming their several plans for revenge, Joy wasn't just sitting about, waiting for them to act, she was already attacking again. Always ahead and always wrong-footing her enemies came naturally to her; as much part of her genetic make-up as eye colour.

Having only just begun to think what she would do in retaliation for Joy's publication of Sam's little pensions error, Susan was suffering another blow from the same source courtesy of her new presidency.

The Crabbes, smarting at the loss of the village hall, now faced more trouble from Susan angered by their underhand Committee meeting. And they hadn't yet got over that trouble with the Council planning department concerning their nice new sign for the post office.

You have to run fast to keep up with the Siptac.

And the Crabbes, already nettled by Susan's attempted seizure of the Church Committee and Joy's take-over of their village hall, were now at risk of losing another part of their empire. Although they didn't yet know it, their hold on the village store was about to be tested to its limit and perhaps a little beyond.

Then there was the trouble with Dave and Stan at the pub. Joy hadn't allowed Jo's allegation of beer watering to be forgotten. And how about that little topless issue? – Sally hadn't forgiven her old friend and Jenny wasn't yet ready to overlook those photographs.

It seemed that wherever one looked in Coldstow, one found growing ill-will and trouble and there, in the background, were the Siptacs. It was hard to believe they had lived in the village for less time than almost anyone else. But none of the tormented souls thought of withdrawing from their wars, even though they were losing every battle on the way.

* * *

Susan was sitting in her kitchen again, having returned from her meeting with Rene Crabbe in the village shop. She was, as ever, complaining. Sam was enjoying a cricket commentary on his personal radio and half listening to his wife; a trick he had perfected over decades of married life.

"Those Crabbe sisters are the most underhand, sneaky pair of witches you could hope to meet."

"Have you met many sneaky witches?" he asked.

"Don't be silly Samuel, I'm not in a mood to put up with it."

He just stopped himself from saying *'You never are in the mood for anything'*. Sam still had a little of his youthful sense of humour but Susan had none whatever. She simply didn't understand anything that wasn't serious.

"So, what have the Crabbes done now?"

She shrank from telling him about the Garden Club's clandestine meeting to remove her. But as she spoke, she talked herself into believing what she wanted to believe. – A common human trait.

"It's nothing specific but she's rude and the sister's an idiot. They shouldn't be in charge of the shop. I'd bet they're fiddling the takings. It's supposed to be a community thing; it's our money they steal."

"You don't know they <u>are</u> stealing do you, dear?".

"Don't split hairs. They ought not to be selling food; it's not hygienic and think about all the food miles – they buy in the supermarket and drive back to sell it here. Someone ought to do something. I wonder if the Council knows about them."

Sam suddenly felt worried. This sort of talk meant she was going to make trouble for someone and that usually rebounded and ended up with trouble for both of them. Susan wasn't a slick operator; things generally went wrong whenever she was involved.

"I'm sure the Council people keep a check on places that sell food. Leave it to them dear, do."

But it was too late; Susan was making plans – she wouldn't stop now, not until it was all over and they were both crying over the spilt milk.

Susan was a clever manipulator but no match for Joy Siptac in guile and she didn't have Joy's luck. - Some people are born achievers, others not.

* * *

"There's bound to be something illegal going on here."

The thought had almost been spoken aloud; she had to remind herself to be careful. This was dangerous ground.

Camera-ready phone concealed in her coat pocket, Susan had walked over to the place she now thought of as The Witches' Store. She casually wandered into the car park and had a little poke about in the rubbish waiting there in bins to be collected or lying about on the ground. She couldn't tell which bin belonged to the shop and found nothing that was obviously criminal but she took a few photos anyway. She would zoom them for scrutiny later.

She photographed the new Post Office sign (hadn't the Council said it broke the law?) and the head height blood stained overhanging gutter.

Closer to the witches' lair now, Susan studied the goods standing outside the shop doorway and took a few more pictures for good measure. The most promising was a view showing a small pile of dog mess close to a sack of carrots but she wanted something better. She had hoped to find enough useful and damaging evidence outside the shop but it wasn't to be, so she marched in.

It was midday; the Crabbes had retired to their cottage for lunch, leaving Jenny in charge of both shop and post office. Apart from looking up to see who had come in, Jenny took no further interest in Susan and carried on with trying to balance the Post Office accounts. – A task she found impossible – it was as if someone always pilfered a little money or, perhaps, some stamps every week and the discrepancies in the ledgers grew ever larger accordingly.

Susan had got round to the Post Office counter when she heard Jenny muttering over her arithmetic. Interested, she asked:

"What's the problem Jenny? Money gone missing has it?"

"I wouldn't go that far but it's the same every week, I'm always short and I can't work out why. It's frustrating and you can't just ignore it. The Royal Mail demands that books balance and, if they don't, the Post Mistress has to make up the difference from her own pocket."

"Does Rene do that then? I mean, put her own money in each week?"

"I don't know that she actually does that but the ledgers say she ought to. The thing's a bit of a jumble so I can't see the whole picture."

Susan thought this might be useful and tried to look as if she was reading a shopping list while she made some notes.

"So how much are you out then Jenny?"

"Oh, a few hundred in different places; cash in hand a bit short, stocks of stamps and so on not tying up with what we ought to have on the premises, a couple of worthless IOUs in the cash box each week that I can't honestly include as money in hand. That sort of thing, you know. I don't like the idea that I'll have to explain it all to some Royal Mail inspector one day. I'd as soon be shot of the job before it all blows up."

Susan moved away to resume her pretend window shopping and, while Jenny turned back to her awkward arithmetic, she took some pictures of doubtful sell-by dates, a dead mouse just visible behind the big refrigerator and Rene's battered old working shoes sharing a shelf with the inedible locally made cakes.

Not much, but enough to be going on with.

* * *

'To:

Heads of Planning, Trading Standards and Public Health and Safety

Elcester District Council
Town Hall,
Elcester.

Dear Sir and Madam,

I do not subscribe to the modern belief that everyone should report on neighbours who fail to observe minor rules and regulations, but there are some criminal acts that one just cannot stay silent about.

I refer to the activities of two incompetent, and doubtless criminal, shopkeepers plying their trade in the village of Coldstow.

On the principle that a picture paints a thousand words, I enclose various photographs showing just some of the matters which you will doubtless desire to investigate on receipt of this letter.

Whilst writing to you I also draw your attention to possibly fraudulent activities by the proprietors of this same establishment as evidenced by the unbalanced financial Post Office accounts and, no doubt the trading accounts of the shop.

It is high time that people in positions of trust are made to realise they cannot get away with riding rough shod over their local community.

The population of Coldstow village demands that you take the necessary action.

Yours faithfully,

A Concerned Resident.'

Playing safe, Susan showed her letter to no one and sent it off to the long-suffering Council.

* * *

The Head of Department was looking through her post on the following morning and discussing the day's tasks with her staff.

"We've got another troublemaking letter from those nosey parkers in Coldstow. It's not in the usual Siptac style – nothing like so clever. It's rather childish. Read it through and let me know what you want to do."

Later in the day:

"I've looked at that Coldstow letter. It's a bit strong – I'd love to hear what the Crabbe sisters would say if they saw it. It's a pain but I suppose we shall have to look into some of it at least. If the sender had given a name and address, I would have written back saying the photos show nothing illegal and any problems with Post Office accounts are that body's affair, not the Council."

"Well, here's a suggestion for you: Write your reply, address it to "A Concerned Resident of Coldstow" and put it up on the village hall notice board."

"What shall I say?"

"Oh, just something bland like:

'To the Concerned Coldstow Resident who has drawn the Council's attention to alleged breaches of the law.

We are able to confirm that the Council is satisfied there has been no breach of any food safety regulation that comes under Council control.

Matters of accounting that do not relate to public funds do not come within the Council's remit and cannot be investigated by this department. If you have any issues to raise, these should be addressed to the correct Authority.

The Council trusts that this reply has brought these matters to a satisfactory close.

Signed'

If that doesn't get rid of it, the next stage is the usual notice threatening fines under some rule or another – there's always something to scare people with."

"That wouldn't satisfy me if I'd written to the Council but it's a good first shot at putting all that nonsense to bed. – Make Mr Concerned Resident see he's facing an uphill battle and probably a public one."

"That's the thing. But don't assume you're dealing with a man. That letter was written by a woman for certain and as a matter of fact I think I know who."

And the Head of Department was quite right; she did know the writer; Susan had crossed swords with her not long before over a Tree Preservation Order on Council land. The experience still rankled.

* * *

The Council's notice was a matter of great interest in the village but, at first, no one, apart from Susan, understood exactly what it was about. She was angered by the feeble, laissez faire response; also a little frightened. She hadn't expected a public reply to her letters and felt rising unease about where matters were going.

Joy Siptac had her own ideas about the notice and, as always, she was right. First, she reasoned, this was troublemaking directed at someone with a business, and probably a public one. Otherwise how could the Council have been asked to involve itself in its finances?

There were several businesses in Coldstow and nearby. Dave and Stan's pub and Jack's, a few farms, a farrier, the village shop… And, at that point, Joy saw it all; not quite correctly but near enough.

The target was the shop. It sold food. And it was a community affair and shop finances were a community matter. The shop meant Rene and Louise; so they were the ones under attack.

Apart from herself, Joy could think of several villagers who might want to cause a heap of trouble for the Crabbes but there was only one who had the sort of mind to go about it in this way. So Joy got there in a single mental leap; Susan had written to the Council, probably about some food hygiene issue and, evidently, either Post Office money or the shop takings.

She thought a little longer. The money issue must be the Post Office side of the business; the Council surely wouldn't have ducked a complaint about community shop money, but the Post Office was controlled by a separate authority – exactly as hinted in the Council's letter.

Joy wondered how Susan had discovered anything about the Post Office accounts. That was clever, almost up to her own sneaky standards. Now, the question was, how to make use of this nugget?

Joy never let grass grow under her feet. She walked down to her very own village hall and stood staring deliberately at its notice board. It wasn't long before a few idlers appeared in the hope of a bit of gossip. She waited until she had a dozen in her audience, then said, as if speaking to herself but just loudly enough in her clothes peg voice for everyone to hear:

"I'm surprised at Susan writing to the Council like that. If she had something to say about the shop, why not speak direct to the Crabbes; they're nice people."

It took less than five minutes for Louise to learn that Susan Repplington-Smythe had been sending complaints about her shop to the local Council and another five minutes to find, and tell, sister Rene the news.

So the wars escalated. It wasn't in the Crabbes' nature to slash their enemies' tyres, nor would Susan have stooped to poisoning Rene's soup – although she might have poisoned food in the shop. They were, all of them, much sneakier. Coldstow isn't a nice place to live but it can be interesting, even exciting, at times. You never know what its residents will be up to next.

Chapter 12

Repair for broken people.

The weather was turning much colder in the autumn evenings and Dave had been obliged to light the fires in both bars. Being cash strapped, he had left this until too late in the afternoon. The damp, steaming logs concealed most of their own feeble flames and did nothing to uplift early customers.

He sat in the usual broken chair with his pint of Old Amber on the small side table and Freddie sleeping under it. He had finished his last grass cut in the churchyard for the year and received the usual unsmiling glare from Rene by way of reward, and to cap that, Susan had appeared and given him a lecture about leaving it uncut for the benefit of Coldstow's wildlife.

It was hard, thankless work. He had to tell Rene to find someone else. No more mowing next year, and no more Susan lectures. He drifted off into a half dreaming state as his mind wandered over the day's small events. He suddenly remembered something and reached into his pocket, pulling out a screwed up sheet of stiff paper. It had obviously been soaked by recent rain but was quite dry now.

He had picked it up as a piece of litter to put in with his own rubbish for the next collection but, for want of anything better to do, he gently flattened it out.

It was the Vicar's notice about her meeting on the day she died but it hadn't been near the Church notice board. The paper had been rolled tightly and apparently thrown into long grass. In fact it had been closer to the village hall notice board than the

Church's. He read it through. Something puzzled him. He just couldn't think what.

"I thought I'd find Freddie here. I've been looking all over. I've got a present for her. I haven't got one for you because you're not my friend any more. I waved when I drove past the church and all you did was look bright red and play around with your grass machine. I imagine you're going to marry it one day. I hope you'll both be very happy."

"Oops, sorry. I didn't see you. I was probably thinking about Rene Crabbe and Susan Repplington-thing."

"Well, if you prefer those two to me, I'll save you the trouble of getting me a gin and tonic and buy it myself. Shall I go and sit in the other bar while you indulge your dreams?"

"Dreams my foot! Rene's been her usual rude, ungrateful self and Susan's just given me her umpteenth lecture on why I shouldn't cut grass. I'm tired of them both."

He went over to the bar and ordered her cocktail while she sat down at his table and enjoyed a mutual loving session with his dog as the best substitute.

To her pleasure he was holding two menus as he sat down again.

"I was just looking at something I picked up in the graveyard."

"Not a spare body I hope; I don't think Dave would approve and I'm sure Stan won't."

"No, it's just a village notice but I think there's something wrong here, although I can't work out what."

He spread the paper on the little table for her to see. The writing was still clear and she had no idea what could be wrong about it.

"Where was this? It's odd that anyone would take it down, then screw it up and throw it away. That's not the sort of thing that people who handle church notices do. They're tidy people with scruples about litter. – Aren't they?"

"As ever you have a point there Watson; I hadn't thought of that."

They sat and thought in silence for a while until she caught

Stan's eye and called him across to place their order.

The Happy Fireside had a small and unexciting menu but it didn't matter very much to either of them what they ate when they were together. The company was all.

Later he returned to his puzzle.

"You see there's a patch on the notice we can't read. Perhaps that's the key and I think I know how to deal with that."

"Don't hold me in suspense. What's the plan? Are we going to ask for an exhumation?"

"Not just yet my overkeen young friend, and keep your ghoulish ideas to yourself – pubs have ears, as the Crabbe sisters discovered when they tried to give Susan the heave-ho from the Garden Club. And, by the way, your admirer is in the public bar and he can't stop looking at you."

Involuntarily she turned half round and caught Sam staring straight at her. Her colour changed and she felt cold anger at seeing him there, intruding on a happy evening.

He saw it all; reached out a friendly hand to hold hers. She snatched it away; furious with herself and apologising at once, but it was the very last thing she would have wished for. The first physical contact and the moment had been lost.

"I'm so sorry. It's because I was happy and he spoiled it. Now I've hurt you and I wouldn't want that for the world."

He said nothing in reply, she wasn't the only one trying to put the past to rest and it was just as delicate a journey for him.

"Anyway, my plan is to go over to one or more of Fiona's other parishes and see if her notices are still on their church boards. If we can find one, we shall know what this one's missing."

"Can I come?"

"I'm not going alone. There are wild and scary things out there in churchyards, and I need protection."

She felt massive relief: no permanent damage done.

* * *

The following morning they drove in his car to Ewer where the church notice board had nothing on it except a list of services – out of date now with Fiona gone and no one yet to take her place. They searched the ground nearby but found nothing, so they moved on to Spattersleigh.

Better luck here; Fiona's notice was still on its board. Jokingly behaving like sneaky children, they opened the glass door and pulled out the drawing pins, posting the folded notice through the open car window before casually sauntering around the graveyard, and then the church itself, like sightseeing tourists.

Lastly, for good measure they visited Sideleigh. Here, too the notice had survived and they stole it.

"Sheep as a lamb. If we're caught it will help our defence that we're kleptomaniacs and can't stop ourselves. We oughtn't to get more than six months, and there's remission of course."

Having been tempted by the pleasant tavern in the village square, it was late afternoon when they arrived back at Coldstow. She had some work to do for her clients, spending the rest of that day and part of the next at her desk, and he gave his own garden some of the care it had been missing recently. In fact it wasn't until the next evening that he sat down to study all three notices.

Concentrating on the faded area of the Coldstow version, he could find nothing of interest. But, once he started to read the Spattersleigh notice, he realised what bothered him. It was simple: the wording was different! He spread out the Sideleigh copy – give or take natural handwriting variations, that was the same. The Coldstow notice was the odd one out, and in no small way.

He stared at the wall of his study, covered with photographs of the construction jobs he had worked on, but seeing none of them, as he thought about what this might mean. He had the shadow of an idea, no more. It needed developing.

Placing all three notices side by side, he switched on both desk lights and studied them.

Most probably handwriting experts tell in less than one minute whether two documents are by the same hand. But that's their job: without experience or knowledge of the subject, he had no confidence in his ability to recognise forgery.

But between the Coldstow version and both the other notices there were clear differences. Differences that did not appear between the other two. What was more, the Coldstow handwriting was variable as if the writer had struggled to avoid reverting to her, or his, own natural style.

Here was forgery for certain and it looked very much as if the two similar notices were genuine, the third was false.

The text differences were disturbing. If Fiona had written the two similar notices, she hadn't been responsible for the third. It seemed someone had wanted to tell the world their vicar did not believe in God. If true, a saddening thought. If not the truth, then it was a gross lie. To suggest that someone is deliberately false about their religious beliefs, especially a senior member of a church, is surely a dreadful thing and there it was: Fiona Abbot does not believe what she claims and teaches.

He stared at his wall again. Why do this? Who could gain from it? He could think of several unpleasant villagers who would certainly not go this far and just a few who might, but none of those had any evident motive.

He needed more information.

* * *

The young curate was living in the vicarage alone, apart from Katie, the middle aged housekeeper, who cheerfully performed tasks that required a team of skilled servants in Victorian times, when wages were low and clerical incomes substantial.

He had driven there on the following morning with no idea of what he might learn. But if you're at a loss, he thought, follow a different path, talk to new people, just do something to restart your mind.

It was another rare, brilliant, sunny autumn day; almost cloudless. A stiff breeze whisked shoals of leaves around in eddies and took them, high over his head, away into the distance. It was a day for doing and enjoying. He was always happier to be out of doors, whatever the weather, but that day was special and he rejoiced in it.

There was an amazing number of discordantly coloured flower bouquets lying by the front door of the old building and inside the open porch. Yellow and white chrysanthemums mostly, bunches of roses, mixtures of lilies and ferns. Wondering that Fiona had become so popular in her short period of office, he bent to read the cards – surprised and saddened by seeing they were all from the same three people: the young curate and two names appearing together that he didn't know. The messages were all similar expressions of love and regret.

The main door was open. That helped; at least someone was willing to see visitors. He walked in, feeling that the old house had lost its soul to a modern world that cared nothing for the past. Church buildings ought to have a spiritual feel; here there was none. Better, he thought, to have sold the place to someone who might have loved it and built instead a bland, modern rectory which the Church would have been able to heat.

He called out to let anyone know they had a visitor. There was no reply and he wandered further into the building; stopping to call and listen again with the same result. His search took him to the vicarage study. Again, its door stood wide open. He left it for later inquiry. If he couldn't find anyone when he had looked through the other downstairs rooms, there might be something of interest there.

The kitchen was wonderfully warm thanks to the massive oil fired range making its quiet ticking noises and occasionally bursting into a steady, brief roar. But still no life, not even a church cat. He had relied on speaking with the curate and hesitated to search on his own. The thought of being found poking about in the dead woman's papers with no possible excuse wasn't pleasant. But needs must...

Despite its open door, the study was warmer than he expected. This was a comfortable bright room with views across the front lawns and away to the distant moors. The massive old desk and captain's chair were inviting and he sat down to his task. There were papers everywhere, reflecting the strange and discordant mixture of Fiona's activities and, perhaps, her confused mind.

Much of it was correspondence from an assortment of charities, mostly political, but some were conventional children's aid organisations and institutions fostering green policies. There was nothing in this to help him and he began to work his way through the desk's drawers. Oddly, these were mostly empty. He registered the fact, tucking it away for future thought, and moved on to a large, overfilled letter tray on the floor, evidently put there for want of available desk space.

This seemed to be the vicar's filing tray and here, at last, there were handwritten notes and messages between Fiona and the housekeeper and just two written by her curate. He reflected on this and concluded that most non-verbal communications between the younger women were probably emails but the housekeeper might have been unwilling, or unable, to follow modern ways.

He pocketed a couple of handwritten memos from the curate and two notes from the vicar with replies overwritten by the housekeeper. He had hoped for something more substantial in Fiona's handwriting but those would have to do if he found nothing better.

A few photographs hung on the walls of the old study, mostly historical and showing vicarage life in better times. Among the crowded garden fetes, village teas and a couple of tennis parties were two recent pictures showing Fiona at her ordination and another with her family; he photographed both; at least he now had some pictures as a reminder that she had been a human being, not just a crime victim.

There were three tall filing cabinets in the room; the drawers were unlabelled and he worked through each of them systematically from top down. Most of the content related to matters occurring during the old vicar's tenure and held no interest. He found nothing to aid him in the first two cabinets, but the third was a small gold mine.

The top drawer was full of private correspondence, mostly between the old vicar and his parishioners but one section had several letters to Fiona from her bishop. He was interested to see that the Bishop of Middleton was her uncle. He thought that explained a lot – Fiona's rise in the clerical hierarchy had surprised, and offended, a good many people but she evidently had the high level connections for that not to matter.

He opened the bottom drawer which at first seemed to contain a stack of unused stiff A3 size paper and nothing else. But, beneath this, he caught a glimpse of colouring. Taking out the overlying unused sheets, he uncovered two handwritten parish notices, apparently drafts of the ones that were now lying on his own study desk. Saying a quiet prayer for forgiveness, he folded one and tucked it in his jacket pocket.

It was time to leave; he felt he had ridden his luck to its probable limit; the open doors were warning enough that there was someone about the place. But he was wrong, good fortune had already run its course. A quiet cough, and there was the young curate standing in the study doorway. He immediately wondered how much of his activities had been seen, or heard - filing cabinet drawers aren't silent, particularly old ones and he had been so busy that he hadn't been conscious of the noise he made.

"Who are you?"

"I'm the man who cuts the churchyard grass. I called in to check if the church wants me to carry on doing it next year."

"Why would we not?"

"Well, there seems to be some idea in Coldstow that the grass ought to be left to grow – something to do with wildlife."

"I see. What were you looking for just now?"

Yes, that was the question he didn't want to answer.

"I can't answer that. It's something I need to know."

The curate looked at him steadily. This went on for so long that a desire to run out of the building and away across the fields and woods to some place where he could bare his soul and body to God started and grew in his mind. It became near unbearable and still this child stared; a penetrating gaze that searched his soul.

"I do not think you are evil. At least your answer is an honest one. I have seen you before, talking to Mrs Redfern. She was here yesterday asking some odd questions. She said the two of you are looking into Fiona's death."

"That's correct. Look, I'm sorry if I worried you but I did try to make someone hear when I arrived and I couldn't find anyone…"

"So, you just decided to have a rummage while the coast was clear."

"Yes, exactly that."

"I like your honesty. We could get on. Now tell me what this is about, and do not take me for a fool."

The voice was clear and firm. Close-up now, he realised with a slight shock that this was a young woman, well educated and certainly no fool. For some reason that gave him more confidence.

He talked openly about his suspicions; his concern that the police were on a wrong track, the risk that their main suspect might even be wrongly convicted and the decision to look for evidence that might point to the true killer. But he said nothing about church notices.

She had a strange, rather old fashioned way of expressing herself and he liked her for it. He could imagine how much Fiona would have valued her.

"Thank you for telling me. I shall think it over and we may speak again if I believe it necessary. In the meantime, if you will show me the papers you took from the study, I will decide if you may keep them for the time being. And, as you seem unaware of it, my name is Greta."

"I thought you were Fiona's curate – her helper."

"I was her helper. New vicars generally need help."

He took the various papers from his pockets and spread them out for Greta to see. She picked each of them up and studied them in turn. When she came to the handwritten notice, she looked at him but said nothing.

"You may have all of these until you no longer need them. I wish you and your friend good fortune in your enquiries. God will guide you."

She turned and walked away toward the kitchen. He had been dismissed.

* * *

Early that afternoon by prior arrangement, they were sitting at their favourite table in the garden at Jack's.

"We need to tell each other beforehand whenever one of us is going off digging. Agreed?"

She laughed.

"So, we both got caught moonlighting for clues to impress one another. Yes, agreed. And what did you find?"

"You first."

"I had a nice chat with our curate – did you know it's female by the way?"

"Of course, Sally. I knew it all along."

"Liar. Anyway, she didn't tell me much but it's clear she's got her head screwed on properly. I did learn that she doesn't think Joy killed her vicar friend. She seems to have done some Siptac studying since the police latched onto our Joy. The outcome is Greta doesn't believe they've got the right man or, in this case, woman. I quote: *'Mrs Siptac has character problems but she isn't a murderer.'* A brief but perfect summing up, I think you'll agree. Now what do you have to top that? – Not that it'll take much."

"The first thing is that I have a great hunger – no not that, you shameless woman. I mean a hunger for lunch; I'm starving."

Going to the bar and looking back to her sitting at their table, he suddenly thought how special she was and how lost he would be without her. He hadn't admitted that before and he cursed himself for letting it happen, after all his care. – More grief sometime in the future for sure.

Burying that thought as fast and deep as he could, he ordered their usual drinks and chose a couple of meals from the special menu. – Jack's specials are generally reliable, even if the shepherd's pie and both curries all look much the same. For most people the chips are the best part and they really are very good.

Sitting down again, he said:

"I spent yesterday evening looking at those church notices. I'm sure just one of them is in a different handwriting. It's a good forgery and I'm no expert but I think the whole thing's a fake. It looks to me as if whoever wrote it got tired of the task in places and lapsed a bit. If two are by the same person and one's a bit of a mixture of styles, that probably means Fiona (or maybe our Greta) did both the consistent versions and A.N.Other wrote the Coldstow notice. I wanted to be sure about it so I went over to the vicarage this morning, meaning to pump the curate for whatever I could get out of her. But I couldn't find anyone and the doors were open so I wandered in. The vicar's study door was open so…"

He stopped to take a drink and she butted in.

"So you went in and poked about. I wish I'd been there to keep a lookout and give lots of false alarms to have you jumping out of your skin."

"Thank you, remind me to leave you behind on my next burglary; in fact I did some out of skin jumping but that was later on. No one appeared while I was having a rummage and I found some samples of Fiona's and Greta's handwriting. And, best of all, another copy of the famous notice. I haven't yet had a chance to look at any of it."

"You mean to say that you walked off with the vicar's papers and not even a qualm. You're the coolest customer of all time; and all done in bright sunny daylight too. Now, I'm glad I wasn't there; you're going to need me as your obviously clean living and innocent character witness when your case comes up. Why didn't you go the whole hog and take a removals van to clear the whole place while you were at it? And I notice it's Greta now, not just 'the curate'. How many girl friends of yours am I going to have to dispose of so as to have a clear field?"

Again, she hadn't meant those words to come out, at least not in quite that way. But, had she known their effect on him, she would have said much more.

They broke off from their detective work to eat lunch and order coffees. When Sam's pretty and pert barmaid was out of hearing, he returned to her questions and his burglary.

"Because I can't go stripping a vicarage of all its contents;

it's a religious thing that you wouldn't know about because you weren't brought up proper like I was. And as to girl-friends; the field is quite clear for you just now but I must warn you; it may not stay that way. Grab it while you can. I've just seen Susan whatsit Smythe ogling me from the public bar, or maybe she's ogling you. One never knows these days."

"In that case I'll just pop next door and ask Susan which of us she prefers and if it's me whether she'll come out this evening. Unless you need me for anything."

"Well, I do need you, so Susan must wait. To continue: I was just about to leave after my rummage through the vicar's drawers when Greta appeared. More accurately I noticed her standing in the doorway and she could have been there for some time; I'd been too busy to notice."

"So what did you do, Sherlock? Skip out, leaving her to call the police?"

"I was tempted but she just asked me what I was up to and gave me a long stare – it was quite unnerving. Then she suddenly changed, became almost friendly. To cut a long tale short, I showed her the paperwork I'd nicked and she said we might keep it as long as we needed it. I think she's as concerned as we are to find Fiona's killer and she doesn't believe it's Joy. She's done her own research in that quarter, as you found out."

"You're saying we can have anything we want out of the vicarage to use in this investigation?"

"No, she didn't go that far. She just gave the ok for the papers she looked at and we need to examine them next."

"Well, let's do that this evening. We can spend the afternoon taking Freddie to the seaside; it's high time she had some proper attention."

Freddie enjoyed her walk along the sands quite as much as the happy couple in her charge. The fourth ice cream cone went to the one who finished theirs first. Freddie cheats at this game by dispensing with the use of her teeth.

* * *

Sally hadn't been into his study before; he had forgotten it would be new to her.

It was larger than most people would expect a study to be; an upstairs room that ran the length and width of a separate annex. Generously lit by rooflights that came down to waist height, the high first floor level gave extensive views in three directions: north across his own woodland, south over the village lane and open fields to the distant sea and, on the west side, across his own garden to Downes farm.

This light and airy space with its modern easy chairs, his old desk and the soft grey carpet delighted her immediately. If she had imagined his office, this was exactly what she would have pictured. And pictures figured strongly here – photographs of his work, marine paintings and a few portrait photos. - She longed to ask about these, but it wasn't yet the time.

He spread out the various papers on the top of a large plan chest and they both bent to study them, heads almost touching and each acutely aware of the other.

"Why did you take these memos from Greta?"

"I'm not sure but I must have been struck by something."

He looked at the most recent note, reading aloud:

"Let's see:

'Dearest Filly, I took a call this morning while you were out. From a man called Reppington Scythe or something like that. He wanted the Bishop's email address for sending some charity notice. I gave it him – couldn't see why not.'

And another one:

'Filly, I've done what you wanted this morning. Just as you hoped, they're all hopping mad. – Should make for an interesting day in Coldstow. Are you quite sure about this?'

Well, that one looks more than merely interesting. Fiona's winding up some people and expecting trouble on the day (I presume it's the day she died). We can ask our little reverend curate what it means I suppose. Apart from that one, I don't think there was anything that grabbed me as being special; I was simply looking for samples of Greta's handwriting. It's clear from these that she didn't write any of the notices; her writing slopes the opposite way and it's more graceful."

They turned to the Church notice taken from the vicarage and he placed the other three copies beside it for comparison.

It was immediately clear that this latest version was little different from the notices at Spattersleigh and Sideleigh. Apart from variations to be expected between handwritten texts, the only difference was a change of layout apparently intended to make better use of the page size.

He switched on a pair of desk lamps and studied the handwriting minutely. He spent so long on this that she walked across to his desk and sat down in his chair, swivelling it gently back and forth as she watched him at work, absent-mindedly playing with papers and allowing herself to slide into daydreams.

"I'm absolutely sure now that the one which says she doesn't believe in God is a forgery and the others aren't. So, the next question is: Who's the forger? And then why? Why was it done? It's a lot of work by someone and no return on it unless it's just to irritate the vicar. I suppose that might be all it is. What do you think Brains?"

She got up suddenly.

"I've got to go; something I have to do."

He was frightened, at first for her, then for himself – that was the greater fear.

"Something's wrong; how can I help?"

She waved her arms about as if she was being attacked by a wasp, shook her head violently and hurried out of the room without answering, leaving him bewildered, distressed, horrified.

What was that about? Another sleepless night coming; he knew the signs.

Chapter 13

Empires at war.

"What I want to know is, where did she get her information about the Post Office accounts? They're not public records for every Tom, Dick and Susan Smith to poke their long noses into."

Rene was speaking and Louise half listening as she ate breakfast.

Rene continued, thinking aloud:

"Those accounts go to the Royal Mail and nowhere else; apart from our own accountant, and then only when she asks to see them - which she hasn't done so far this year. That leaves only us and Jenny; I'll question her when she gets in later. If she's working with the enemy then…"

"Then what, Rene? Are we going to kill her too? Like you killed Fiona?"

"For goodness' sake Louise, you're going to get us arrested if you keep on like this. I told you: I had nothing to do with the vicar's death."

"Of course not; anything you say dear. I know when to keep quiet."

Rene glared at her sister, feeling just for the moment, that she really would like to murder someone, and that one not far away.

She sat and thought for a while, then set off to open the shop and wait for poor Jenny, who was even then leaving her home for the same destination. Jenny, however, was completely unaware of the trouble she had caused and thinking of nothing more than her never ending task of keeping both shop and proprietors in order.

"Ah, Jenny, I want a word with you."

And good morning to you too, she thought, but stayed silent as she walked into the back room behind Rene, who was speaking without turning to look at her employee.

"Louise and I have been targeted by someone in the village who has been telling stories to the Council."

Rene turned and waited to see what effect this had, but Jenny remained silent, giving her just a lofty eyebrowed questioning look.

"As you don't seem interested, I shall not waste my time with long explanations. The fact is that we have been accused of mismanaging sub-Post Office money. In particular that the accounts do not balance."

"Well, they don't, as I've told you umpteen times, and they won't balance until you put back into the business the money needed to square things up."

"I don't know anything about that. What I do know is that someone, who I suspect to be you, told this troublemaker a pack of lies that amounted to accusing us of fraud."

Jenny felt herself going through the same temperature and colour changes she experienced on the day of her row with Sally Redfern.

"I did nothing of the sort. She wormed it out of me that the figures don't agree. That is the truth and I stand by it. It's not a matter for concealment and I'm not going to lie for you. Anyway, I've seen the Council's answer on the board; your whistle-blower was making a lot of complaints about the shop; not just the money side of the Post Office. It's obvious you've upset this someone in a big way and they've decided to have their revenge by stating a few home truths. You have only yourselves to blame. And, by the way, I resign. You can run the shop all on your own from now and you can also do your own accounts – I wish you luck with that impossible job."

And, with that satisfying speech, Jenny walked out.

It wasn't at all what Rene intended.

In every organisation there are doers and parasites, sometimes there is just one doer and a positive host of the other sort. It is a doer's task to deal with problems and to carry out all the regular day-to-day jobs that are called for by the business, whatever it is. The parasites take the credit – that is their task and part of the whole process. No matters can get done without at least one doer and no one will appreciate what is done unless there are parasites to tell the world theirs is the achievement.

In Coldstow's village store, Jenny was the sole doer. Lacking her to do the detail work, Rene well knew the Crabbe shop empire would wither and fade to nothing, nor would that take long.

It took all the pride swallowing that Rene was capable of. She followed Jenny up the lane toward her home, calling after her like a squawking hen and frequently tripping over her own feet in her hurry. Jenny got to her front door first but Rene was up to her before she had it open. Jenny turned to face her pursuer, ready to fight now on her home ground.

"Well, Miss Crabbe, what do you want now? We surely have nothing more to say to each other after your accusations against me."

"I do understand how you must feel Mrs Allen and I do apologise if I gave the impression I am dissatisfied with your work. That isn't the case at all. It's just that we, Louise and I, had just learned about Mrs Repplington-Smythe's shameful activities and I reacted in a moment of ill-temper. That was wrong of me. I quite see that my complaint is entirely against her. Will you please withdraw your notice and stay on at the shop?"

And, digging ever deeper into this unfamiliar world of grovelling, she added (to her own disgust):

"We, I, need you, the shop won't run without you."

Jenny couldn't let this go on. It was frankly revolting to see and hear.

"Very well Rene. I will stay. But I want a twenty per cent increase in salary – and I shall require you to bring my pay up to date immediately; some of it's almost six months overdue. And you must pay into the Post Office the shortfall in the accounts. That has to come from your own money, not out of the shop till, or there'll just be the same black hole in another place. I'm not going to cover for you any more on this. If the cash situation isn't put in order, I shall tell your accountant I'm not going to be involved in the book-keeping any more and why. That'll force her to do an audit and make an official report – your business won't survive that."

As she agreed to these distressing terms, Rene was telling herself that she wouldn't keep her promise. The shop was hers (well, almost) and she wasn't going to be told how to run it by an upstart servant.

And so Rene's little war with servant Jenny was entirely lost and still there remained the pressing need for revenge on Susan Repplington-Smythe.

The day passed in Coldstow's Community Store much as it usually did, save for the inevitable sly comments. A few customers bought a few items, others stood about outside hoping to pick up, or foment, the odd bit of gossip that might enlarge upon the Crabbes' misconducts or the issues hinted at in the Council's public letter.

It was an opportunity not to be missed by the Siptac who, during the day, appeared off and on from nowhere, made the occasional spiteful comment in her clothes peg voice, then disappeared to the same place, taking her floppy orange busby with her and leaving a little more trouble behind on each occasion.

"Good morning Jenny. Have you managed to balance your books yet? If you haven't, you must tell the Royal Mail, but of course you know that. I've checked the Rules; I can help you there or I'll do it for you, if you want."

"Good afternoon Louise. Have you cleared up your mouse problem? I think I've just seen one under your refrigerator. Or it might have been something larger – I hope it isn't what I think it is."

"Good afternoon Rene, I see you're still keeping filthy old shoes in the food display. And the cakes aren't covered. I expect Susan's informed the Council already. If she hasn't, surely someone will. The public has to be protected."

And at last, the underlying aim came to the surface when the

Crabbes, Jenny and everyone else had grown tired of the constant barrage and heartily sick of seeing the Siptac's busby bobbing along on its way to and fro.

"It's too much to expect a couple of old ladies to manage a place of this size and keep up to date with all the latest regulations as I do."

"I'm perfectly capable, thank you Mrs Siptac. By the way, how is your husband's little flirtation with his barmaid going on? I'm surprised you don't mind about it, but then we all live in these modern times with their modern thinking and modern ways.

It would distress me if my husband was in a bar every night spending my money on a mere girl much less than half his age. I wonder what she sees in him, apart from your hard earned money. It's certainly not his looks although I suppose you're used to those and hardly notice any more."

Sensing defeat in this little skirmish, Joy wandered away, taking just a moment to pick up a vile looking cake and pointedly read its sell by date before dropping it in apparent disgust on Louise's offending work shoes.

That awful day in Coldstow's Community Store and Post Office came to an end, as all bad things must. The shop closed at five thirty, when the loungers and gossip-hunters drifted away for want of any further grist to their mills. The Crabbes went home to refresh themselves with tea taken from the store and consider what was to be done.

"I think this is one occasion when we deserve an evening out with dinner and a glass of wine at the Jack's as Good as his Master."

"I'd like that Rene. Can we afford it?"

"Of course. I'll take the money from the Post Office till as usual."

"Haven't you been told not to do that?"

"It's our Post Office and therefore our money."

An hour later, the sisters were sitting at a discrete table in Jack's restaurant. The intended two glasses had expanded into a bottle of the best white wine that the pub had to offer and they were waiting for the waitress to come and take their orders for food off the main menu. None of the cheaper "todays specials" had appealed to either of them.

"Well, there's a thing. Look behind you, Rene."

"What am I supposed to be looking at?"

"It looks very much like a naughty husband having an evening out while the cat's away. In the Public Bar and not a care in the world who sees him. He's a lad and no mistake; it's a different woman every week. And just see at the bar on this side. – that's another of his little flirtations. The famous Sally Redfern. And, as the Siptac woman might say, wearing a bra for a change. Quite the modest one all of a sudden."

Rene looked as directed. There, as Louise said, for all to see was Samuel Repplington-Smythe attempting to put his arm around the pretty and pert barmaid who was trying to gather up empty glasses while keeping the amorous Sam where he belonged – out of reach. Suddenly the girl seemed to give in. She turned to Sam, put her arms around his neck and kissed him full on his lips. Had she seen across the bar what Rene was doing? - We shall never know.

When it came to opportunities, Rene was as quick witted as Joy Siptac. She had her phone out of her bag and camera-ready before Louise had finished speaking. A few moments later it was back where she kept it and the nice waitress was taking their order.

"I believe we have reason for a little extra celebration Louise. We shall enjoy our coffee liqueurs and a pudding each I think."

* * *

The choice had been between email and a hand posted envelope. Hand posting had won on the grounds that, barring any late night witness, it was untraceable. The disadvantage was the possibility that the wrong person opened it. They decided to take that risk and, in the event, all went very well. – If destroying two people's lives is a well thing to do.

* * *

On the following morning, Susan saw the envelope lying on her doormat among the bills that arrived by the more usual post.

'From a well-wisher. A happy evening out in the pub for our famous fraudster.'

She read the typed words before unfolding the pictures. But they weren't a disappointment when she saw them. In fact they were really very good, considering the problems of artificial light and general activity in a busy pub. Sam had been still at just the right moments.

She stood, shocked and silent, for one long minute, wondering how much more trouble she could stand from her wretched husband and who might have been the picture taker. Her immediate thoughts took her to the Crabbe sisters but then she felt sure neither of them had the necessary skill. She couldn't even imagine them with a mobile phone. - It doesn't do to underestimate your enemies.

She sat in her kitchen, waiting, yet again, for the source of all her misfortunes, and when he appeared, she wondered why she had ever married the man and, once married to him, why she stayed so.

Not for the first time, Sam was hung over. Neatly dressed and freshly shaved he could look reasonably attractive, unless you came very close. But now, he was simply awful to see, nor was the smell appealing.

He sat down, evidently expecting her to produce breakfast.

In its place she silently spread on the table in front of him the four enlarged photos so kindly printed by Rene and delivered in the early morning hours by Louise. He said nothing – there was nothing he could have said that would have made any difference to what was coming.

The mime continued; Susan pointed to the door; Sam rose and left.

* * *

The Crabbe sisters watched Sam walking away down the village lane, head bent, unkempt and incompletely dressed. It was a sad sight but the sisters had no sympathy to give.

"I think we may say that the proper person opened our little gift Louise."

"Yes. We don't need to kill her now, do we Rene?"

* * *

Perhaps it was the activity of some malevolent fate, or mere coincidence. On the same day that Susan opened her hand-delivered, typed envelope in the morning, he opened another in the afternoon; the letter inside was written in a cultured, feminine hand.

'My dearest Grass Cutter.

I find I haven't the words to say what I want so much to tell you. I can only hope and trust that you, with your kindly understanding, will already know what's in my heart without my clumsy efforts on this page. But I must try.

Fingers crossed (if that's possible with a pen), here I go:

I've loved every minute of our time together; a gentle, unhurried, happy, getting-to-know-one-another courtship. It's what I wanted and dreamed of ever since… well, it doesn't matter since when.

But every day I wake up scared that this is the day it's all going to go wrong. Yes, I know, that's weak and cowardly. I can hear you saying:

"You will never get what you want if you shy away when it counts."

And you would be right. I know that, but I still couldn't trust myself, or maybe I didn't trust your love.

The other day when I sat with you in the office, I watched you at work and loved you more than ever. Suddenly I was horribly frightened; I knew if I stayed there for one more minute, I'd shout 'I love you – say you love me. Say it now.'

But I couldn't do it - you must understand - how frightening that would have been for you – how destructive to us both.

Now you know how I feel. At last I've managed to declare myself, trusting, hoping you feel the same and will tell me so.

And now, the most dangerous part; the throw of the dice that settles all for good, or for terrible:

I shall be in our favourite bar tomorrow, and again the following evening. Come to me then if you will. If you don't then, my friend, I shall ask no more of you, I shall leave this troubled place to start a new life yet again.

With all my love.

Your very own Watson.'

He looked at the date – it was written three days ago. He felt sick. Why hadn't he looked at his mail before? Normally he didn't miss a day. Perhaps he had foreseen something like this and been scared.

He sat down at his desk, gently swinging one way and the other, just as she had done a few evenings ago. The room smelled slightly of her familiar scent; his papers lay just as she had left them. He wanted to freeze everything and hold it all just as it was; for ever.

Hours passed before he rose slowly from his chair and walked stiffly out of the room, downstairs and across his dark garden.

* * *

It was the second night when she had hoped he would come. Sam had played his last games with his barmaid friend; the Crabbe sisters had tottered unsteadily back to their cottage and the bar was closing. Sally paid her bill, picked up her handbag and walked out to the car park. Her hopes, more accurately her expectations, had been destroyed and she had no clear plan; she hadn't thought she would need one.

She returned home and, like an automaton, started to pack a case. She would leave straightaway with enough necessaries to stay in hotels while she decided what to do. The house could be sold later. It was four in the morning when she drove away with a feeling of deadness in heart and mind that had nothing to do with want of sleep.

* * *

By the time he woke from troubled dreams and painfully realised afresh that he had lost her, she was far away, breaking contact with her life in Coldstow.

In time, she intended to look for a new job and another place to live but before any of that, she half decided to take a wandering holiday in the States. – In that case, no amount of searching would have found her. But something happened and the American tour idea was discarded for two reasons; first there was an unmissable job opportunity; secondly, Sally came across a couple of good friends.

* * *

His search wasn't easy; she hadn't meant it to be and he really knew very little about her past life, her family or her previous home, only that she had come from Sussex, or perhaps it was Surrey, and that her surname was Redfern. If she had been, or still was, married, she had never mentioned any other name.

But he did have the registration number of her car; she had bought it new from a dealer in the Home Counties and the sales manager let slip enough from her records for him to learn where Sally had lived at that time. Perhaps she had some romantic sympathy with the lost soul who pressed her so hard for help, or maybe she was simply careless about dealership rules.

It got him nowhere, however. The house she had lived in for a short time was a rented property and it had changed hands twice since then. The latest tenants didn't know any Sally Redfern and they made it plain they didn't care either. But the neighbours had known, and liked, her. It was from them he learned some more of her history. They kindly invited him in and offered tea while they chatted as if they were all old friends. He found himself wondering why no one in Coldstow had ever been that kind to him in the years he had lived there. The difference between West Country ways and the South East perhaps.

His new friends had no idea where Sally might be found. They thought she had been married to someone and left him for some reason but they didn't know what. It was all very vague and unsatisfactory.

He tried some more possible leads; local shops, a couple of sports clubs and then no more. He realised he didn't even know exactly what she had done for a living. Technical author, he thought but that wasn't enough to take him anywhere.

He returned home after a couple of fruitless days, not giving up, but taking time to think.

He collected Freddie from her favourite kennels. She made it plain she was missing Sally and gave the kennel staff a cheerful goodbye while ignoring him. He knew this would go on until she decided it was time to forgive the unkindness of being left behind. He would have to work on that with some extra treats and an invitation to sleep upstairs at the end of his bed, but there was nothing he could do for his own pain.

It seemed little had happened in Coldstow over the previous few days and, for want of anything better to work on, the spiteful ones who had noticed Sally's absence made the most of it.

Unsubtle and insensitive as ever, Susan asked him if he had fallen out with his "dear lady friend" and invited him to call in at any time for "tea and a chat" while the Siptac put it differently:

"I suppose your little Sally has got fed up with you and gone off somewhere to do a bit of topless modelling. Pity she hasn't the figure for it."

He ignored both women but made a silent vow to stay well clear of Susan as long as Sam was away and a personal promise to deal with Joy when the time was right. It would come, but when it eventually did, he was to find himself playing the strange role of Siptac rescuer, rather than avenging angel.

Once home, he made an effort to think more clearly.

Remembering her mention of a family solicitor, he fished around to find the firm's address.

'Dear Mr Clarke,

I have been trying to locate Sally Redfern, a friend and neighbour of mine from Coldstow. I recall her mentioning your name as her solicitor and a friend of the family.

Would you be willing, please to pass a letter on to Sally on my behalf? I am not asking that you undertake anything that would compromise your position in any way.

Please be assured, I am simply trying to reach a friend; I think she will vouch for me if you speak with her.

Yours sincerely.'

It was painfully difficult to get even that far. Every sentence had been written and rewritten until the letter stopped making sense when he re-read it yet again.

He took Freddie for another reflective walk and imagined what Mr Clarke would think on getting his awkward letter. Probably he would be disgusted by it. Worse, suppose he passed it to Sally and it disgusted her? On his return he gave it to the office shredder and the machine showed him what it thought of his silliness.

He was coming to believe that she really didn't want to hear from him. – That being so, he decided at last it would be wrong to continue; the thought that he might offend her horrified him. At that, he abandoned his search, but he couldn't stop his mind migrating to subjects it wanted to think about, or torture him with.

* * *

It wasn't in his nature to do nothing and mope in a corner. Whatever had gone wrong in his life, and there was plenty, he had always faced his troubles squarely and got on with the tasks in hand. So he returned to his investigation into the deaths of Jo

Downe and Fiona.

He did this without the help of her enthusiasm and cheerful humour, but with all his old determination. He liked to think he was doing it for her. That comforted him.

175

Chapter 14

Secrets of an inn.

It was time for the bank manager's monthly review of the Happy Fireside's finances.

With Jo's departure and the manager's "suggestion" to move away from locally bought ingredients in favour of a cheap ready meal caterer, the figures were looking a good deal better and, as Dave pointed out, Christmas was around the corner – even Coldstow's pub might expect to cater for a few seasonal parties.

So, the manager looked as pleased with the success of her advice as bank managers ever do look pleased about their less profitable customers.

"I think we may have turned a corner, David. It's such a pity you didn't take advice earlier. I hope you follow my suggestions in future. I'm always here to help, you know."

Remembering the manager's distant behaviour as long as the Happy Fireside was evidently on a road to certain ruin, Dave didn't know anything of the sort. Well, at least she was friendly now, so he set out to ride his luck.

"We want to improve the business and that's where the Bank can help…"

It was a full hour later when Dave left the bank and walked down Larkston High Street, a little surprised, but very pleased, to have got the loan he wanted.

He sat down with Stan who had been hiding in a corner of the Blue Bowl Café, trying to spin out his cold coffee under the impatient eyes of its proprietor and two of her regular lunchtime diners kicking their heels by the entrance door.

"I got it; all of it. She swallowed the figures we put together; I wish we'd massaged them a bit more. She must have been putting gin in her tea or something, I've never known her smile before."

"Perhaps she fancies you – if she does, you'd do well to go back and ask for more."

"Stop that; when jealousy gets the better of you, it doesn't make you any nicer, and things start to go wrong. Remember Jo. Now for the next step."

Over the following few days the Happy Fireside's bank balance grew steadily larger. Surprisingly, in the face of this uncommon liquidity, stock levels fell, unpaid debts rose and the few remaining staff missed their wages.

And suddenly the pub's bank account was empty and David Wood and Stanley D'Arteur couldn't be found. The several workless villagers waiting for the Happy Fireside to open one lunch time were at first puzzled by the lack of welcoming lights, then worried by the pub's locked doors and, finally, angered to discover that Coldstow had apparently lost its main centre of social affairs and the only place where one might buy a drink or enjoy a meal.

The rumours spread instantly – Dave had finally cracked, murdered Stan and legged it with the month's takings, or it was Stan who disposed of Dave after a row about an affair with the local butcher and then killed himself with the butcher's own meat axe, or, more likely than anything else, the pair had simply run away from creditors.

Hearing loud voices and even some shouting, he left his house and walked toward the pub. A couple of eager gossips buttonholed him to tell what they knew, and a good deal they did not. He turned away, going around to the rear of the building and the untidy piles of sundry barrels and crates typical of such places.

Hidden from sight, just beyond an abandoned refrigerator, one of the rear doors was unlocked. He opened it and walked in on the stone-floored corridor toward Jo's one time territory; the kitchen area. The only illumination came from three fire exit signs and what little daylight got through the still-curtained windows. It was warm there, and a small oven was hot – they hadn't been gone more than an hour.

The corridor was carpeted now; he walked on, emerging between the two unlit bars which, more than anything else, emphasised the strangeness of that silent place. He looked into the two empty tills and glanced at the rows of optics, all empty apart from a couple of obscure spirit bottles.

But he found what he was looking for. There, under the counter, were not one, but two, almost empty whiskey bottles. The first, he thought, might have been the bottle he had last seen on the day Jo died, or something almost identical to it; he didn't recognise the label, but he wasn't a whiskey drinker. The other was a familiar brand. He managed to slide the awkward things into his deep coat pockets and turned to leave.

For no very good reason, he went along the corridor toward the narrow back staircase, not returning the way he had come. At the top of the stairs he hesitated, looking at the closed doors and wondering if he really wanted to know what was in those rooms.

"May as well complete the search, I shan't get another chance, that's for sure" he thought.

The first was a neat en suite twin bedroom, light cream in colour with dark green curtains, quietly waiting with its small television and tray of tea making things, all ready to serve paying guests that would never arrive. Then two more equally tidy guest rooms, both decorated in the same cream and green theme – singles this time - and a separate shared bathroom with its pile of clean white towels. All the rooms were warm and welcoming and that was the total of the Happy Fireside's paying accommodation.

A closed door across the corridor led into the proprietors' quarters. It wasn't locked.

He looked briefly into what had evidently been Dave and Stan's bedroom – a large suite with its own bathroom. In marked contrast to the guest rooms, this was untidy. Plainly the drawers and open wardrobe had been stripped in a hurry. The bed was unmade, the floor littered with discarded clothes and personal items. The room itself looked tired and dated; no recent redecoration here and the carpet was worn bare in places. Dave and Stan had lived their innkeeper's lives without money or luxury.

He turned away quickly and opened the last door on this floor. As he expected, this was the pub's "conference room". As far as he could remember, it hadn't been used since the village hall had been built, and it showed it. The place smelled musty but, like the kitchen, it was warm. Dave wasn't concerned any longer about heating bills.

The windows were all curtained and the place was faintly lit by two more exit signs and a skylight. For Coldstow it was a surprisingly large room, probably at one time the upper area of a large cart shed built at the side of the farmhouse itself. The bare wooden floor stretched ahead of him. There was a small bar on one side and a stack of bent metal chairs.

Even in the poor light, he could see the room held nothing to interest him; he crossed to the double doors on the far side and walked down the wide staircase into the pub's reception area. He could hear voices from the crowd gathered outside and turned to find his way out by the hidden unlocked door. He saw no one as he walked slowly back home with the bottles bumping against his hips.

That evening he returned to his office, partly to do a little work but mostly just to sit in his chair and touch the papers on his desk as she had done. Her perfume could hardly be sensed now, but he liked to think it was still there. With his troubled mind, this was not perhaps a wise thing to do but he could not stay away. The room was becoming central to his being.

He had brought his stolen bottles with him and now stood them on his desk, unsure what, if anything, they had to tell; even wondering why he had taken them. If there was a clue here, how would he know? Sitting there with Jo's murder on his mind, he thought of Chris Downe and the worry that his friend might have been wrongly caught up in her murder. - A curious parallel with Joy Siptac's entanglement in Fiona's death and Joy was probably quite innocent of that, too.

After what had happened to him recently, he had half forgotten his vow to clear those two innocents. That promise wasn't for the sake of friendship but because it was the right thing to do. No one else seemed to be making any effort to find the truth behind either death, police included.

He was sure she would have expected him to finish their investigation. Well, he would do just that; for her as much as anyone. In truth, also for himself but, being him, he wasn't likely to admit that.

He called Chris's number and for once got through. Could they meet tomorrow evening at Jack's? Chris sounded pleased. Perhaps he was just as lonely and lost.

In the meantime, he turned back to the enigmatic bottles. He couldn't resist it. He fetched a glass from the office drinks cupboard and unscrewed the cap from the one with the unfamiliar label. If he was right, this was probably the criminal offence of interfering with evidence. But of course he had already gone too far; the bottle ought to have been left where it was, under the bar at the Happy Fireside.

He poured half a glass and sipped. He knew nothing about whiskey himself. Not liking that particular spirit, it was natural he would think it was unpleasant; that proved nothing. He drank off the remainder of the glass; if he wanted to know how it would affect him, it was pointless to pick at it.

* * *

He woke late the following morning, still in his office chair, feeling ill and vaguely aware of a night's torment by savage dreams. Surely one glass of whiskey ought not to have such a vile effect.

He rang Chris again, suggesting they met at his own house instead of Jack's. But Chris needed to be at the farm that evening so they agreed to meet there at seven. At least that kept matters private; Jack's was too public and dangerous.

* * *

Chris appears to be even younger than he is. It's something to do with his pink face and a slightly wide-eyed look, as if he has just been astonished by some pleasing revelation. On the rare occasions when he removes his flat cap, his fair hair makes him seem even more youthful, but don't be fooled, he is a strong man and very good at his tough farming job. Having cruelly lost his parents when he was much younger, he has had to manage the Downes empire alone and he has done it very successfully.

Apart from his wellingtons, indoors and out his uniform has ever comprised a dull green zip up all-in-one overall bearing numerous indecipherable stains, thick grey socks and his farmer's flat cap. Very likely he has on any number of garments out of sight, but there's no way of knowing what, so one must assume that what one sees is what one gets.

Chris is never embarrassed about his appearance and, looking at his friend that evening, he thought:

"The man's always completely natural; pretence isn't a part of his world. I can't imagine him doing anything underhand, unless it's filling in his agricultural grant forms and he simply wouldn't see any wrong in that."

They sat down in the room where Jo had lain after she died; in fact, it might have been where her life ended. He realised suddenly that he didn't know exactly *where* it had happened – here, or in his car – an upsetting thought.

As ever, they talked about their common interests, about the world's problems, farming and politics. Eventually they came round to Jo.

"Chris, I've got a question or two about Jo. Are you OK with that? Say if not; I won't push it; you're the only friend I have in this bloody place and there's no way I'm going to lose you."

"I'm OK. If I don't want to answer anything I'll say so and we can let that one go."

"First off, I was down at the Happy Fireside soon after Dave and Stan skipped. A back door was open and I had a look around the place – call it natural curiosity – after all it's not every day your local publicans disappear."

"You're a cool one. I heard about the crowd in front of the pub; if they'd seen you, you might have had a deal of explaining to that clottish Constable. He's a menace and definitely not one to invite into your life. So, I imagine you found something in your rummage, or you wouldn't be telling me you broke in."

"Correct. Although there was no breaking about it; the place is wide open to the world. Making the shortest possible story of it, I found two whiskey bottles under the bar. I think Dave used one or other of them for Jo's drink on the day we lost her."

"Did you by Heaven? – What makes you think you've got the right bottle? It's quite a while since then. Surely the original would have been emptied and thrown out long ago?"

"I don't think so. Jo had her own whiskey under the bar and Dave served her from there. And he put the bottle back afterwards; I was there at the time. Of course neither of them may be *the* bottle but, on balance, I think I'm right. There were several brands set up on the bar optics. Jo's wasn't. Both those bottles were kept separate for a reason."

"So where does that take us?"

"I'm not sure. But last night I drank half a glass from one of them and, either I'm allergic to whiskey, or that bottle's been spiked. It sent me to sleep in a chair for a solid twelve hours during which I hallucinated nightmares and I'm not the sort that normally has them.

And we may not be short of a motive. I wouldn't have made anything of all this, except that Jo had been telling everyone in the bar that Stan and Dave were watering drinks and short-changing customers over food. She may have had something more to say which Dave didn't want to come out."

Chris sat silently digesting this for so long that his friend wondered if it was a sign of guilt and what he would do if he was suddenly faced with an admission to Jo's murder. But after a while:

"That was brave and foolish of you, old friend. If your suspicion's right, you could have been killed. You must have known that. I'm glad you got away with it. But, for my sake, if not yours, please don't do it again. So what's the next of your looney plans?"

"I'll leave the next one and come back to it later. This is where it gets a bit difficult."

"I'd like to know what you'd describe as very difficult. To me, none of this is easy by any stretch."

"On the night Jo died, I picked her up, put her in my car and drove her over here. I couldn't find you anywhere. The only person to ask was someone driving a loader. Nice enough but I thought he was looking at me a bit strangely; suspicious of me perhaps. Maybe nothing in that but my puzzle's about you, Chris. While I was here, you turned up apparently looking for Jo in the Happy Fireside. Why didn't I see you on my way here?"

"Does that matter? Do I have to explain where I am twenty fours a day?"

"Steady! If you don't want to answer, you don't have to, and I won't mind. We agreed that, remember?"

"All right. Sorry, I'm just tired; but it's nothing sinister. I wasn't on the farm when you brought Jo here. I was on next door's land. – Pat Westleigh's place. The cattle in one of the sheds got out; they'd spread themselves over Westleigh's and I was desperate to get them back. Pat has his knife into me for something else. The last thing I needed was a cattle trespass problem with him; he's small, spiteful and looking to make trouble. So, I had everyone out there rounding up cows as fast as we could. I'd have asked you if I'd known you were about. It was late when we finished and I was worried about Jo. She'd had that nasty text from Dave and I should have been with her that evening. She deserved that. When we found the last of them, I left my people to get the cows back under cover and went straight to the pub. If Jo was there having a row with that idiot, Dave, she might have needed my support. I didn't take the route you were on at all."

"Understood; I don't know any of the Westleighs. What's your problem with them? They're your closest neighbours; not good to have a feud there."

"I'd rather not say, except that it's a family thing and it goes back a generation to my mum and dad. God bless them, they didn't deserve all that trouble."

"Fair enough. Now back to the bit I skipped earlier. I've had a funny experience with Jo's whiskey (assuming that it *is* hers) but I don't drink the stuff. You do. Are you ok to give it a try yourself? If it has no effect on you, perhaps we can put a line through the people in the pub that night as murder suspects. – Maybe."

"You ask a lot. If I'm to die, I'd rather it was for a better reason - like saving you from your daft ideas. But I'll do it. After all what's my life worth compared with your self esteem? Have you got it with you?"

"Indeed I have. If you like to fetch a glass – a small one I think!"

He watched Chris pour. Despite the warning, he filled the glass, and it wasn't a small one. He drank; a sip first, then most of the rest.

"Stop! – Please!"

They sat and looked at each other for a while. Chris felt rather dreamy and said so, then, without warning, he leaned over to one side and immediately began to snore. That was all, no excited babble and none of Jo's thrashing about. He woke up later, having slept for just an hour while his friend watched over him.

"I suggest you go to bed, Chris. We'll talk again soon."

"What about trying the other bottle?"

"I don't think we should risk it; what we need is a professional testing lab. But I reckon the other is ordinary whiskey – one had to be. What brand did Jo drink?"

"She wasn't very fussed; generally the least expensive on offer at the Larkston supermarket."

He returned home, more puzzled than ever and wishing he knew a competent doctor with a good knowledge of drugs, alcohol included.

He ought to have gone to bed then himself. It had been a long, hard day, and poor rest the previous night, but he couldn't resist going into his office once more to sit there, picturing her, and trying to recall her perfume, although it was quite gone by then. It was becoming a habit, half painful, half soothing, pathetic and unstoppable.

* * *

'Mr Kenny Selliford
Technical Publishing Manager
Historical Scientific Publishing Ltd
4071B Southampton Row
London WC1

Dear Mr Selliford,

I refer to our telephone conversation today when you kindly offered to pass my letter on to your author, Sally Redfern.
As you will see, I have left the envelope open so that you may know it contains nothing that might cause Sally any distress. The opposite in fact.
Thank you so much for your help in this.

Yours sincerely,

Greta Abbot.
The Vicarage, Sideleigh, Elcester'

Chapter 15

A garden empire flourishes

Susan was coming to terms with a life alone. For most of their married life, Sam had been an embarrassment to her, letting her down in company, undermining her efforts to dominate and manage the local community and to be admired and respected for her high ideals; eventually bringing down her small empire by his crimes in the pensions department. Perhaps his greatest sin up to then was to be caught for that.

All these things she had tolerated, yet liking him ever less and longing to be shot of him. By the time they moved to the village, she had reached an age where one must despair of escape. The years ahead are too few, the effort too great.

But Sam had found it in himself to commit just one more sin. The one that she could never forgive. A girl, easily young enough to have been the daughter she never had. And an affair carried on in public - the open insult to her. No, it was more than anyone might bear.

It might have been different if there had been a flaming, one-sided row; words said that had been held back for twenty years now out in the open at last. But it hadn't happened that way. There had been no clearing of the air, just that mime sequence, and now she was without him. So she sat again in her comfortless kitchen, lost and missing him, not for any love on her part, but through the painful silence and loneliness of friendless Coldstow. She had often imagined herself throwing Sam out of the house but always in her thoughts this opened up a happy future at the centre of a kindly community with friends and, in her most secret hopes, a partner who would value her as Sam never had.

Susan didn't have either Joy's cleverness or Sally's natural warmth, and she knew it. But she did have grit and the determination to come up fighting when things went wrong for her, as they so commonly did.

She again thought over the social openings Coldstow had to offer. Susan wasn't the sort to enter a public house, except with a chaperone. Besides, she had no idea how to strike up acquaintance in such places. The thought of trying made her cringe. As to sports, she had never been keen on playing games of any sort, and her effort to push her way into church management had fallen at the first hurdle.

There remained the Garden Club. Well, she was its President, and you can't get higher than that in any organisation - can you?

Susan was the president who wasn't wanted, who had clung to office by the narrowest vote only just after her election. Not a very solid base from which to relaunch her life. However, being what she is, that thought didn't come to mind as she planned her social career in horticulture.

* * *

'Coldstow Garden Club
Outing on 5th November

To all our members.

You will be pleased to learn that I have arranged an outing for the entire Club on Saturday 5th November.

We shall be going to the RHS garden at Bridesley.

I have arranged a coach to take us all which will be waiting for us outside the Happy Fireside public house (no hope of an early cocktail, I'm afraid as our transport will leave at 8.30 am sharp!)

We shall spend the day at the garden and you can enjoy lunch there in the Society's Acer Café which I'm told does a very good shepherd's pie.

Don't worry about the cost; the transport is on me.

I look forward to seeing you all on the day.

Your President.
Susan Smythe'

Some of the usual troublemakers had gathered around, even before Susan had finished pinning this to the village hall notice board watched by the angry eyes of Joy Siptac from her upstairs eyrie at home.

"She just doesn't get it, does she? That'll annoy the whole lot of them; she's treading on toes as always. President means figurehead - and a silent one in Coldstow. You get elected and you keep out of things until someone tells you to make your speech at the next AGM; then you retire the next year."

"I think it's kind of her to do it and she's paying for the bus. I'd like to see everyone go, only I'm busy on Saturday."

"So are most people on Saturdays – it's when you take the kids shopping or have a lie in if you don't have any. I'll bet the coach runs empty. She doesn't even seem to know the pub's closed down."

Susan had never fully realised what spite underlies (and underpins) Coldstow life. Half the village had already decided to get up early on the day just to see poor Susan set off alone for a day in a garden well past its summer best.

But, in the event, a reasonable number of people did turn up for the trip. This was almost entirely because the villages of Ewer and Spattersleigh had no garden clubs of their own and commonly looked to Coldstow for horticultural entertainment. In fact, the hopeful travellers outnumbered the spiteful loungers who were denied the pleasure of watching the President taking her solitary day's outing in a bus sufficient for forty.

And Susan's day started well with managing the club members into their seats, managing what they looked at from the coach windows on their journey and managing their disembarkation at their destination. People even listened politely to Susan's carefully rehearsed eco-lecture on the bus.

From there, things started to go slightly wrong. The club members weren't minded to stay in a single group and all Susan's efforts to keep everyone together while she took them round the garden and told them at each stop what they were looking at, came to nothing.

The group was composed almost entirely of women who knew one another. So a number of sub-groups formed; these wandered off in various directions and, like milk spilt on a kitchen floor, were soon distributed all over the place, including the garden coffee shop, where five of them spent the entire day talking over one another in ever louder voices.

Three people did stay with Susan, a couple and a small, frightened lady on her own.

The couple comprised a thin, trembly old man and his very overweight wheelchair bound wife who had chosen that day to wear an amazing assortment of brilliantly coloured clothes and scarves. Unfortunately for Susan, the wheelchair was found unsuitable for garden wandering and the lady insisted, in a very loud voice, on having one of the electric chariots supplied by the RHS. The transfer from the first vehicle to the second was not effected easily and the embarrassment of it all wasn't eased for Susan by having a small crowd of onlookers who gathered to watch the entertainment and listen to the fat lady's language.

It transpired that, presumably through death, the solitary lady had recently lost her husband and this was "her first time out". She latched onto Susan like a burr on one's clothing, literally and embarrassingly going wherever Susan went throughout the day and frequently bursting into tears for no apparent reason. The contrast between the two women was stark. The widow's clothes matched her skin colouring and she spoke in whispers that Susan only half heard.

"Would you like some tea Mrs Callow?"
"… haven't been since he … thank you"
"Come on then, we can sit here."
"… first time out ……… thank you."
"Don't you like your tea Mrs Callow?"
"…… haven't met anyone since …… my daughter doesn't care ……
need the loo ……..."

Oh, God, thought Susan; *what did I do to deserve this?*

But she had done nothing to deserve it, save to organise a group outing for common, everyday people. It's not you Susan; it's just people. Don't let it get you down.

And she didn't let it crush her. Her quality shone through and, even though the Acer Café was closed for "maintenance work" and getting Mrs Archer from her hired wheel chair was even worse than dropping her in, her organised day was, broadly, a success.

There was no need for any lecture on the return journey as almost everyone was asleep and if that isn't a sign of a happy day spent, what is?

When the coach arrived at the Happy Fireside, someone made a little speech of thanks and Susan received the first applause for her efforts that she had ever known. She was on her way to becoming a little more human and a lot more likeable.

∗ ∗ ∗

Coldstow was so used to the business of revenge between its residents that it was taken for granted every fresh unkindly act would be countered by another, and slightly more spiteful, response. - Like a singles tennis match where the ball is returned back and forth between opponents. But what happens if the ball suddenly goes missing?

Having, as they thought, delivered a highly effective blow against Susan, the Crabbes had been waiting for some time to receive the counterpunch. But none came and the sisters didn't know what to do. There are no written rules for the management of Coldstow's little wars but it is an understood thing (understood by all except the Siptacs, that is) that you wait to be hit before lashing out again. Otherwise you don't know where you are in the battle sequence. The tennis game can't have two balls in play.

Susan had got past the inconvenience of losing her Sam and started to make something of Coldstow life. This was quite enjoyable and, after a very short while, she stopped blaming Rene and Louise for what had happened and quite forgot to settle her score with them. So, the Crabbes were puzzled.

Rene voiced the sisters' joint concern:

"I just can't understand it. The Smith woman ought to have taken a swipe at us by now."

"Perhaps she's retired hurt – can't take it any more."

Rene shook her head.

"I don't think that's it; she's not the type to give in; you only need to think about what she must have put up with during her marriage - and she was still coming up fighting when they got here. No, either she doesn't feel the need for a counterblow for some reason that we don't know or she's got something really huge planned. - I wish I knew what."

"I thought we were going to kill her; we ought to have done it by now; it's no good sitting around waiting for the sky to fall in."

"I wish you wouldn't Louise. Times have changed; it's not so easy nowadays; you've got to realise that."

But Louise couldn't see this at all and said so.

The Crabbes would have been less worried had they known that Susan was really quite grateful for the way things had turned out, although she would never have admitted it, even to herself. Her Garden Club presidency was successful and she was enjoying a life free of Sam.

Despite mutterings of "pushy woman" and "plant ignoramus", Susan was becoming accepted, if not liked, by most of the Club members and even some of the Committee. Her willingness to foot a few bills from her own purse had not gone unnoticed among the mean Coldstow residents, where any freebie was sure to be grabbed with no thanks the instant it appeared.

And there were other reasons for her popularity. Quite simply, she earned it.

Susan had the gift of getting what she wanted and if she wanted something for "her" club she generally got it, whether it was a well known garden presenter for an evening talk, access to a private garden no one else had been able to achieve or free gifts at a local garden centre. Among the local parishes, Coldstow Garden Club functions became widely known and well attended, which is more than may be said of either its church or its village hall events.

But pride precedes falls and jealousy is a powerful emotion, perhaps the most powerful of all.

* * *

Joy Siptac was watching Susan being busy yet again at Joy's very own notice board.

"I'm not having this."

"What's that Mrs S? Can I help? Can't have you being upset, can we?"

She glared at him, more deeply suspicious by the day. Everything Harold said had a touch of sarcasm about it now, and his foolish smile didn't reassure her any more. She decided to test him.

"Yes, you may help, Harold. Go over to our notice board and tell the Smith person she can't use it. It's only for official village hall business. Oh, and make sure you have that bit of paper taken down and put somewhere it won't be read.

On second thoughts, bring it back here. I may want to make a complaint to the Council."

This didn't suit Harold at all. He was quite willing, for the benefit of a relatively peaceful life, to perform any amount of sneaky tasks Joy wanted done but, facing up to anyone wasn't for him at all. Besides, he liked Susan, despite her complete lack of dress sense and make up. In fact Harold was quite attracted to her. Such things can happen, even in innocent little West Country villages. It's more about personalities than beautiful skin, although skin does matter – eventually.

Harold wondered if he dared give his wife a blunt refusal and bring to a head his simmering dislike of her. It was sure to happen some day. But he wasn't ready. That awkward fact left him with the immediate problem of how to deal with Susan and her troublesome notice.

He walked slowly over to join the little crowd that had gathered around her. It was a nice sunny day – the sort of day that Octobers and Novembers occasionally bless us with, as if the gods are apologising for what they are about to do to us in January, if not before.

And Susan gave him a smile as sunny as the day. Yes, she had changed. What had Sam done to her all those years?

His own face lit up as if she had switched it on. Here was Harold bearing a genuine smile; nothing like his usual vacuous grin. And he looked taller without his usual stoop. Yes, she thought, he isn't the same; she wondered, but only for one moment, if Joy had become less spiteful recently.

Harold's message removed any doubt that his wife had turned over a new leaf.

"Look, Susan, I'm really sorry to say this but there's a message from my wife …"

She spoke quite gently, not the old Susan at all:

"I quite understand Harold. Joy doesn't like me using the board for Garden Club business. I don't want you to get into any trouble on my account. I'll put the notice through a few letterboxes and word will soon get around."

He grinned.

"That's for sure. You probably don't need to do any more than whisper your message in your own kitchen; it would be all over the village in minutes. Thank you for your understanding, Susan. Between you and me, she doesn't deserve it."

He hadn't meant to say that, but it was out now and you can't vacuum up careless sentences to make them forgotten history.

"I don't know about that. Harold, you're not a member of my

club but why don't you come along to the meeting? You can read all about it on this."

She handed her notice to him and, Joy, watching from her favourite window, smiled one of her spiteful, satisfied smiles for a job well done. He had been told to get the notice and there it was done.

Harold took the poster and read it carefully, memorising the details for later.

"Thank you, Susan; I'd like to come. In fact, I will."

* * *

Joy read it as carefully as Harold had done but with a very different purpose. She looked for means to make trouble; he looked for a way to spend an evening in more attractive company.

"She was very nice about it; she's going to post her notice in letterboxes instead."

"Yes, very nice of her, I'm sure. I shall have to check if that's allowed. She isn't a post-person; I can't think the Royal Mail would allow such things."

He couldn't bear this.

"Of course she can deliver her own mail. People in the village do it all the time at Christmas. You can't stop her; it's not fair"

She looked at him astonished. The man was talking rubbish. She was so incensed that she became quite incoherent, and that was rare for her. Joy prided herself on the cold detachment she brought to the manipulation of her numerous victims.

"How *dare* you? I'll stop anything I want to stop and you won't stop me stopping her. You'll do as I tell you, Harold Siptac and you can start by stopping your chatty meetings with the Smith woman or I'll know the reason why."

Harold stared at her for a moment, trying to make sense of all the stops and stopping his wife was broadcasting about the room. Whatever it meant, this much was clear: he was being told to put Susan and her nice smile out of his life and he rebelled, at last.

"I shall do as I please, Joy and you will just have to accept it. I've had enough, no - more than enough, vastly more than enough, of you pushing me about. It stops right here. And for your information I shall be going to Susan's meeting. She invited me and she smiled at me as you never do."

Harold walked out, intending to ease his mind with a couple of ales at the Happy Fireside.

It wasn't until he reached the pub that he remembered it had closed. Rather than go home, where only spite awaited him, he set out to walk the rest of the way to Jack's, soothing away his anger with thoughts of his friendly barmaid.

* * *

Back at home Joy sat very still holding Susan's screwed up notice in fingers white with the force of their grip.

* * *

The same enigmatic message went out to their separate addresses.

'Dear Sally and Chris,

We are all agreed, then. The Hart and Sceptre, ten am this Friday.

Love, Greta.'

Chapter 16

Investigators at work.

With the disappearance of the Happy Fireside's proprietors, Jack's pub was more crowded than ever but he found a spare corner and claimed it for the two of them.

By the time Chris Downe arrived, he was trying out one of Jack's new draught beers and finding it less to his taste than his usual Old Amber. It had been a difficult day; Freddie was in one of her uncooperative moods and he had spent a tiresome morning trying to persuade her to pee followed by an afternoon of office work that he had resented keenly on a rare sunny autumn day. Paying work was one thing, but hours spent on his own accounts and a VAT return to finish were hateful waste of good outdoor time and he roundly cursed the country's government for it. He was sure it would rain tomorrow.

And Chris was in no happier mood. The police had visited him again to go over and over his movements on the day of Jo's death. Apparently they had at last started to consider the possibility of murder and, of course, they began with the husband.

It was no help for Chris to tell them Jo and he hadn't been married. At first, that was irrelevant as far as the Detective Chief Inspector was concerned. Later he decided it was suggestive of another motive – perhaps Jo had made threats to force a marriage or… or…

There seemed no limit to police flights of imagination. Chris had been worn down by the interrogation and it showed in his tired face.

"What we need, old friend, is a decent meal and a bottle of red wine. My treat."

"Can't refuse that; I'm sick of my own cooking, and everyone else's since I lost Jo. It's a puzzle to me what people do to decent raw food before it reaches a plate. It's enough to make you sell up and take residence in a good hotel."

"Why don't you? If anyone's got the money to do it, you have."

"Same to you; you're not short of the means. You should have married Sally and taken her away from this rotten village. I suppose she wouldn't have you; that's what comes of being a hermit."

His friend immediately changed the subject, with the result that Chris learned what he needed to know.

"What are you eating? I'll pick the wine – can't trust you farmers to do that; you don't have palettes."

They moved into the dining room where they ate and talked in easy friendship, with only the faintest shadow cast over him by the mention of her name.

Their talk turned again to Jo. He was at a standstill in his investigation; the doubtful whiskey appeared to have very different effects on different people. Perhaps there was nothing more in that bottle than stale spirits. A few days ago it had seemed he was making progress when he searched the deserted pub. Now there were more unanswered questions than ever.

Chris had been silent for a while:

"I've been thinking about this poison theory. I don't believe for one moment that Jo meant to kill herself. Angry people don't do suicide; they turn outward against the world, not inward on themselves. Do you want to kill yourself when you're having a spat with the Siptac woman, or do you want to kill her? Alright, don't answer that. The point is, bumbling doctors and policemen apart, we both think Jo's death was caused by something, or things, she ate or drank. Not being suicide means it's either accident or murder. If it was a slow acting poison, she ingested it (is that the right term? – Why doesn't the medical profession speak English?) before she set off to tell Dave what she thought of him.

If it was fast acting, it happened in the pub and, unless you can remember her having anything different, the source was one of the whiskey bottles under the bar and we can take that a bit further because in that event, the culprit's Dave.

Question – why would Dave want to end Jo's life?

Answer – (Just a suggestion): Dave heard enough of Jo's revelations about watering beer and cheating the diners to warn him there might be something else on the way and, whatever it was, he feared it so much he took the extreme risk of killing her in his own public bar.

Only a fool would do that. That's where Dave the murderer theories come unstuck because (a) Dave isn't a fool whatever else he is and (b), it presupposes he had a bottle of poison waiting under the bar ready for use. – It's just not reasonable.

And there's something else that we've learned from our Let's-See-If-We-Can-Kill-Ourselves schoolboy games. – The wretched stuff affects people differently; if it *is* poison then it's hopelessly risky to use as a quick murder weapon."

He had already followed the same lines of thought and come to much the same conclusions.

"I agree, but all that does is to take us round in a huge circle and prove to ourselves that we've solved nothing, not even the approximate time the act was committed or even that there was an act. Where do we go now? Answers on a postcard, please or whatever the modern equivalent is – I haven't seen a postcard for years."

"Oh, I think there was an act alright. Maybe we need to start somewhere else. Perhaps we should try asking what the motive may have been. Given it wasn't me wanting a clear field to hook up with a new girl friend - and, believe it or not, I loved Jo a lot more than I love myself, it's terrible being without her – then what would anyone gain by killing her?

She had no real money, just some modest savings, and the car I gave her. Maybe the possibility of inheriting something from her mother. But that won't be much, the old girl's been living in a care home for the last five years; I'd be surprised if there's anything left there. I hadn't given her a share in the farm although I intended to one day. Being a typical farmer, I might never have got round to it; the bloody cows take up too much of my life to have time for anything else.

And, before you ask, yes, she did leave a will. It was made long before she came to Coldstow and I get nothing. As if I'd want to."

They fell silent again and finished the wine. He fetched coffees for them.

"We can't give up Chris, we owe her better than that, poor dear. Suggestion: research the motive angle. You can look into how matters stand with Jo's mum. Has she run through her cash? How old is she? Well or ill? Has she come into any money that Jo would have inherited? Did Jo have her own solicitor? Has he anything to tell us? Did she have enemies - not counting the wretched Dave, that is?

It may seem pointless but unless we gather every bit of information we can, there's really nothing to work on. At least more knowledge may strike out some of the expanding list of possibilities; we've got to get that under control. And I'll go back to whiskey bottles, Dave and Stan. I don't suppose their skipping from the pub has any bearing on all this, do you, Chris?"

Chris' mind had begun to wander.

"Not unless they had a batch of dead bodies in the cellar that Jo was going to tell the world about. I wonder if they're still there?"

"Who might still be there? Stan and Dave?"

"You're not listening, I just wondered if the Happy Fireside cellars are choked with bodies waiting to be found by the next publican."

"If there are, I'll bet the new owner won't stay long, although it could be a draw for ghoulish customers. Turn the place into a gold mine; perhaps you should buy it; expand the Downe empire."

For the time being, that was how things were left, but he worried about Chris and how he would stand up to more interrogation by the police. His young friend was as physically strong as his tough job could make him, but it was mental stamina he needed. Hopefully he had enough.

* * *

Against his expectation, the following day was, again, bright and sunny; almost cloudless. At seven thirty in the morning it was cold, much colder than the day before. This was one of Nature's busy days; a day to live and to love living. A brisk wind with a lot of north in it had risen in the night, stripping some of the trees bare and reminding the world that autumn is brief and precious, winter neither.

He stood, patiently for once, waiting for Freddie to finish her performance and marvelling, as he did every year, at the shapes and colours spread across the lawn, lying in drifts against walls or spinning through the air on their way to decorate anything that needed it. He blessed his decision years ago to plant so many maples.

Breakfasts and walk done, he invited Freddie into his car, where she promptly fell asleep, and set off to Larkston and the vet.

* * *

Freddie had her booster injections and took the offered half of the vet's ham sandwich by way of a well earned little reward for bravery.

"She's three kilos over her ideal weight, she needs to cut down on the treats."

"*You* tell her. She's the one that does the eating, not me."

The vet turned to the dog:

"Freddie, you're the intelligent one. I want you to get him under control; he has to stop giving you so many treats. I know it's hard but you have to be cruel to be kind. He'll be all the better for it. Training, training, training, that's the key. You must realise humans are slow learners and some, I mention no names, are slower than others."

He turned to Freddie's manager;

"And you, my old friend, are looking very underweight. You should eat more. Hermit life isn't good for anybody."

"And you need to get out more. Take in the sunshine. Sitting in here looking at dog's bottoms won't get you a tan."

The three of them went out together to say goodbye in the sunshine. He left his car and they walked the short distance into town.

The Blue Bowl still had a few tables out on the pavement and they were comfortably sheltered from the wind. He parked Freddie and went next door for a paper. By the time he returned, Freddie's group of admirers had evidently discovered she liked ice cream.

"It's dangerous doing that, she took an old lady's hand off only yesterday. Just because she felt like it; no warning at all."

The little crowd drifted away.

The friendly waitress took his order and slipped a small cake Freddie-wards. He ignored the deed.

Their mid-morning snack included a raspberry cone and a vanilla one. Freddie chose to eat the vanilla cone first, keeping her favourite for last. Afterwards, she sat watching him, unblinking, silently pleading for a bit of whatever else might be going.

He drank his coffee, absolutely refusing to pour any into the saucer for his starving friend. Refreshments over, they both settled down for a restful half hour in the sunshine.

He woke to the noise of chair legs scraping on stone.

"I am sorry to wake you. Can we speak?"

It took a few moments to recognise her. It was the first time he had seen Greta without either collar or cloak. Fair haired and naturally beautiful, now she looked her probable age – perhaps twenty six or thereabouts, certainly not the nineteen years he guessed when she first appeared in the parish. It was partly the clothes, of course, and the make-up.

She was a smart dresser; there was money in the background, and she wore her money well. The sort of graceful woman that only other people know, but she wasn't distant. He was an accepted part of her team, whatever that team might be about.

"Of course, please do. Can I get you a coffee? I'm going to have another one."

She accepted the offer – just a nod. She probably received so many gifts that the occasional coffee meant nothing.

"How are you faring Greta? Are you managing to cope with all those parish tasks on your own or has a new vicar been appointed?"

"Quite well enough thank you, yes and no in that order. But I did not spoil your rest to force you into small talk. How are you getting on with investigating Filly's death? I am relying on you; the police are hopeless. I have no faith there."

"The answer to that is: I'm getting nowhere much and progress isn't helped by losing my right hand. That doesn't mean I'm not still on the case though. Greta, I really don't think you should rely on me in this. The police have infinitely more resources than you and I. In fact I'm looking into another death and I'm bogged down there, too."

"Yes, I know about Jo Downe and I am sorry about Sally; you need her help. But right now, I want you concentrating on my problem. The police won't act unless someone does their work for them."

Greta rose to leave just as the drinks arrived. She ignored them.

"I have something that may interest you. I think it should."

She dug around in her nice, expensive leather bag; it looked brand new. He wondered if she used her designer handbags once, then threw them away or, more likely, gave them to some foreign aid charity.

"Forgive the question: why are you so concerned about this? Why can't you let the authorities do their job? And why did you just call it 'your problem'?"

"Filly was my sister; for all her faults, I loved her. I still do. God does not strike a line through love just because someone dies."

He watched her walk away, confident that she had got him doing exactly what she wanted. He thought he wouldn't be the only one.

Sitting there in the sunshine and wondering if he could possibly absorb a third latte without bursting, he slipped into another of those half waking, half dreaming reveries that had become such a common feature of his life since he lost her.

Some small part of his mind must have been alert or he would have missed seeing Sam Repplington leaving a shop on the far side of the high street. Sam wasn't alone. Jack's pretty barmaid walked beside him, moving like a young colt and looking more like a daughter than what she was. But he could understand the attraction, if you were that way inclined.

He watched as the couple wandered down the street, arm in arm, window shopping, before turning into the Headless Swan. They seemed completely bound up in one another; a strange conjunction. Lunching together, he supposed – not cheap either.

He paid his bill, extracted Freddie from her pleasant biscuity dreams and turned down the main street to see where Sam had come from. It was an estate agency. Intriguing, he thought, but not much help for solving the problems in hand.

He walked back toward his car with her envelope lying in a jacket pocket waiting for him to remember it.

Chapter 17

Change partners!

'To all members and affiliates of Coldstow Garden Club

Meeting This Saturday

Please note that our meeting will now take place this coming Saturday at 6.00 pm in Ewer Village Hall and not in Coldstow's hall.

This is due to unforeseen circumstances and I am sure everyone will join with me in thanking Ewer for its kind hospitality in making its lovely facilities available at such short notice.

Please pass this information on.

Susan Smythe
President'

Susan's notice was delivered to individual addresses and, as she expected, this proved to be just as effective as the village hall noticeboard, which she had decided to abandon to its spiteful owner.

Having learnt about the meeting from one of the Coldstow gossips, Joy reacted very simply by writing her own letter, but under Susan's name, telling everyone that the meeting was cancelled altogether. Unusually for Siptac trickery, this proved to be a mistake; perhaps she was losing her touch.

"Come here Harold.

You will take these letters and deliver them to their addresses. No, it is not a mistake that most of them are in other villages. Just do it."

Harold dutifully picked up the bag of mail and went out to his car. He drove across to Spattersleigh where he just chanced to meet the CGC President.

Susan had just chanced to bring a small picnic and some tea which they each enjoyed very happily in the other's company.

Later, they just chanced to empty Joy's mail bag in Susan's recycling bin before he went home to report a successful mission. Joy made a pot of tea for them both by way of celebration and to show Harold that she could be nice if he did nice things for her.

But it was rather too late for that.

* * *

The club meeting was a fairly ordinary affair but Harold enjoyed it more than anything he had done with his wife in the previous twenty years. The combined experience of being away from Joy and with Susan quite went to his head.

On his return late that evening Joy met him at their front door.

"I suppose you spent the night at Jack's with your lady friend behind the bar. I won't have you making a fool of me Harold Siptac. This will stop – NOW! From tomorrow, you will take me with you when you go out in the evening unless I say otherwise."

Harold decided he would make sure Joy felt "otherwise" whenever possible; and she hadn't said anything about going out in the afternoon.

The next club event was to be a whole day affair and Harold had made his plans. But the storm was already looming and coming indirectly from another source.

* * *

At one time photography was a clumsy and complex activity. Awkward cameras, film that got itself exposed and spoiled when one wasn't looking and the final nuisance of having it developed and prints made. That printing took time and money. What disappointment after all the effort to find the lens cap had been left on or that Uncle William had lost his head somewhere out of the frame.

Now, all that's gone, people are taking pictures all day and every day, happy in the knowledge it costs nothing and able to preview their photos in an instant. If Uncle W loses his head, just take another picture; take a movie of him if he keeps doing it.

There had been few, if any, people at Susan's evening meeting without phones and their useful little cameras. By the end of the night, there was any number of shots recording, well, everything, including the cheerful faces of speakers and their appreciative audience.

And the Crabbe sisters had enjoyed the evening as much as anyone else.

"This one, I think Rene. Our dear Susan looks quite radiant with her new man friend and he seems to have lost his jacket and tie – very casual if I may say so."

"Put it in the pile then, we don't want to be mean. Dear Joy would never forgive us if we kept any just for ourselves"

So it was that, a few days later, Joy collected from her front door mat a flat envelope about the size of the one she had once delivered to poor Jenny.

"HAROLD SIPTAC!!"

That shout could be heard throughout Coldstow, and some distance beyond. Some who heard it immediately went inside and loudly slammed their doors. Others stayed very quiet and still, not wanting to miss any part of what was coming and a few (the local constable included) grinned and went on with whatever they were doing. By unspoken consent, all lawnmowers and strimmers in the village were switched off.

* * *

"I think we have made our point very effectively, sister."

"Yes, Rene, I think so. Do we still have to kill her?"

"Hush, child. God will have his way, we are just his instruments."

* * *

The unseasonal warm, sunny days continued and the nice young couple's children (Annie 3, Didi 4 and Nikki, 6) had spent a happy morning in his garden making the most of the paddling pool he had bought that summer and earning their keep by bathing Freddie – several times. He had handed the three of them back just after midday; for once, declining their mother's offer to share the family lunch. He had tasks to perform that afternoon.

By subtle degrees the Happy Fireside pub was starting to look dilapidated. He wasn't sure what distressed him the most. Perhaps it was the rapid increase in West Country mould on walls and paintwork. The pub's sign seemed a little lopsided, but it might have been that way for years and he just hadn't noticed. Certainly there was more trash about the place – a couple of smashed bottles, a leaking rubbish bag that attracted local cats and, inevitably, a smashed window – that promised ill.

He entered by his hidden door, seeing no sign that anyone had come that way since his previous visit. Without wasting time on the ground floor, he ran nimbly up the main stairs, crossed the great meeting room and reached the owners' accommodation. Here he stayed still for a full minute, gathering courage for what he had to do.

He opened the bedroom door and began a far more thorough search. Every aspect of what he was doing was unpleasant to him and the musty smell, more intrusive since he had last been there, made it worse; nauseating even. *"It's just damp and lack of heating"*, he told himself; what else could it be?

A small pile of letters and odd papers looked interesting, He pocketed them to be gone through in detail later when he had the time.

He finished going through the bedroom, making a systematic and thorough job of it; he wasn't coming back a third time.

The bathroom was large, with a vast, aging jacuzzi. He loathed those things, they seemed designed to be incapable of thorough cleaning, full of unreachable places where filth might settle and remain for the life of the plumbing. The stench was worse here than in the bedroom.

He ran through the contents of two bathroom cabinets, opened an airing cupboard and carefully took out the bedlinen and towels. He returned everything in the same order and closed the cupboard door.

Still nothing had come to light and he wasn't even sure what he looked for; he was simply doing his job; the job he had undertaken for Jo's sake and perhaps for another's. At least when this was done, he could draw a line through one of the possibilities.

He finished in the bathroom and left it open as he retraced his route to the door onto the main corridor. He took a last look around; trying to sense the room's history, recent and past. It still told him nothing. Maybe there was nothing to tell.

Downstairs he stood silent again on the ground floor, summoning courage for the last task.

It was clear which door led to the cellar – it was the only one locked. His sensible side told him that was enough; he might leave now with conscience clear. He couldn't be required to get past locked doors. The other half of him, that belligerent side that had caused so much trouble through his life, said *"Find the key or break the door down, just get on with it. You're wasting daylight."*

He remembered a rack of keys at the back of the public bar. But when he looked, it had been stripped. He wondered why Dave would do that. If he meant to return, what could be worth the risk of getting caught by the pub's creditors?

There had to be other sets, partial or complete. But where? He searched the kitchen, two larders, the saloon bar. Still no luck. It was growing dark in the early autumn afternoon and now he had another problem; a car stopped close by; steps and a voice calling.

"Anybody there?"

He smiled with relief.

"Inside Chris, come round to the back, I'll meet you."

"What the hell are you doing in here? Next thing I know you'll be up for house breaking or pub breaking or whatever the coppers would call this. Anyway, here I am, as instructed, and whatever it's about, you've got my support. What are we going to do?"

"You might have started by apologising for being late. This isn't a job for one person. And if <u>we</u> are going to do anything, <u>we</u> can't do it until I can find a key to the cellar door. It's locked and its strong."

"So am I. Let's see this impassable thing."

They went in, Chris stood looking around and constantly sniffing.

"Why does this place smell so foul? Damp, stale food and staler spirits? It's not that long since they skipped off. The place can't have rotted in that short time."

He made no reply but pointed to the cellar door. Chris immediately threw himself against it and fell down the full flight of cellar stairs. The lock was a feeble hardware store thing, quite new and poorly fixed – Stan and Dave's typically inadequate efforts to make the cellar secure. There wasn't anything they could get right.

There was a light switch by the now open door. When he reached the bottom stair, his friend was back on his feet, rubbing his shoulder.

"Why can't I take you anywhere without you embarrass me?"

"Because I like to embarrass you; I don't have many pleasures in my life; your one of the few I've got"

"Well, try to curb your eagerness for any more amusement. This is serious stuff and I don't need a one man wrecking crew about me."

"What are we looking for?"

Yes, he thought, good question – anything from a couple of bodies to a scrap of paper.

"How should I know? I'm just looking and hoping to gather a bit more information."

"You can't gather *more* information because you haven't gathered *any* yet. You should read up on your Alice in Wonderland."

"Oh, shut up. You work your way around clockwise from the stairs; I'll go the other way. And don't doze off."

They were each about half way around their allotted search areas when Chris swore softly.

"I claim the prize, I think."

He walked slowly across the room, fearing what he would see. But he had to look, this was why he had come here.

It wasn't what he expected.

"That's quite some still. And full bottles of whiskey on shelves over here – peculiar names on the labels. These two weren't doing things by halves. I wonder if it all went into the bar upstairs or were they selling it by the bottle?"

He picked one out.

"The Crabbes sell this label in the shop. Makes you wonder, doesn't it?"

"If they got it from the pub? I doubt it; the sisters hated them. I suppose Rene might have been tempted by a bit of easy money, but with Jenny on the accounts it would have been difficult."

"Anyway, I'm taking this. It's the last opportunity to grab any evidence here. Let's finish our circular tour and go."

They turned back to their search.

"Some papers here. Looks like invoices and delivery tickets for their little scam – equipment, bottles… I'll have these too."

"We aren't looking to catch bootleggers. We want whoever killed Jo – remember?"

"Yes I do, Chris, and I also remember that Jo's death might be linked to whiskey in this pub."

"Point taken."

They climbed the cellar stairs and reached the rear corridor.

Followed by his friend, Chris made his way to the kitchen, drawn there by its association with Jo. He stepped in and closed the door, wanting to sense how the room had been when it was buzzing with activity, and she the centre of it all.

He turned to leave and unhooked a cloth bag hanging on the

back of the closed door. He waved it as if he had found a trophy.

"Jo's bag. We'll take it with us."

They returned to the unlocked back door and stepped out into fresh air. Glad to leave the Happy Fireside to decay in peace, they walked together back to his house.

He poured them both a beer.

"I want your view on something."

As instructed, Chris took the opportunity to do a little needling:

"If it's about your love life, keep it to yourself. Better still, tell Sally."

"That's below the belt. I lost something I didn't know I had, and it's painful."

Yes, thought Chris, now it's right out in the open. We progress.

"You said you want to show me something?"

He led the way across to his office and Greta's photographs spread out across the plan chest.

"I saw Greta in town. She's given up being a nineteen year old boy curate and become a modern, moneyed sophisticate. Impressive – she managed me into a corner anyway. Apparently her idea is that I solve her Filly's murder and the police stay out in the cold. I told her no and she said yes. So I said yes. You don't refuse a woman like that anything. She handed me these pictures and walked off as if she'd done the hard bit and it was over to me for the loose ends.

Oh, and she owes me a coffee; two actually. One head isn't getting anywhere but, with you, now there are two (one and a half anyway) and we all know that's better. So what do you make of these?"

With his reading glasses on, Chris suddenly looked older and far wiser. He spent a full ten minutes on the first picture.

"I can't see the clue, if there is one. I take it that it's a picture taken the day the vicar died, hence all the people. What does the other photo show?"

"No more interesting than the first as far as I can see, but have a look yourself."

Chris spent another five minutes in study before returning to the first picture and scribbling little notes.

"What have you got?"

"I don't know that I've got anything. It just seemed a good idea to identify everybody in the crowd that I recognise."

"Where does that get you? Trying to see who's two timing who? Recognise any of your farmhands skipping off work?"

"Well, you're in the picture, or Freddie at least. But no ice cream van."

"Then it's not her. But you haven't answered the question. What's your idea?"

Chris thought for a moment.

"It's essentially a picture of people. Assume we're supposed to spot a particular person – perhaps someone you wouldn't expect to be there. Approaching it logically, we need to pick out each individual and try to identify every one of them. Those we can't name go onto a short list and we move on from there."

"Can't see it myself. We don't know whether Greta's telling us to look for someone local or a stranger. But I suppose there's no harm in listing the guests attending the party. You carry on with your photo; I'll do this one."

They worked on accordingly, spending an hour in their separate studies before calling it a day and driving over to Jack's for a bar meal. Chris left him then to see if he still had a milking herd. Happily, he had.

Despite the late hour, he returned to his office and sat for a while wondering how he had come to miss Jo's bag during his search of the Happy Fireside; it must have been obvious enough.

He worked on for a while; as ever, finishing his day by sitting in what he now thought of as her chair and hurting himself again with another bitter-sweet reverie.

∗ ∗ ∗

Living a secretive life in their rented cottage, Stan and Dave were getting on one another's nerves. They were in the middle of one of their regular rows and Stan was feeling spiteful.

"It occurs, Dave, that you may have done something very stupid, and I'm not going to carry the can for your mistakes."

Dave had no idea what his partner was talking about and would have preferred not to know. But he dared not ignore it. Stan could be dangerous, especially when he was riled.

"What are you talking about now? What mistakes? Please don't start your troublemaking again."

"I'm talking about the evening when Jo Downe died. It was you that gave her that last drink."

Dave felt as if his heart was shrinking. This was the shadow he feared. He had worried that Stan would reach this point eventually and now here it was. But he would play it out to the end.

"You're speaking in riddles. Is this an accusation of some sort? Make yourself clear Stan."

"I watched you pour her drink; I saw where it came from. It wasn't from her own bottle – and it killed her."

Dave stayed silent. This was exactly the point he had been torturing himself with since it first occurred to him.

Stan wouldn't let it lie.

"Well, did you kill her? DID YOU? ***DID YOU?***"

The man was becoming hysterical.

"For God's sake, Stan, stop it. Of course I didn't kill her. I just wanted her to calm down, to stop shouting her accusations in front of everyone."

"So you gave her a massive dose of alcohol. That's what killed her, and it makes us murderers!"

"Nonsense. It doesn't do anything of the sort. Jo killed herself either deliberately or by accident. Anyway we didn't make her drink it."

They both went silent as they realised the enormity of it all. This wasn't another little domestic row any more, it was suddenly taking over their lives, overwhelming and sending them reeling into a totally alien world.

Dave struggled to think: was there anything they could do to make this thing go away, or at least save them being drawn ever further into the police investigation?

"We have to get rid of the still and any other evidence that's lying around the Happy Fireside. It won't guarantee our being left alone, but we'd be stupid to sit on our hands doing nothing."

The early hours of the following morning saw the two of them at the rear of their old pub. Stan was fiddling with a massive bunch of keys; fear was making him clumsy.

"Try the small door; we never used to lock that one."

It still wasn't locked; they were inside and standing in the rear corridor by the door to the pub's cellar. Stan was key fiddling again and trying to hold a torch with the spare hand he didn't have.

"Don't look now but someone's been here already. Someone large and desperate for a drink apparently - the lock's broken."

"It's nice to know you're able to make jokes, Dave. What do we do now?"

"We go down and have a look of course; it's why we came. What else?"

The cellar seemed as they had left it. They looked at their old still and the counterfeit bottles.

"We can't take all that away; there's far too much to carry and where could we put it?"

Stan was right. Dave had forgotten the size of it all, and the weight.

"All we can do is take the paperwork."

But even that was impossible. Stan's voice was suddenly higher pitched:

"So the police know about it all and they've taken away enough evidence to send us to jail."

But Dave disagreed.

"I don't think it's the police Stan. They wouldn't have left the rest of it; certainly not the alcohol. No, this is someone else. I wonder who and why?"

"We may as well take a few bottles and deliver them to the usual place; we can always do with a bit of pocket money. And we can take the pipework. Without that, it won't look so obviously like a still."

That, at least, they could agree on.

* * *

Rumours in Coldstow generally have some basis in truth, but not necessarily very much. Gossip about the sale of the village pub was no exception.

The fact that the Happy Fireside was up for sale had been easily discovered; most of Coldstow spent at least some part of every day checking what was new on the property market within a radius of twenty miles or so and scrutinising the interior photographs on maximum enlargement. The gossips were spreading the news within half a day of Morgan and Morgan (Commercial and Leisure Department) putting their ad on the major property websites.

And the price was surprisingly low, reflecting perhaps that this was a creditor's sale and the bank didn't want the place hanging around and deteriorating into a liability. Naturally the Bank, being a bank, judged things aright so the pub sold speedily and that, too, was easily found out from the internet.

But there, gossip ran out of fact and imaginations had to fill the gaps. According to one source, the place had been sold to a big brewery which wanted to modernise the place and add a Pizza franchise. Another story had the buyer as a developer with plans for sixteen houses and a block of twenty flats. Yet again, some said the Council had plans for a recycling depot.

If one owned a property in Coldstow, each spiteful rumour was more distressing than the last with the result that the truth, when it came out, was not just a spicy nugget but a considerable relief.

He might have set the rumour-mongers straight but saw no reason why he should. That day in Larkston had told all. Morgans the estate agent, Sam and the barmaid, free flowing money, an obvious celebration; it was all there for anyone to read and he had read it perfectly.

All that remained to be seen, and so complete the picture, was Susan's reaction when she learned what she had on her doorstep.

But, in fact Susan was less concerned than the nosey parkers would have liked her to be. By then her presidential activities and a developing romance were filling both her time and thoughts. In short, she had moved on, but jealousy is a powerful emotion and so is the desire for revenge.

Chapter 18

Trouble at the inn.

Beginning with the mindless task of clearance from cellar to attic, there was much to be done in bringing the Happy Fireside back from the brink of dereliction, and the builders were constantly finding further problems. Lacking experience and skill, the Building Inspector was a trifle overbearing and rigidly inflexible with her rule book. The several council departments involved in food safety matters, fire regulations and licencing each had their conflicting, and therefore obstructive, influences on the progress of Cheri and Sam's venture, or the lack of it.

It was fortunate, therefore, that despite her youth, Sam's ex-barmaid partner was a strong and determined young woman with a surprising amount of solid experience in the hospitality world for her age. Even better, Cheri had a nice inheritance which was as yet unspent when she agreed to share in, or perhaps take over, Sam's new venture.

Eventually the works were completed and so disappeared such evidence concerning Jo's death as the place had retained. The pub was restocked and staff re-engaged or, where that was impossible, replaced. At last the Happy Fireside was ready for its opening and Coldstow was already running its usual sweepstake on the probable date of the couple's bankruptcy, even before the pub served its first meal.

* * *

Chris Downe had booked a table for the two of them on the pub's opening night, partly to have a ringside seat for any unintended entertainment (that is, something more than the small and over-loud band engaged by Sam for the occasion) and partly to discuss progress with their investigation, or the want of it.

Unsurprisingly for a restaurant's first night, their meals were delayed, and they passed the time talking about Jo and occasionally chatting with various friends and acquaintances who wandered across to their table.

The unintended entertainment started before any food arrived.

Harold Siptac sat on a stool in the public bar, for a while free of his wife's irritating presence and happily looking forward to a planned discrete meeting with Susan. It might be thought that discrete meetings and public houses belong to different worlds but they had both felt a busy opening night would be safe cover enough for a quiet drink and a modest holding of hands at one of the Happy Fireside's corner tables.

The first part of their plan to go astray was the absence of a corner table. Harold, neglecting to book, had assumed the seating arrangements would be unchanged and space would be available. Neither was the case. The only remaining seats were two tall stools placed exactly in the centre of the public bar and in fullest view of just about everyone attending the Happy Fireside that evening.

The next hiccup was the presence of Mrs Joy Siptac. But Harold was unaware of this as he awaited his lady friend because Joy, unlike her husband, had booked a well concealed table for herself on the far side of the saloon bar.

And the third little disaster was the entrance into the dining room of Rene and Louise Crabbe who had come for much the same reason as Chris Downe, except that they had some prior knowledge, or maybe sixth sense premonition, about forthcoming events.

There is something about the Crabbe sisters that commands respectful silence. Perhaps it is their age or the fact they control most of the controllable activities in the village. Most probably it is simply their presence. Rene doesn't wear a sign saying **'Don't**

mess with me' but she might as well do so and her sister's aura rubs off on Louise.

The noise in both bars faded away to a quiet conversation level as the Crabbes were taken, like royalty, to their table where they affected to ignore everyone else in the room as they studied the menu. Rene chose a beef sandwich with chips and Louise, after Rene had put her off the idea of a curry (*"Unwise in the circumstances, dear"*), ordered the same.

There was no special reason why Harold should feel as he did when Rene Crabbe was nearby, save perhaps for his part in the Siptacs' takeover of the village hall, but he feared the woman horribly. Sat on his prominent bar stool and without Susan to protect him from the world, he sensed Rene's eyes drilling holes in him even before she sat down. He longed to turn and face her, to give her stare back, look for look and glare for glare but he just could not do it. So there he sat, cringing under an imagined evil eye, when, in fact, Rene and Louise, both, were watching poor Sam Repplington being demolished by his customers.

Problems in the Happy Fireside's kitchen and sundry other difficulties, all resolved by his surprisingly capable partner, had passed Sam by. He had the bare bones of a speech prepared for the occasion and came out from behind the bar to be among the customers while he made it.

"Ladies, gentlemen, friends. You all know me and if you don't, you soon will..."

Like Susan and her speech at that awful Church Committee meeting, he had an uneasy feeling there was something wrong about those opening words.

He got no further for the time being; others wanted a share of this and, of course, they hadn't missed his glitch:

"How come we all know you and some of us don't?"

He was saved the trouble of answering this one; a second heckler butted in:

"We do know about you; where did the money for the pub come from, Sam? Been at the pension fund again, have we?"

Sam faltered; he hadn't expected trouble; this was supposed to be a meet-the-benevolent-new-landlord night. These people ought to be grateful to him. But Coldstow is a spiteful place – it's in the soil.

"Now then, I'll make the jokes tonight and you can do the drinking. How's that?"

"We can't see Susan; wife not with you tonight, Sam? Swapped her for a newer model, eh?"

Sam was starting to feel angry; this was all so unfair.

"My wife has nothing to do with anything. Susan's hundred percent behind me, she's just busy doing somebody else this evening."

Poor Sam: blunder after blunder and still they kept coming.

"Who's she busy doing it to, Sam? What's his name? Wouldn't start with an S, would it?"

As if he hadn't made a big enough mess of things already, Sam promptly put his foot in it again.

"None of your business. And for your information his name begins with H, so you can be quiet.

Now, with your kind permission, I've just got a few words of welcome, and then we have a surprise for you ...."

"What's the surprise, Repplington, old man? Harold Siptac going to give us a talk on wife swapping and photography?"

"Don't just sit there Harold, tell us about it. Does Joy like being photographed? Can we see the pictures?"

Sam's anger faded, chased away by cold despair. His grand welcoming was lost beyond recovery and fate hadn't finished with him yet.

* * *

Joy Siptac had stayed half hidden in her niche beyond the saloon bar long enough to hear her name taken in vain and, incidentally, to mark down for future attention the troublemaker responsible. But just at that moment there was a little task to perform.

She left the saloon via the door bearing silhouettes of two little people. Here a well lit stone flagged corridor ran away in both directions; to the left a door on one side with a little picture of a figure in trousers, then, cutting across the corridor, a closed door marked **'*Kitchen – Private*'**. Another sign, facing her, showed a skirted figure with an arrow to the right. Joy walked confidently to the left and without hesitation opened the door to the Happy Fireside's cooking facilities.

⋆ ⋆ ⋆

Constructing a new kitchen requires a good many trades, all working in essentially the same place at much the same time and they really don't get on very well. Tom, the floor layer gets in the way of Josh and Phoebe, the electricians, who forget to tell Tom until too late that the large cooker cable has to go under Tom's tiles. Phoebe saws a cable slot for the cooker in Luke's new plaster and the cooker installer finds the slot is on the wrong wall. The wall tiler, Eddie, finishes his tiling by working into the small hours and goes off on his touring holiday in the States. The following morning, the carpenters move a doorway, hacking Eddie's tiles off one side of the new opening and leaving a strip of bare wall on the other.

And everyone, but everyone, hates the poor plumber who cuts, drills, hacks and hammers away to make paths for his cold water pipes, his hot water pipes, the central heating, the gas supply, the new drains and so ever on until it is really quite surprising that he isn't murdered and his body buried under the new floor – but that would spoil the floor tiles and of course no one would wish to do that.

But the Happy Fireside's new kitchen had been finished at last, and just in time. The skilled trades were away to war with each other in much the same way on their next job and the new proprietors, their new chef and the several new members of staff took possession of their nice new toys for the first time. And, being new, of course everything was sure to function perfectly. - Well, actually not.

Extractor fans are wonderful pieces of equipment – when they work but neither fan was working on Sam's opening night.

It was hard for Joy to see into the steam filled room. There were two, no, three, women there. One of these, thin, red faced, white aproned and evidently the cook (or chef, as she prefers to be called), was growing more frustrated by the minute over the vast range that had caused grief since the early afternoon. – A lesson to us all, as if we needed it, to place no reliance on electrical equipment working first time out on its own.

Chef doesn't cope well with problems, especially those that catch her off guard. She used to work at the hotel in Larkston's square, cooking and serving the bar meals and occasionally standing in for the head chef in the restaurant when needed. But her employers never quite got round to promoting her; she just couldn't cope with stress. She is fifty three and just then, looked some years older – her wrinkles aren't her fault and she looks quite attractive when she smiles but she wasn't doing that on the opening day, so she appeared rather grim. Her grey hair is mostly hidden under her chef's hat but when she puts it up, it suits her and a trace of make-up suggests she would, and does, scrub up well for a party. She is one of Sam's "discoveries". In fact, she was thoroughly discovered by him some time before Stan and Dave quit the Happy Fireside.

Lily, the other woman in a white apron, is the real worker in the Happy Fireside's new kitchen. A dinner lady in the now closed Coldstow primary school, she takes each disaster as it comes; handles it with confidence and moves on to dispose of the next. Lily is short and nicely curved, looks thirty, is now forty years old but as active and constantly cheerful as she was at twenty. She has a round, red-cheeked face and fair hair imperfectly covered by a blue and white striped kerchief. Fellow workers and customers like her at once. No catering organisation should be without one.

As Joy arrived in the kitchen, Lily was competently preparing various cold starters, stopping both "Chef" and a vast pan of French onion soup from boiling over and dealing with the numerous problems that Sam left in his wake whatever he had been doing and wherever he had been doing it. Right then, as Joy appeared, the current disaster was the absence of bread rolls - a mistake simply explained – Sam had forgotten to buy any.

Cheri, the working partner in this venture, had been ducking back and forth between customers and kitchen, taking orders, smoothing ruffled feathers and sharing with Lily the job of clearing up after Sam.

"Perhaps we should tell them soup's off?"

"Not in quite those words Lily. Anyway, the starter menu looks thin as it is and it's the only one that's hot. Half the diners have ordered it. I'll find some bread; leave it to me. Now, how are the mains doing Chef?"

Chef had suffered that day and it wasn't getting any better. Apparently the mention of main courses was the last straw:

"I've had enough; enough of this bloody cooker, enough of bungler Sam, enough of it all. Sorry it's not either of you two. I'm off and if you've got any sense so will you be. Let them whistle for their dinners. Serve the greedy little wretches right, missing their caviar for once."

It had been decided between the two proprietors and their cooking team that the menu for the Happy Fireside's re-opening day should be essentially simple; four starters, four main courses and a rather wider choice of, mainly cold, desserts.

A short list and an easy run for their first night. - All that required was a smooth-running kitchen and some happy diners. Well, the guests were still enjoying themselves out there at Sam's expense, so that was one box ticked. But producing their simple menu out of a new kitchen with all its teething problems and a new team to run it was proving to be another matter altogether.

Patient and resourceful as ever, Cheri, the peacemaker stepped in. Yes, it was hard, Chef - I'll see everything's put right by tomorrow, Chef – you've been so patient, Chef – we all admire you for your skill, Chef … and so on.

And Chef consented to stay – on promises of more help, more pay, more praise even.

Through the steam, Joy Siptac stepped forward like an orange haired pantomime character appearing from a puff of smoke. The clothes peg voice spoke:

"Can I be of use? It looks as if you need a hand."

It's an odd quirk of human nature that one's first reaction to a stranger's offer of help is to refuse it. Perhaps this is because we like to prove to ourselves that we can manage or, maybe, we doubt strangers and their motives. Something of the sort may have entered Lily's mind and one should always listen to one's doubts.

"Who are you? Didn't I see you in the bar just now? Customers aren't allowed in here; I'm sorry, you'll have to leave."

"I was trying to find the loo; I got lost; your signs don't comply with…"

Joy stopped herself just in time. Old habits die hard but just then she wanted something from these people.

"You'd do well to let me help. I'm used to this sort of work. *(This was partly true, but restaurant kitchens aren't quite the same as the Siptac microwave)*. Just show little old me what you need doing and I'll work away quiet as a mouse."

It was for Sam's partner to decide:

"I shouldn't be allowing anyone to work in here without the proper checks. - But we *are* shorthanded; perhaps I can bend the rules just this once. So long as you keep quiet about it, I'll take up your offer. You can help Chef; we pay by the hour and you wear the kit provided – over there by the door."

So Joy donned a white apron and with some difficulty perched a little white cap on top of her wobbly hair, then, without a word of discussion with Chef, she took over management of the soup. Not much of a task but it suited her very well.

∗ ∗ ∗

He wasn't an impatient man but Chris had been working outdoors all day, as farmers do. He needed food and good quantities of it:

"I don't think much of it so far. If my steak doesn't appear in the next ten minutes, I suggest we go to Jack's. There's still time."

"Wait a bit longer. You won't get as good entertainment there. And I want to know what Joy Siptac's been up to: she was lurking in her corner out of Harold's sight, then she was gone and now she's back again, still hiding."

"I don't like the woman but I suppose she's allowed to have a pee sometimes; at least she can't be spoiling anyone's life when she's doing it."

"I'm not sure about that. I can imagine… Anyway, you don't go to the loo bareheaded and come back wearing a white cap."

Chris perked up. Making his way to the bar, apparently to buy another round for the two of them, he stared directly and deliberately at Joy.

"Nice cap Joy. New fashion is it?"

It took her perhaps half a second to be certain he was addressing her, another half second to work out what he was talking about and just one more to put up her hand and discover her headgear. For those few half seconds the Siptac was lost for a reply but, as we have seen, the woman has plenty of grit.

"I can't see it's any of your business Mr Downe, but I always wear this when I'm inspecting catering establishments for the Council. It's the Law. And if that's your Chelsea tractor in the car park, its number plates are obscured with some filth or other. I shall have to report it."

"Go right ahead Joy, be my guest. It will have been worth it to see you looking so cute."

She stared after him as he walked back to his table. Joy hadn't known she was cute. She fell into a little daydream.

The trouble with the Siptacs of the world is they have no sense of humour.

"Well, what's the story behind the pretty cap, Chris?"

"Oh, we wronged her, she's been inspecting the place on behalf of the Council and they make her wear a silly hat for the job. She told me I'm going to be reported for having a dirty car and I told her she's cute."

"Are you sure it isn't your dirty mind she's reporting?"

"I expect that was it. Now look who we have here – one Susan Smith, Smythe or Repplington arriving to join her Harold, in fullest public view. That should give our Joy something to chew her nails."

"Indeed. – I wonder at Harold choosing to sit there, so high and obvious. Didn't think he had the courage. And Susan doesn't seem bothered either. Lucky she wasn't here earlier to hear her name being bandied about. She looks quite radiant. Young love!"

"If I know this rotten village, it won't be long before someone tells her, plus a few fanciful additions. In fact I suspect her silly clot, Harold, is already doing just that – see her colour's changing!"

And Chris was quite right. Silly clot Harold wasted no time in giving her a blow by blow account of Sam's speech, from its bold start to the final fade out, plus everything his hecklers contributed along the way. Being able to share troubles with a friend is one of life's blessings but Harold simply dumped the whole burden, and he felt better for it. Susan did not.

Hardly noticing her change of mood, Harold pressed on with his evening, happy now to be immersed in their small world and busy himself with ordering meals and drinks. Susan had been hungry when she arrived, but no longer. If she could have done so she would have left for home, but, as we've seen, she, too, has grit and she wasn't going to allow the local crowd the pleasure of gossiping behind her back.

Public bars are awkward places to sit and eat. Little elbow room, small space for all the necessary crockery, condiments, plates and glasses and then there's the nuisance of other customers doing all the things that people do at bars from just standing around and talking close to your ear to shouting orders at the bar staff over your head. So, vegetarian Susan wisely chose a simple toasted sandwich to go with her shandy. Foolish Harold selected something that was less appropriate in the circumstances.

One must hand it to the Siptac. For shear nerve she has no equal.

Having performed her sabotage, Joy ordered a snack meal at her discrete table. Soup of the day and a minute steak with chips; whether she consumed any of her starter is uncertain – she did leave a good deal of it. At all events, her bar receipt confirmed she had been served a full portion and what one ordered, of course one must have eaten.

✳ ✳ ✳

Their steaks had been remarkably good and they were relaxing over coffee in the saloon bar.

"By the way Chris, how have you got on with your photo from Greta? – I've identified some of the people in mine but it's hard going – too many are either half in and half out of shot or they're pointing the wrong way. I can't recognise them by their backs. And there are some who seem to have no heads. – Explains a lot about Coldstow locals but no help to us."

"About the same as you, I guess. I'm stuck on the faceless ones and there's another unhelpful batch that I just don't know, face or not. Our Filly seems to have attracted quite a few followers from elsewhere. Perhaps we ought to join forces and run through what we've got to date. See who we can eliminate – if any."

"Agreed – tomorrow night?"

But he couldn't make that evening and it wasn't until a few days later that they met at Downes Farm.

✳ ✳ ✳

The Happy Fireside's re-opening night was drawing to a close. Some drinkers remained at the bars; most of the diners had left, a few still sat lingering over coffee and conversation. So far, on balance, Sam and Cheri might have considered it a successful evening but the little problems kept coming.

"Can we go home now? I'm feeling rather full and I need to use the loo."

"Use the pub's loo; it's just beyond the door over there."

"The powder room's got a queue out into the car park and the men's is the same, or I'd use it. ***I NEED THE LOO!!***"

And variations on that same conversation were being repeated around both bars. Further, not a few diners had skipped the dessert course and left early. One had been violently ill in the car park; another was sick in her car before she got home.

They sat and watched, astonished, as the epidemic spread.

"It's like watching a biblical plague get under way. I expect a host of locusts next."

"It's a plague alright; a plague of food poisoning or itching powder – look at the three at that table. They got up as one and they're dancing around on the carpet while they wait for their bill... Now they've gone leaving their credit card behind. – Such is the rush of modern life."

The entertainment ended after another ten minutes or so. Chris paid the bill and did not forget his credit card. They both left, taking their time and chatting in the car park for a while. Both of them drove the short distance home at gentle speed.

But neither had soup that evening. Nor did Rene and Louise, Joy, Susan and half a dozen others.

Sam, Cheri and Chef were ill to varying degrees and so were Harold and most of the remaining customers, including all the hecklers. So that was one silver lining to set against Sam's several clouds.

Chapter 19

Police encounters.

Elcester Police Station is a featureless 1960s brick and concrete building with ribbon windows to the upper three floors. The existence of a basement is hinted at by the tops of a few further windows peeping out just above the level of the front car park. We need not enquire just now about the purpose of the basement but Joy Siptac has visited there in the past and can tell more about it, if anyone wants to know.

A wide concrete stairway leads to the double entrance door under a flat roofed porch. Up to that point a visitor might as well be entering a council library, a museum or any other public place of pleasure. Past that door, no one could make that mistake. There is nothing inside Elcester Police Station to offer anyone other than a masochist the hope of a good time.

He ran lightly up the concrete steps; the main door was wedged open and he arrived, a little breathless, at the front desk. The sergeant stared at him for a long moment. There was no conscious intention to bully; the policeman looked at everyone that way, including his own family. It was habit born from training and practice.

"Yes sir, what can I do for you?"

The way it was said, the words might as well have been *"what can we do to you?"*

"I'm here to see Detective Chief Inspector Cardler. - He knows I'm coming; I've got an appointment."

He suspected he was overdoing this – another minute and

he would be babbling; two more and he might confess to being someone the police were looking for.

The desk sergeant continued his stare. His attitude was hardening. - Innocent people didn't ask to see Cardler; no one would be that stupid.

"Wait over there. I'll see if he's in. And don't wander off."

He walked away intending to lean against a wall - until he saw the filth on it. He stood a little distance off, waiting as directed.

And he waited a long while, time enough for feet to go numb, for him to count the number of stained tiles on the floor and then the bricks in the wall behind the desk sergeant. He had left his phone in his car or he might have made some use of the time. He edged toward the door, half decided to abandon the venture.

The sergeant didn't like that.

"Just wait there, Sir; he won't be long"

It was tempting to ignore the man and just leave but he wasn't going to try again. Another visit was unthinkable.

"I've got other things to do apart from waiting here. I'll give it five more minutes."

He got another glare but ignored it. Apparently the softening up system had been worked to its limit. The sergeant made a phone call and suddenly, DCI Cardler was available and there was a uniformed someone to take him upstairs.

The first floor was as depressing as the reception area. A bare red brick corridor lit by steel framed windows along its entire length and some sort of composite grey floor suitable for the sort of traffic a police station might expect. The spacious office at the far end of the building contained a few grey filing cabinets, some uncomfortable looking chairs, a small, untidy grey desk and the Chief Inspector himself, a large, sloppily dressed figure standing with his back to him and looking down into the street.

The door closed; he stood waiting for the man to acknowledge him. Throughout the time he was there, the policeman never turned to face him. The conversation began without any of the usual formalities on the part of either of them. They might as well have been longstanding enemies for all the regard they showed each other.

"You've been poking your nose into the death of Mrs Jo Downe. That's police business and you will stay out of it."

"You should do some basic homework; Christopher and Jo Downe weren't married. I haven't been poking my nose, as you put it, into police business. You lot did nothing to look into her death. It's not police business if you've dropped your enquiries, as you surely have."

"Be very careful what you say. I could have you held for questioning right now; suspicion of withholding evidence, tampering with evidence, trespass on scene of crime."

"So hold me. You haven't any grounds, and you know it. As far as you're concerned Jo's death wasn't murder, so there was no crime, there is no criminal evidence for anyone to withhold or tamper with and there isn't a scene of crime to be trespassed on. Anyway, what evidence are you talking about and where was the scene of crime – the pub, Jo's home, my car?"

The other man continued to stand by his window, silent, evidently thinking, then:

"You can go. Remember what I said."

"I didn't come here to be told I could go. I came to tell you that in my view Jo was murdered and why I think so. She deserves a proper enquiry into her death, not just a sweeping under the carpet exercise by a lot of lazy coppers."

He regretted it as soon as it was out. Not much chance now of getting the man on side, and without him, this lonely job was going to be harder than ever.

No more was said by either of them at that meeting and he walked back down the bare concrete stairs, across the reception area with its unpleasing desk sergeant and out into welcome fresh air.

"I need two things," he thought, *"a bath and a bit of luck."*

He had one more task. The bath must wait but he might hope for luck.

Turning down a side street, he entered the Western Press offices. The young archivist gave him a cheerful welcome.

"I expected you an hour ago. Been trying to find a parking place?"

"Something like that. No difficulty parking, just took a long time to escape the police."

The girl smiled. She had known him since before she left school; his jokes were often obscure, but she gave as good as she got.

"I've looked out what you asked for and found you a pokey office to do your poking about in. If you promise to stop riling the local Force, I'll find you a cup of tea. Is Freddie with you?"

"Thanks - a biscuit would be welcome. And no, Freddie isn't with me today, she decided to stay in the car when I told her there wasn't any ice cream on offer. - She has to save her strength for the big things in life."

She brought his tea and stopped to see what he was doing.

"Funny thing: you're the second person interested in that; asked for copies, too."

That got his attention.

"Who was it?"

"I can't recall her name. Nice mover, sexy. Sorry, I've got to get on; work's piling up."

He wasn't fooled, that sudden switch told all; his friendly archivist had caught herself saying more than she ought and put up the shutters. Strange, those weren't adjectives he would have used to describe Greta. He thought no more of it at that time.

On his way home across the moor he stopped to take patient Freddie for a long walk over one of their familiar circular routes. The dog wanted it; so did his mind.

Feeling a need to be among any sort of company, so long as it wasn't Coldstow's spiteful gang, he stopped again before reaching home to have lunch alone at Jack's. The waitress's warm smile made him feel a lot better about the human race but that feeling wasn't going to last long.

* * *

Of all crimes, those that cause the deepest harm are the personal, invasive ones. Physical attack and rape are perhaps the worst but having one's house broken into and thoroughly searched is as damaging as property crimes get. The knowledge that someone has brutally entered your home, examined every personal possession and learned the intimate details of your life is, of course, far worse than the physical loss.

He had got back to his house late in the afternoon. It was raining and the late autumn daylight had almost gone. In the darkness, he saw nothing wrong until he reached his front door, even then, being unprepared for it, he was slow to accept that the pale splinter of wood on the ground was anything sinister.

The door was closed but it opened as he touched it. There were more splinters on the hall floor and some twisted ironmongery.

He took Freddie back to the car and shut her in on the back seat, then walked quietly back to the broken door. Uncertain if anyone was still inside the house, he worked carefully, opening the door wider and slipping into the hall. He left all the lights off and collected a small torch from a shelf under the stairs.

After listening carefully for a full five minutes, he switched on the hall and landing lights and immediately sprang up the stair. With astonishing speed he literally ran from room to room, noting in his passing the turmoil everywhere but not stopping to check.

Nothing found so far, he ran back to the ground floor and repeated his room by room sprint. Again, nothing.

Still without examining the damage, he took out his mobile phone and rang Elcester police station.

"DCI Cardler please. Tell him it's the man he spoke to this morning about Jo Downe's death and it's urgent."

This time he didn't have to wait long for the Inspector's voice

"Well, what do you want now?"

"Tell your bully boys in blue to ring me before they break into my house next time and I'll leave it unlocked to save the cost of a new lock. That's all."

There followed a slight grunt at the other end and the phone went dead.

"And to hell with you too." He thought.

There was nothing he could do about his broken lock until the following day but he spent the next two hours carefully checking certain particular concealed spaces in the house, generally putting things back in order and binning what was unrepairable. Strangely, nothing seemed to be missing except some notes made at an earlier meeting with Chris.

By ten o'clock, he was ready to go to bed; it had been a long and unsatisfactory day, and much still to be put right. He made some coffee and sat in his kitchen, playing ball with Freddie and rewarding her catches with small pieces of carrot, proving that they didn't always ignore her doctor's advice.

* * *

Lost for a few moments in a private and crime-free world, he almost missed hearing the sound of the buzzer at his broken front door.

He had been ready for trouble as soon as he knew he had a late visitor, but he didn't need the kitchen knife.

"You can put that away. I haven't come to arrest you. Not tonight anyway. Are you going to ask me in or shall we talk across your doorstep?"

"Detective Chief Inspector Cardler, as I live and breathe. Yes, do come in. You can gloat over what your lot did while you kept me waiting about this morning."

The policeman silently looked through the downstairs rooms. A finger pointed upstairs sent him to check the rest of the house. He returned to the kitchen and watched Freddie playing with her friend.

"Would you like some tea Inspector, or something stronger?"

"I'll take the tea – thank you."

Neither of them spoke until the tea was made and both were seated at his kitchen table. It was the first opportunity he had to look at the man face to face. Typical police, he thought, hard, rather red face, clean shaven, close cropped grey hair, head and neck moulded in one like a bullet; a big man wearing a sloppy grey suit, a nicely tailored shirt and, surprisingly, fine Italian leather shoes. – Altogether an enigma; the outer shell ill at ease with the inner, perhaps.

"You probably won't believe it, but I had no knowledge of this. If any of my lot are involved it's for reasons outside the Force."

"If you say so. But why did you come here tonight? And why alone?"

"Alone because I want to talk without it being official. I'll come to the why in a moment. First I've got a couple of questions."

"Funny, I hoped you might have begun with an apology."

"I've got nothing to apologise for; I told you we didn't do your break-in."

"I was talking about something else; your desk sergeant kept me waiting an hour after our appointment time this morning; it was plainly a softening up job and I didn't like it. Also it did occur that it might have given someone a chance to pop over to Coldstow and rough up my life a bit – a warning to stay out of police matters, perhaps?"

"OK, you're right about keeping you hanging about and I apologise but that was nothing to do with damaging your place. I repeat; not us! Now I want you to tell me why you're so sure Jo Downe's death was murder and what you expect from me, because you obviously wanted something this morning, at least you did before you lost your rag."

He looked steadily at his visitor, trying to decide whether the man was genuine or thoroughly crooked; it had to be one or the other. There really wasn't any choice; he needed help and he couldn't see it coming from any other source.

"Jo was angry the day she died. The pub had sacked her from her chef's job just to save money and they did it in a rotten way. There was a lot of sympathy for her over it. First, angry people don't kill themselves. Second she was there to give the landlord a public roasting and she was enjoying it; people don't kill themselves when they're getting that much satisfaction.

So she died by natural causes, accident or murder – there are no other options. She was fit and healthy – a little overweight perhaps but aren't most of us? That doctor's bloody useless but she knew Jo's medical history – she wasn't liable to pop off suddenly. But that's what happened. There was something very odd about her behaviour just before she collapsed. She'd certainly had some alcohol before she arrived but she wasn't blind drunk. It was after she had a drink in the bar that she lost the plot."

He hesitated for a moment, still unsure how much it was safe to say, then continued; no point stopping now.

"It's common knowledge now that she had barbiturates in her system. I can't see she took them deliberately. Jo was no fool; she wouldn't have mixed alcohol with her drugs. And I go back to the doctor. She missed the drugs first time round. That was a sloppy examination but everyone based their thinking on it and it seems they still do – your lot included. What I'm after is the truth; her partner's the best friend I have. At one time he was under suspicion and I hate to see that; he loved Jo as much as any man loves his partner."

Cardler wasn't impressed. His policeman's brain objected to all of it.

"Alright, so the investigation might have been better done by everyone. But you haven't even suggested a motive or the how or the who."

"The motive I don't know; maybe someone feared she was about to blab something they didn't want generally known – Jo was pumping out some awkward little disclosures about the two pub owners that night. More to come possibly. Or perhaps she was in somebody's way – an inheritance possibly. How should I know?

The how is another matter. I reckon the killer added barbs to her whiskey and, after she drank the mixture, removed the evidence. It was either done at the farm or in the pub. She had her own bottle at both places. The drug could have been added any time before the murder, maybe days before. As to the who, I've got my own ideas but I'm not prepared to say more just now."

"Ok, ok, you've done a lot of thinking and I can see some logic in it. The fact is, after you came to see me this morning, I looked into the case again; I reckoned if you were that keen on your theory, I ought to take you seriously."

He was grateful for that much. Surprisingly, Cardler went one step further:

"I've got my own investigation to make. I'm not prepared to tell you about that but I might (I emphasise 'might') be willing to get some answers for you if doing that doesn't cut across police work."

"I suppose I can't ask more. What I need is some lab reports. Can you feed something through your system for me?"

"What is it?"

"It's more a case of 'What are they?' – 'They' are different samples of spirits. I can give them to you now. In fact I had them with me when we met this morning to scratch each other's eyes out. I don't want to say what I'm looking for. I need a completely independent lab report on them all."

"Good God, how many are there? Do you know what that sort of thing costs?"

"Just these four. And what's the police budget for, if it isn't solving crime?"

Cardler was softening:

"You'd be surprised – everything from helping old ladies find their cats to humouring amateur detectives with bees in their bonnets. By the way, you'll need a crime number for your insurance claim. Ring me tomorrow – I'll make sure there's no delay. And leave your front door untouched for the fingerprint team tomorrow."

"Have a beer before you leave? – Peace offering."

"I will. Accepted as offered."

Chapter 20

Mutual help.

Stomach pains, from whatever cause – food poisoning, hunger or physical strain - are miserable ills to bear. Some of the Happy Fireside's opening night diners might have preferred being burgled to suffering cramps that lasted through the night and, for many, on into the following day.

It hadn't taken much detective work to identify the cause. Wise after the event, people remembered the onion soup had tasted slightly strange and wasn't it an odd colour? Doctor Ledger attended to some eight cases and another five elected to suffer unattended at home – the good doctor having lost some of her patients' trust following her incompetence over Jo's death and the gossips' inevitable malevolent stories.

But whether they consulted their GP or not, none of the sufferers was minded to let the matter rest as far as the proprietors of the Happy Fireside were concerned.

So half a dozen residents and two outsiders consulted with their lawyers and, out of public duty, Joy also wrote to the food safety team people at Town Hall.

"We've got another complaint from the Siptac woman in Coldstow. This one's about food in their local pub. – The one that's just reopened."

"That's a full set in one month – she's reported the village shop for selling out of date laxatives and the Jack's as Good as his Master for short measuring spirits."

"What shall I do about it?"

"Send a reply saying we're looking into it and get your friend in the planning department to find some breach of the Planning Acts at her house. There's always something.

It's time she had a taste of her own medicine."

* * *

They had arranged to meet at the Happy Fireside a few days after the soup episode. The pub's kitchen was closed pending the outcome of investigations and the place was almost empty. They sat at a table in the saloon bar with Greta's photos in front of them. Chris was making his report:

"I've done as agreed. This is the list of people I've identified and I'm sure about; they're all certainties either because you can see faces or something familiar – companion, clothes, dog, that sort of thing. The next is people whose faces I can see clearly but I don't know and the third is people I can't identify but I might know if their faces were clear. Everyone's numbered in the picture and those are the numbers in the three lists. It's probably all useless – there's a lot I can't name."

"Don't despair Chris. We haven't finished the job yet. Next task is to swap photos and lists and see if we can fill in any of each other's gaps, and perhaps identify people who appear in part in both photos. Two half pictures might be enough to name a few more."

"Ever hopeful, aren't you? I know I was all for it before we started but I can't see now where we're going. Modern murderers don't wear wide brimmed hats and black cloaks, any more than burglars wear striped vests; it's just not the fashion nowadays."

"No, but whoever it was, I'm sure the killer's in at least one of these pictures or Greta wouldn't have thrust them on me."

"But if she knows who it is, why bother you about it? Why not just go to the police?"

"Beats me. I can only repeat: she doesn't trust them, and she was very strong on that."

"Well, give me my homework Sherlock, and I'll do as you say.

I only work here. What about a meal at Jack's?"

He sat silent for a while. Sherlock – that was what she had called him. Now Chris was doing it; a strange coincidence, half disturbing, half comforting, as if his friends were there with him in spirit. It wasn't the first time that thought had come to him.

Cheri walked across to their table and sat down uninvited. She looked washed out, nothing like the competent, cheerful and colourful young woman who managed the opening night.

"Can I interrupt you both?"

"Be our guest, we were just boring each other with our fishing stories."

"You were here on our disaster night – did you see anything I ought to know about?"

They both felt uncomfortable; put on the spot like this, it was going to be difficult to avoid trouble one way or another.

"Such as?"

"Such as anyone playing about with the food or just someone acting strangely."

Neither replied, but Cheri pressed on:

"And such as a local woman who left the saloon bar hatless and returned with one of our kitchen uniform caps on top of her hairdo."

Chris wasn't going to lie to protect Joy Siptac and he wanted to help. Whatever happened to spoil the opening night, it wasn't Cheri's fault, or Sam's for that matter.

"Yes. I did see her, it was Joy Siptac, but I can't tell you any more than that. We were in the public area all the time."

"I think she poisoned the soup. She came into the kitchen before we started to serve up and offered help – it was all pretty hectic just then and I said yes, provided she didn't make an issue about kitchen training. She put on the uniform and went off to help Chef. She didn't stay long because, when I looked in again, only Lily and Chef were there. I thought that was a bit odd but didn't have time to investigate. What I can't believe is that apparently someone called Siptac reported us to the local authority for breaches of hygiene regulations. Surely no one would foul up the food and report it themselves - it's beyond anything."

Chris felt sorry for her. Cheri was learning about Coldstow the hard way.

"Not for Joy Siptac; I'm not telling you this but that woman would do anything for spite. – Has she got her knife into you, or Sam perhaps?"

"I can't think she has a grudge against me; Sam possibly, but I don't know the history and don't want to. Whatever it's about, the customers shouldn't have suffered. I'm not going to let this go."

"Good for you, I, no, *we* wish you well Cheri."

"Thanks. - By the way, what's the photo about? You seem puzzled by it."

"We're trying to identify everyone in it – it's a sort of game to keep two old blokes off the street."

"Can I play? I could do with a bit of entertainment."

Chris looked at him and got a nod.

"It's a picture from a sort of fete day in Coldstow. We have to name everyone in it. See the numbers? These are three lists I've made: people I've identified, those I can't name and some that I can't make out because they're wandering about with their heads cut off. You're in there – having a rare day off from slavery behind the bar at Jack's."

Cheri said nothing as she studied the picture, then turned to Chris' lists. She went back and forth for some time before:

"Well, I've got a few you haven't. I come from Ewer and some of these guys are old neighbours and family friends. Can I add their names to your identified list?"

That done, she returned to study the picture again.

"I don't know names, but these two by the hall door are church people; and aren't the furtive two without heads the pair who used to run this pub? They're carrying things. Does that make them murderers?"

"Who said anything about murder, Cheri?"

"You didn't. But I'm not stupid; this picture was taken the day the vicar died, that's plain. But it's before it actually happened; or before it was discovered anyway – no police about, and people are wandering around in all directions. Coldstow would have rushed to those skips when her body was found, poor thing."

Cheri stood up and started to walk away but turned back:

"Don't mind me. I shan't tell anyone what you're doing. I hope you work out who did it; the police can't, or won't."

Later that evening they were back in his office.

"Well Chris, that's as far as we go. We've identified most of them. We're left with five we can't name because there isn't enough of them to see and another five with faces we can see but which none of us, Cheri included, can recognise. I wonder what Stan and Dave were doing in the picture."

He photographed the picture and zoomed it.

"Bottles! I wonder where they're taking them. – Best guess; the Crabbes' shop."

"Well, that's one question settled; that still was working hard; sales across the bar *and* supplying the local shop. Those two were in deep and so were their customers. I wonder when that's all going to come out. Watch this space."

They both laughed. It was a relief to fall back on a piece of good solid Coldstow criminality and meanness.

"I wonder how far apart those pictures are in time."

"Why didn't I think of that? And, Chris, what time of day were they taken? We know the first was before Filly died. This one's slightly later: look at the shadows – one of that day's few sunny periods."

"But what's the significance?"

He got up, stretched and went away to make coffee in the small office kitchen, and to think, before answering.

"I'll tell you what the significance may be: the second one's before the murder was discovered but after the murder itself."

"How do you make that out?"

"Second photo, bottom left hand corner – what do you see?"

"A lorry; probably moving as it's a bit out of focus."

"Not just any lorry – it's a skip truck; in fact <u>the</u> skip truck; the one that came to take the skip that was hiding the body."

"So?"

"It's guesswork, but bear with me for a moment. Suppose we're looking at before and after photos; the first shows the killer in sight before or soon after the deed; by the time the second was taken he, or she, has got away; as anyone would. – It's just a premise to try out. If it's correct then we should look at who's in picture 1 but isn't in 2."

"Are you suggesting whoever took the snaps knew what was going to happen and cold bloodedly recorded this for future use? That's unbelievable; it would mean A.N.Other knew the killer's plan in detail. Why take photographs that don't seem to prove anything? They aren't enough for blackmail, surely."

"No Chris, I don't suggest that. At least one of these photographs was published in the local paper. I've seen a copy at the Western Press office. Probably both of them were taken by the same press photographer and I expect there would have been a lot more again that didn't get used. Photography's cheap and they make sure they don't miss anything. Anyway it's got me thinking on different lines; lines I'm not comfortable with. I need to sleep on it."

Chris puzzled over this for a moment before giving up and returning to the subject.

"Before you take to your lonely bed, I've done my research on Jo all as agreed. Her mum died four weeks ago. She and Jo used the same solicitor who's dealing with the estate. I managed to speak to him; not easy to get information from a stone but I did learn the trust fund that met the old girl's nursing home fees falls in now and what's left goes to Jo's estate. But there's nothing much left – less than ten thousand anyway.

Mum had nothing much of her own; in total it can't amount to a sum worth killing for. Jo's will left everything she had to her husband, - she hadn't got round to changing it - so he stood to gain something, but he isn't poor. There's no motive there as far as I can see.

As to enemies; Jo had none to my knowledge. Most of the villagers here are pretty unpleasant, but Jo wasn't one of their targets.

And a bit more information: Jo's carry bag that she left in the pub had some papers. One was a letter addressed to her from a different firm of lawyers with advice about 'going to court as a next step' in her divorce - she kept that a complete secret. And the rest of the paperwork is mostly delivery tickets for food from catering companies that Jo's written her comments on – none of them complimentary. It looks as if she was gathering evidence on the poor food she had to deal with. - I felt very sorry for her."

"That fits with papers I found in Dave and Stan's bedroom after they skipped. There were two letters from Jo to Dave, about the quality of the food she was having to cope with. Basically she was threatening to leave her job and tell what she knew unless they went back to buying from a decent source.

All this is hard on you, Chris; try to think of something else for a while. You have to move on."

"Physician, heal thyself. I told you Sally was your cure."

"You're as bad as my doctor; I feel worse every time I see him, so I don't consult him any more."

And Chris thought:

"Nearly ready to be pushed over the edge, can't be long now; I wonder how it's going to be done."

* * *

The date is Friday the twenty fifth of November and the scene is a large and comfortable sunlit sitting room in an English county town hotel. It is 11.00 am and the place smells of good breakfasts and cut flowers, as a quality hotel should at that time of day. And this one has been looking after people, and doing it well, for over two hundred years. The room, at the front of the building, overlooks the tree lined main street, the generously wide pavements and the three cars parked in the visitors' parking bay by the hotel entrance. In the Autumn sunshine a few tourists are viewing an unusually small Norman church which stands in its green graveyard opposite. The high street is busy but, apart from a ticking longcase clock and occasional quiet voices, there is no sound in this room; traffic noise can't get past the double glazing or the hotel's old stone walls.

The owners haven't got round to redecorating this year. The place shows the marks and scars of twelve months use, but this only adds to the aura of comfort. Tall cream painted Georgian windows and gracious internal joinery need to bear the signs of use, like the richly patterned dark blue carpet which plays its own part in pleasing both eye and ear.

Three people are sitting in a remote corner of the room, two in a deep settee, one in a leather armchair. Coffee and an assortment of biscuits have just been set for them on a low table. They will have an early lunch together a little later on before returning to their homes and work. For one of them a one hundred mile journey; a mere fifty or so for the other two.

Their easy talk and relaxed positions show them to be good friends. They have been here regularly for some weeks now. The subject of discussion is always the same; it is a matter of concern to each of them, although they have slightly differing reasons for their interest.

The man spoke:

"I still think we should do more. It's too much to ask of anyone without help."

The very smart young woman in the leather chair reached over to pour the three coffees:

"I can't agree; he's got a good enquiring mind. He will get there with what we've given him. I need it to come from him and so does he."

"I know. You think it's a way to repair his own mind. God knows what he'd say if he thought we were manipulating him to that extent."

"We are all in God's hands. He doesn't make mistakes about people."

The other, older, woman spoke for the first time:

"We talk about him as if he's a machine. I hate that."

"Sorry, I didn't mean to be heartless. We all care. Just give him time and he'll get there; truth will come out because it must.

We promised each other to keep watch over him and that promise stands no matter what happens or how long this goes on."

The second woman spoke again:

"So long as we stay close and meet frequently, I suppose it's alright to let him work alone. But if I think he's at risk I shall act on my own, even if neither of you agree."

"Of course, if he falls into danger, we shall all be there for him. You won't be alone any more than he will."

The conversation became more general. After lunch the three of them studied a few documents and photographs; their earlier discussion continued where it had left off until they parted on the hotel steps and drove away to their separate destinations.

Nothing needed to be said about their next meeting. The time and place were fixed, unchangeable.

Chapter 21

Interrogations.

Cardler was suffering another migraine courtesy of Coldstow and its little difficulties. He had a particular distaste for anonymous letters.

'If you want to solve the murder of Jo Downe, look into what Joy Siptac was doing on the Happy Fireside pub's reopening night.

Well-wisher.'

The inspector couldn't see how something that happened long after Jo Downe's death could have any bearing on it. And he certainly did not want any more of the Siptacs – either of them.

But he was bound to follow it through, particularly after the Elcester police work at the start of the case. He wished that amateur detective in Coldstow to hell and a speedy journey. But he was quite wrong there: the anonymous writer was someone else entirely and the motive for it wasn't an enthusiast's desire to help the authorities; it was good old Coldstow troublemaking at its most spiteful.

In any case, what was he supposed to investigate, and why didn't the letter say? He picked up his phone.

"I've got your supposedly anonymous letter about Mrs Siptac. I don't like this sort of thing. If you've got information about a crime, come out with it."

The phone stayed silent for a time while he thought.

"Well, hallo to you too, Chief Inspector – and I do recognise your voice, so at least you're not anonymous. I haven't the first idea what this is about; if you think I'm the sort that sends unsigned letters to the police, we've both sadly misjudged each other. And I thought we'd got over our mutual distrust."

It was the policeman's turn to have a quiet think.

"Mm. Sorry if I'm wrong. Listen to this…"

He read the letter over the phone.

"So why think I wrote that? It's not my style and it has to be garbage, what's Siptac's food poisoning act to do with Jo?"

"I don't know anything about food poisoning; tell me."

"I assumed you would know. A lot of people were ill after the local pub's opening night. Apparently it was caused by the soup. Perhaps I shouldn't have said it was done by Joy Siptac but it's pretty certain she was the culprit."

"Ok, leave it with me."

* * *

It didn't take long for the Chief Inspector to have a word with his friends at the local council and to learn that one Mrs Siptac had been complaining about quite a few matters, including food poisoning and the sale of out of date goods in the local shop. He summoned his desk sergeant:

"What's the name of that incompetent constable who covers Coldstow district?"

"PC Mabbtree."

"I want to see him. Two o'clock; Coldstow's pub car park."

The DCI arrived promptly at three that afternoon together with one of his detective sergeants. By then the uniformed local man had been waiting at the Happy Fireside's front door for an hour and a half, getting ever colder and, incidentally, bringing the pub's afternoon business to a halt.

Cardler met Cheri in the public bar, introduced himself and wasted no further time on niceties.

"You had some cases of food poisoning the other evening.

What can you tell me about it?"

"I can't tell you anything much. Everyone who ate the soup was ill and, so far as I know, everyone who didn't was fine. Is this a police matter? I thought we'd been through all the enquiries from the Food Safety Team. In fact we've been cleared to re-open; they didn't find anything wrong with our kitchen. It's a bit of a mystery, and, I may say, it hurt us badly. It was our opening night."

"It's a police matter now. We've had information suggesting the poisoning was deliberate. Did you see anything unusual that evening; anyone behaving suspiciously, anyone around the food when it was prepared or served that shouldn't have been?"

"Before I answer, I'd like to know what this information is and who passed it to you."

"Can't tell you that, Miss. Please answer the question."

"I don't know anything for certain; I do have suspicions but I'm not going to get someone in trouble who may be innocent. And don't threaten me; I don't buckle."

"Fair enough, let me put it another way. If I mention some names, tell me any that were here that evening and that you couldn't vouch for. I'll start with Rene Crabbe."

She made no response.

"Louise Crabbe… Susan Smythe… Harold Siptac…"

Still nothing from Cheri.

"Joy Siptac?"

"I can't vouch for her."

"Ok. I've named her, not you, and now you tell me why she's not on your goody list."

"Joy Siptac came into the kitchen shortly before we began to plate up. We were shorthanded and very busy. She offered to help. It's no secret that I bent the rules by agreeing and she went to see Chef. She was stirring soup when I last saw her. Soon afterwards she'd gone and I didn't see her in the kitchen again. Later she was in the bar and she ordered soup. But I don't think she ate any. If she did, it was very little."

"What else can you tell me?"

"Nothing, except that I noticed she was being watched very

closely by two of the other customers from when they arrived up to the time Joy left. There's probably nothing in that but it looked odd."

"Names?"

"Sisters; Rene and Louise Crabbe. They keep the village shop. I gather they aren't best friends with the Siptacs."

He asked to see the chef and her assistant, Lily. They confirmed Cheri's information but had no more to add. Sam, when questioned, could tell the police nothing of relevance except that Joy had a habit of doing unpleasant things.

"And perhaps that habit might include poisoning people" thought the detective, *"and I'll bet that's the connection our anonymous informer wanted made - Jo Downe. And, again, poisoning anyone within reach without caring who. Maybe Jo was killed just for the pleasure of killing and not because she was Jo."*

These were unpleasant thoughts but, to the worldly-wise policeman, not impossibilities. Joy had been at the Happy Fireside's bar on the night Jo died, now here she was in the forefront of suspicion for a mass poisoning in the very same pub. – *"I don't care who I kill, it's just fun to do it"*.

Next for interrogation were the managers of the village store. He chose to deal with them separately.

"I'm investigating the possibility that someone deliberately poisoned food at the Happy Fireside pub…"

He got no further. Rene deliberately tripped him up with her shaky old lady act:

"Yes, I heard that Mrs Siptac was responsible. It's awful; not being able to go out for a modest snack without being killed. I hope you lock her up. We're all at risk of our lives as long as she's free to walk about. The evil of it!"

"We don't yet know there was any poisoning or, if there was, that Mrs Siptac was involved. Why are you so sure Miss Crabbe? And while we're on the subject what do you know about a letter to the police alleging Mrs Siptac's guilt?"

"I wouldn't know about your anonymous letters Inspector; you'll have to ask their author."

"How do you know the letter was unsigned? Perhaps because you or your sister Louise wrote it? I guess it was your sister and you're shielding her."

"Of course it wasn't either of us. What would we gain by such a thing?"

But he had found the pressure point and proceeded to use it without mercy.

"I believe that letter came from one of the two of you. More specifically, your sister."

"Absolutely not. Louise is a complete innocent."

He turned the screw; "If you won't tell the truth, I shall have to arrest both of you."

She couldn't let Louise become caught up in this. Her sister had always been a trifle weak minded; Rene had spent a lifetime protecting her.

"Alright, I sent that letter. You can leave Louise alone."

"Why point the finger at Mrs Siptac?"

"Because she deserves it and because she certainly caused the food poisoning. We watched her that evening. She left the bar and came back later wearing the sort of white cap they wear in kitchens. Someone we saw speaking to her must have told her she was still wearing it because she suddenly snatched it off. And she ordered the soup but didn't drink any. Proof enough I'd say, wouldn't you?'"

"Do you know what she added to the soup? Would it have been laxatives bought in your shop, perhaps. - A sale of out of date medication that's even now the subject of official enquiry?'"

Rene stayed silent. A silence that was, as she would have said, proof enough.

So Joy Siptac was arrested for the second time. Not, at this stage, for involvement in any murder but on charges quite serious enough and Cardler hadn't yet dismissed the idea that poisoning might be habit forming. There were plenty of examples in history.

* * *

The news that Joy had been re-arrested reached Coldstow within ten minutes of it happening. Possibly the long-standing friendship between his friend the Desk Sergeant and PC Mabbtree had something to do with that. The fact of her incarceration was correctly reported but the reason was open to guess, and the gossips duly made their guesses and stated them as truths.

It was variously rumoured that Joy was held for the murder of Jo Downe, for murdering the vicar, for murdering husband Harold (who hadn't been seen for twenty four hours and must therefore have been done away with) and for attempting to poison the whole village to death. Delicious news all of it.

Having done no more than take Freddie out for her mid-afternoon sniffing session, he heard all these rumours from their various sources and rightly deduced the only reliable element was that Joy was back in jail for some crime that had more to do with soup than either whiskey or skips, but whatever the spiteful woman had been up to, it had got her back into trouble. She really was very difficult to help. He was tempted to leave her to stew in her own juice. Protecting Chris and serving mistress Greta were tasks enough.

The thought of another encounter with Cardler wasn't pleasing, but he had to move on.

He called his least favourite Desk Sergeant but the DCI was out. On the spur of the moment he decided to leave no message. Information seemed to leak from Elcester Police Station as if it had no walls; better to work alone.

* * *

It is midday in the Hart and Sceptre hotel. His friends have finished their weekly review and, again, aired their worries about him. Lunch beckons. They don't know it yet but his two female guardians are to learn a little more about their protégé today, something that will explain much and confirm their judgement to be correct – not that they need it.

The older woman is now sitting in the armchair. She seems a

little different; perhaps it is her dark hair – which, like her friend, she wears neatly arranged on top of her head today – or maybe she looks just a trifle more worried than usual. But she is smart as ever in her dark suit, cream blouse and blue silk scarf. That discrete jewellery she wears so well cost a good deal of money. Like her younger counterpart's accessories, her navy blue shoes and bag are quality and evidently new or very nearly so. Her make-up is lightly applied and in perfect harmony with everything else.

As ever in the company of these two, Chris feels he ought to be in another part of the room, like a despatch rider, standing ready to receive their instructions and carry them out in an instant. But they are very kind to him; he has been allowed to sit with them again, and even take part in the meeting, as if he were as wealthy and sexy as they are. – A strange sensation, bearing in mind that Christopher Downe, owner of some eight hundred acres of grazing land, a house, several cottages and heaven knows what else, is as well off as his good friends Greta and Sally, although perhaps not quite as physically attractive.

He just doesn't dress the part. The women know exactly what effect they have on him and they both know that Greta will take him in hand one day when he is sufficiently softened up.

"I don't understand what drives him, Chris. It isn't as if he's a people person; he stays on the edge of things but he's always quietly there when wanted. He doesn't like getting involved but can't seem to help himself."

"I do know the reason. I won't tell you details, but I will say this: he can't bear to see anyone blamed for another's crimes, or for that matter, criminals getting away with what they do."

That wasn't enough by far for Sally.

"You can't stop there, you know. Tell us more; help us understand. We've all earned his trust now; nothing will go any further. You know that Chris."

But the man stayed silent and, after waiting for him to speak, Greta broke in:

"I think it is lunchtime. Talk to us when you feel it is right and not before. Just remember we are all damaged people and we have all found comfort in our friendship. None of us would even dream of doing or saying anything that might hurt each other, least of all our absent friend."

Unusually, they lingered over lunch. Afterwards, by silent consent, they returned to the old hotel's comforting lounge. There, a few couples and a small group of tourists were talking among themselves and, again, without a word between them, they walked together further down the hotel's main corridor and entered a small, empty sitting room on the north side of the building.

The deep armchairs were comfortable, the room warm and welcoming; long tapestry curtains and two full length pictures of ladies in Victorian dress concentrated the eye and mind within the room itself. Unlike their favoured lounge, here the windows looked out on blank stone walls and a small paved courtyard some distance below. This was a place for private talk in which the outside world had no part to play, a room that heard many secrets and where the two ladies on the walls kept those secrets close.

Chris left the room for a few moments.

"Thought we ought to have some tea. Clears the mind."

They sat in silence, awaiting whatever would come. Chris turning over in his mind what he intended to say and the women patiently leaving him to gather his thoughts, however long that might take. They all had work to do that afternoon and people who depended on them to do it, but none of that mattered just then.

The uniformed maid left. The sound of the door closing emphasised their privacy. Silence continued as Greta distributed tea and, at last, Chris spoke.

"You want to know about our Sherlock. If he knew what I was going to say now, I'd lose the best friend I've had since my parents died. I don't have to say more to you on that subject. I'm placing myself in your hands completely."

Neither replied – there was no need.

"He arrived here, I mean in Coldstow, seven or eight years ago. He immediately got a name for being a hermit. You know the spiteful tongues in the village – every sort of rumour was spread. None of them kindly and, as ever, there was the odd bit of truth. I don't know where the true part came from, or if it was just a chance guess by someone. I've had that treatment myself. According to gossip I'm everything that's bad, mostly because my family has money and the locals don't forgive that. And the farm makes smells, we spread mud on the roads and so on. Most recently of course I'm supposed to have murdered Jo.

From the start we had much in common. Both men, both unsociable, both a bit of a mystery and therefore perfect targets for Coldstow. We got to talking about his dog one evening at Jack's, shared our thoughts on life and went on from there. Mostly we've met by chance but sometimes we arrange to have a meal together or one of us walks over to see the other, have a moan about the world and see what we can find in the drinks cupboard. I tell you this as background. It's a friendship that's developed slowly. Neither of us readily trusts people, and with good reason, but I grew to trust him – he's helped me through some bad times and I'm quite sure that trust is mutual.

One evening, at my place, we'd had a few drinks – not drunk but at that stage where your guard can slip a little – I asked him where he lived before Coldstow. He isn't the sort of man you ask personal questions of. I'd always respected that and I could have bitten my tongue then for asking. I didn't get the put down I expected. He was silent for a while, then he told me. It was a village in the Home Counties. I'd heard of it but couldn't think how. Something made me push my luck:

'You have family there?'

I hadn't been thinking of a wife and children, more the sort of general family connections most of us have with our home area, so his answer surprised me.

'Not now.'

'But you did have?'

'I had a wife. She died.'

'Sorry to hear that. Do you want to talk about it?'

'I don't, and before you ask any more questions and destroy a fine friendship, she was murdered.'

He said nothing for a few minutes, then he added:

'I was suspected of killing her. It took me a year to clear myself – the killer wasn't even a man.'

I didn't ask him any more questions. He'd said enough for me to imagine what he went through, and incidentally to understand why he hated my getting caught up in Jo's death and, in spite of her nature, he couldn't let the Siptac woman be suspected of Filly's murder when she so obviously didn't do it."

Neither woman spoke until the three of them had left that very private room. Nor did any of them return there again. The hotel's bright lounge with its open view onto the busy main street remained their chosen meeting place.

Chapter 22

Murder scenario.

Cardler wanted to see him at the station. Not a positive sign, he thought. If this was about test results, he would have expected a more discrete meeting. And, after his previous visit, he had no wish to see the same people again.

But the awkward desk sergeant wasn't there. The young PC at Reception wasn't exactly welcoming but she didn't keep him waiting. He was in the Chief Inspector's own office within five minutes of arriving and he wasn't just expected, apparently he was to be treated with respect this time.

"We've got your test results. I haven't looked at them yet. When I have, you can give me another beer at your place. – Tomorrow evening suit you?"

So, there were two separate matters running side by side. One official, the other not. He wondered if the official business was about Jo, or the vicar. – It was neither.

"Tomorrow's fine."

"You may have noticed we've had a change of staff downstairs.

I'm not going to give you details. This much I will say: I don't allow anyone to meddle in my cases, however well meaning. I apologise for any trouble you had. Officially I'm asking: do you want to make a formal complaint about your break-in? If you do, it will be investigated fully, but not by me. It's entirely up to you. Unofficially I'm telling you my desk sergeant's on long term leave and three members of the Force have brought their career development to an end, not for making any personal gain but out of misplaced loyalty to me. If you choose to let the matter go at that, I'll owe you a good deal."

There was nothing to consider; he needed the man on his side and he wasn't vindictive by nature. But he did want to be sure there were no more incidents.

"I'll take the unofficial option, but just one thing: I want the people concerned told that's my decision; no reason for any vendetta against me. Understood?"

"Understood."

"Incidentally, did you find any fingerprints at my place that matched anyone on your records?"

"I'll check."

That was the end of the official meeting.

* * *

It was eleven o'clock when DCI Cardler arrived in Coldstow the following evening. He was getting used to the man's apparent eighteen hour shifts. They walked across the courtyard to see what beer his office drinks cabinet might have on offer.

"Here's a copy of the reports for you. Your samples don't seem to tell us much. You're going to be disappointed if you were hoping we'd find a tasteless poison only used by a remote tribe in Guatemala."

The Chief Inspector summarised from memory:

"Sample 1; Marked: 'Jo's own bottle under the bar.'

• *Tests shows ordinary decent quality single malt.*

Sample 2; Marked: 'Other bottle under bar - may have killed Jo.'

• *Almost neat alcohol; looks like it's been dressed up to pass off as whiskey – good for blowing your head off.*

Sample 3; Marked: 'Labelled bottle from the still area.'

• *Very similar to sample 2 – dressed up hooch but less violent – probably more water in it.*

Sample 4; Marked: 'Bottle at Downe's farm that Jo apparently drank from.'

• *Different distillery but otherwise as sample 1.*

No barbiturates anywhere, in fact no added drugs at all, unless you count alcohol itself. So, what do you make of all that? Mucks up your theory does it – or not?"

He sat silent and stayed that way for so long that Cardler wandered away to pour himself another beer – all this talk about drinks made him thirsty.

Eventually he came out of his reverie.

"Most of that's exactly what I expected but either one of those tests is wrong or there is, or was, another sample that we haven't got."

"There won't be anything wrong about the reports. We gave the lab no lead. As you can see from the details, we asked for a full analysis; it wasn't just a request to check for particular drugs. I told you: it's an expensive job."

His mind was racing through possible explanations. He had been sure he knew what happened to Jo and he was still sure – or almost so. That evening he had expected to put his theory to the man in front of him and leave the necessary digging to the police. Now he faced presenting his theory short on fact and long on imagination.

He didn't expect his idea to be accepted readily and it wasn't. But the policeman listened; he was good at that.

"I want to tell you how I believe Jo's death happened. It's a longish story; just bear with me."

The Inspector wriggled around in his chair – he was already feeling uncomfortable.

"I agreed to meet. I'm not ducking out now."

"I don't know every detail – I'm guessing the unimportant bits - but I think it was this way:

Jo wanted a divorce; we know that now. As Chris Downe never spoke to me about marrying her, I think she never told him. Probably thought it was better to be free before she raised the possibility. In fact, much as he loved her, I don't think Chris would have gone along with it. The poor woman died having been spared that let down at least. I'll call Jo's husband JH for the moment. JH gets a letter from a lawyer, or maybe a phone call from Jo, asking him to agree a divorce. He can't accept the idea. Perhaps he hoped to get her back one day – or maybe he's a possessive type – 'if I can't have her, no one will', anyway he refuses and she presses the demand.

Things go from bad to worse in his mind; it's clear he really has lost her. He broods on it; thinks about killing Jo and maybe reckons to kill another bird with that stone by ruining Chris Downe's life at the same time.

JH is clever – and whoever killed Jo, he, or she, was certainly that. He plans a murder by poison and hits on the idea of adding her medication to her alcohol. - If he can achieve that and be well out of the way when she dies, there'll be nothing to connect him to her death which will look like suicide. If it works as planned, it's a perfect crime.

He buys a bottle of a whiskey that he knows she drinks, ready for doctoring it at the farm. He reckons on simply parking the adulterated bottle in the drinks cupboard, or simply making use of one already there, and leaving. Depending on what he finds at the farm, he can play things as they come.

Nothing may happen for a week or two but at some stage Jo will start one of her binges, have a few glasses instead of her occasional one, or even the whole bottle, and JH reckons that'll be the end of her. As a bonus, almost certainly, the person to find her will be poor Chris.

I'm guessing again here, but probably JH never did his homework and the mixture in that bottle wasn't enough to kill unless, perhaps, she drank the whole of it in one go. Anyway, she was still upright, and full of bounce, when she reached the pub.

So, JH arrives at the farm. He may have been surprised by the number of people about the place, or perhaps he spied out the land beforehand and already knew how busy it is. Anyway, whether planned or thought up on the moment, he frees a whole shed load of cows and that's quite enough to get Chris, and everyone he can muster, rushing around after Buttercup and her mates. In fact that worked well. Just one problem; Jo didn't join the throng – probably too full of her woes from being sacked by the pub.

So, thinking all's clear, he potters off to the house to do his job. He's almost finished – found Jo's medication in the bathroom or used a drug he has with him; doctored his whiskey, or a bottle that's already there - and suddenly he spots Jo – perhaps doing something outside in the yard. Now he's under pressure; he mustn't be seen; he puts his bottle on the sitting room table and skips out by a back door.

He watches Jo go indoors and can't bring himself to leave. Things are going wrong; he hasn't had time to tuck his poisoned bottle away in the cupboard and leave things to take their course after he's gone; now Jo's already on the scene and every chance she'll be drinking before he's even away from the farm.

It isn't long before she reappears and marches off down the lane on her way to the Happy Fireside. She's probably a bit unsteady and he wonders how much she's had. He ducks back into the house and sees the now half full bottle. Decides it's a piece of evidence he ought to get rid of. – I don't know what he does with it; we may never know.

Thinking on his feet, he takes another bottle from the cabinet and parks it in full view and half empty on the table. He rinses her glass with the clean whiskey. I've wondered if there were any prints left on that glass or the bottle; or if they were wiped clean – we shan't find out now; it's too long ago.

JH stays at the farm desperate to know what's going to happen. Is Jo going to die or not? After a while he hears a car and I appear. I'm shouting for Chris; telling the world I've got Jo with me and need help. His mind must have filled with questions. What's happened? Is she alive? Who is this bloke?

He watches as I wander about calling for help, realises he

can't stay hidden for ever so decides to do the opposite – appear loud, large and obvious on one of the farm's loaders. We meet; he helps with getting Jo indoors but she's evidently dead by then. He volunteers to get Chris but probably just slips away, leaving hardly a memory behind him. The rest you know."

That police mind was out of its comfort zone again.

"Blimey, that's a lot of guesswork and not much evidence to prop it up; you might as well tell me it was all done by aliens from Mars."

"Give me a chance; I've thought about this a lot. Just consider what we have: Jo was killed, that's for sure. It may have been part accidental but she didn't kill herself; we agreed that. She had drugs in her when she died but she didn't take them by choice. In fact she hadn't been taking them for months – I got that from Chris Downe. And they were dissolved in what she drank, but the bottle at the farm was my sample 4 – good clean whiskey.

She went to the Happy Fireside, made a few revelations that frightened Dave, the proprietor, and had another drink there. It's not believable that Dave added anything to the whiskey he gave her. I was there – it came straight out of a bottle kept under the bar, possibly one specially for Jo but, on this occasion, I think not.

I think what he gave her was my sample 2 and you have to compare it with Sample 1. I believe number 1 was Jo's usual drink – nothing wrong with it. Both bottles were together under the bar where I found them. But number 2 was fierce alcohol and not much to tone it down. I think that's the one that killed her. She'd already drunk a good deal at the farm plus her own drugs. On top of that Dave gave her something that sent her over the edge as it might have done to anybody."

His audience was fidgeting; it wasn't just his awkward chair; there was too much guessing here and too few facts for comfort.

"You're not carrying me with you at all; where does this hooch come from and why give it to Jo? And, while we're on it, what's your sample 3 doing in all this?"

"Patience, friend. I'm slow about it, but getting there. The super strength stuff came from a second bottle under the pub's counter. It's alcohol the owners were distilling in the pub cellar. I think they gave it to customers who were too drunk to know what they were drinking or, more likely in this village, some who wanted a drink with that much kick in it and didn't mind where it came from. And my sample 3 came from one of a dozen bottles in the cellar all bearing fake labels. It was dressed up to pass as a cheap whiskey; weaker than the hot number under the bar and probably being sold by the bottle. Incidentally the village shop seems to have some on its shelves."

The DCI grabbed at that one. Here was something solid at last.

"Does it by God! Is there *anyone* in this village who lives a clean life?"

"Well, there's me for a start, and dog Freddie. Well, me anyway."

"If I'm to buy into this fanciful stuff, there has to be more to go on. You haven't shown Jo's husband was anywhere in the area, only some bloke driving a loader when everyone ought to have been playing cowboys round the village. And – and - and, well and a whole lot of other holes that you can't fill."

"I'm well aware of it. If we had sample 5 it could be a clincher."

"What's sample 5?"

"From the doctored bottle the intending killer left at Downe's farm."

"Mm, yes I see that; it might elevate your story from fantasy to possible fact. What do you want me to do? I assume that's what this is all about – dragging the poor old dumb policeman in to do the hard work once the PI's got bored and run out of steam. And by the way, I need some coffee. My head's spinning."

There was another angle bothering the Detective:

"You know what this means, don't you? If you're right, Jo's intending killer is guilty of attempted murder but not more. Dave, the barman is guilty of either manslaughter or murder depending on what the law decides he intended. What's your view on this Dave bloke's motive for feeding his bad whiskey into Jo?"

"He may have hoped to shut her up before she let any more

cats out of the bag. I doubt he wanted to kill; I know the man, a bit weak but no murderer. It was done on the spur of the moment, with no clear thought. And if you're asking what more Jo had to tell; the obvious thing was the still in the cellar."

"So the one who wanted to kill Jo didn't and the one that didn't, did? – Sounds like a storyline from a party game. Heaven help us if all this comes to court."

He watched his audience thinking through the scenario he had put to him. The man was giving it a chance and he couldn't ask more than that; he might not have done as much himself if their roles had been reversed. Eventually the policeman stood to leave.

"I'm not convinced, not at all, but I admit the story fits the facts. Can you recall enough to describe this loader driver and more important, would you recognise him if you saw him again?"

"It was dark; I'm not sure. My mind was on Jo, I didn't even think of murder – why would anybody in those circumstances? And if she was killed, I wouldn't have thought it had been done at the farm, not then. Next step has to be: find Jo's husband, if you can."

"That's something that needs care. We can't just go up to him and ask if he killed his wife – we've got nothing to connect him into this, except your guesses. Even questioning him might be too much at this stage. I'll think on it. You'll be hearing from me."

"Just a thought: does the husband have a police record?"

"You can leave some of the thinking to me you know."

He made their coffees and they chatted quite easily about nothing to do with murders while the policeman fought a ten minute tug o'war. Freddie won.

Chapter 23

Changing partners again.

Two days after their meeting in Coldstow he rang the Station. As usual, the Inspector was out but he returned the call within five minutes. Relationships were improving.

"I've thought some more. Can we meet?"

The Inspector said they could – he named a country pub some ten miles from Coldstow.

The Green Witch Inn sits on a back lane that runs between the small rural town of Hansleigh and Ewer village. This was quite a major highway until late Georgian times but the road has little traffic now and the Witch's status has slipped somewhat from its high days when it might fairly have claimed the right to be described as a coaching inn. Now it is simply a pub; popular both with locals and those tourists who know of it and appreciate a good meal when they get it.

The oldest part of the building is half-timbered Tudor and doesn't seem to have changed much either inside or out since Henry VII died. Later additions, done in the various architectural styles of each successive century, have enlarged the place so that it now seems disproportionately vast for its location. But its good name, for both comfort and food, keeps it busy enough throughout the year, whilst there are always at least a couple of quiet places where people may meet and talk without either having to shout, or run the risk of being overheard, if they wish to be private.

Detective Chief Inspector Cardler often made use of the Green Witch, at times to be on his own and think over his problems, at others for such private meetings as he chose to keep to himself.

It was another fine sunny autumn day; still very warm for that time of year, and he found his host sitting under a sunshade at a large round table in the Green Witch's pleasant garden. He looked rather out of place among the pots of late flowering lobelias and lavender but large plain clothes policemen tend to look out of place wherever they are, especially when away from their home ground.

There were two pints of Old Amber on the table and two lunch menus propped against the glasses. He was getting to like the man. They had a lot in common.

He ordered a curry; the Inspector chose his "usual". This, when it came, was a vast steak pie with a ridiculous quantity and variety of vegetables and a jug of gravy enough for everyone in the dining room behind them.

"I see you're on a diet. Don't miss out on the pudding, will you?"

"I shan't; they know me here. I leave them to choose for me; most likely it'll be the apple crumble. I recommend it; you need building up."

"Shall I start my story while we wait?"

"No, I'd like to eat first, in case you're going to upset me. I don't care for fairy stories and I've got a suspicion that's what's coming."

So they chatted easily about nothing very much, yet learning more of each other than they ever would have done in more formal circumstances and, in due course, they enjoyed an unhurried lunch – dessert included – before he turned to the task in hand.

"Did you locate Jo's husband?"

"No, but we do know him. There's a criminal record; small time; not an arch-poisoner if that's what you were hoping."

"I never expected a history of murder; if my scenario's correct, it was very much a one-off crime of passion by a man who loved one woman too much. What I did hope for was a fingerprint record."

"I'll check. But I don't see that's any help. We need to place him at the scene - Downe's farm in particular, and we're not likely to get lucky now. According to you, everything he would have handled must have been smeared long since - door handles, controls on the loader, drinks cupboard. What else is there? Downes is far too big a place to be lifting prints everywhere; where do you start? And just look at the number of people working there, and all the untraceable business visitors – reps, lorry drivers. No, I'm afraid that's a non-starter unless you've got some special location in mind where he left his dabs and no one else has been there since."

He allowed a long period of silence to elapse.

"As it happens, I think I do have exactly that."

They stared at each other, one calculating if his words were having a sufficiently electrifying effect; the other trying to show no emotion whatsoever. It was almost a drawn game; but the detective had sat upright – no more – it was just enough.

"I think his prints are on my car. – Not the one I came in today. – I only thought of this two nights back but it's been garaged for some while. If prints exist, nobody will have smeared them."

"Stop the suspense; it's killing me."

"Think back to that day when I took Jo back home from the Happy Fireside. I carried her to the car. I needed help to hold open a rear door for laying her on the back seat. At the pub that was Sally Redfern but I didn't take her with me to Downes. It wasn't right to drag her into that situation. I had the same difficulty at the farm. Lifting a dead weight out from a car's back seat and coping with a door that's trying to shut on you is more difficult than you might imagine. Our pretend loader driver held the door and he slammed it shut afterwards. So far as I know, no one's touched the handles or the door itself since."

For all his faults, and he would have admitted to none, the Chief Inspector moved quickly when there was need for real action. And he loved proper police work; something that he felt had been unsatisfyingly missing in this wretched case from the beginning.

"I'll arrange this. In the meantime go home; open your garage doors and don't touch that car!"

* * *

The delightful sight of police swarming over his property gave Coldstow's gossips a fine opportunity to fabricate various stories about his criminal history and they duly excelled themselves. Much of the pleasure faded away however when the law departed without taking him into handcuffed custody. – Hopefully, the gossips agreed, it was just a matter of time.

It was a while later that two casually dressed women arrived at Sally Redfern's house and entered with a key. Missing nothing, Coldstow's nosey parkers perked up immediately – despite their daily internet searches, the fact the place was for sale had escaped them all.

But Sally's house was not for sale, at least not yet – one might almost have thought she didn't intend to leave.

The woman who looked like an estate agent wasn't carrying house brochures, that case contained much more specialised equipment. And the one that Coldstow took to be an interested viewer, prospective buyer and future neighbour was a forensic examiner, working on instructions from DCI Cardler.

* * *

It might be thought that Joy Siptac would take some rest from her troublemaking labours after twice finding herself in police custody, but that would be to misunderstand the very essence of her nature.

Her recent temporary incarcerations had no effect whatever on her enthusiasm for causing as much hardship as possible for those who crossed her, and indeed for almost anyone that did not.

It hadn't taken long for Joy to deduce the role of the Crabbe sisters in her little trouble with the Law about laxatives and soup. As for her Harold and his very good friend, Susan Smith - as Joy called her - there was that very public display on the same evening at the Happy Fireside. That needed avenging.

* * *

'The Postmaster.
*Royal Mail
Trollope Street,
Elcester.
5 December*

Dear Sir,

FRAUD AT COLDSTOW SUB- POST OFFICE

I write to you with both reluctance and sorrow.

Reluctance because no one would wish to see the names of two elderly ladies fall into disrepute, however necessary it may be to have their felonious activities properly investigated and brought to a close.

Sorrow because these crimes do not reflect on the perpetrators alone but upon the good, I may say honoured, name of one of this Country's most respected and admired Institutions, namely our Royal Mail service, the Envy of the World.

It is a matter of no small concern that incidents of fraud in a sub-post office for which you have the ultimate responsibility appear to have been continuous, some might even say, commonplace. We, the Public, are surely entitled to ask how this is.

Does the Post Office not inspect the accounts of its branches? Are there no regular audits to bring the activities of fraudsters into the open and shine the clear light of day into their dark corners?

No doubt upon receipt of the information in this letter, you will at last hasten to make all necessary enquiries and take the vigorous action appropriate for ensuring that these crimes cease and to bring the fraudsters to public justice, not least to discourage others from following a similar course.

*Susan Repplington-Smythe
A well-wisher'.*

Having written her letter, Joy turned her thoughts to Harold.

This was a more complex issue. She found it difficult to admit, but she missed him. The house was uncomfortably empty and, in his absence, she was having to do the many tedious day to day tasks she had always left to him, and all her own dirty work.

To say that Joy loved her husband would be a trespass where none of us ought to go. Many that knew her would say the Joy Siptacs of this world do not love; not even themselves. That is too hard; all can love, but not all in the same way. Let it simply be said that, if asked whether she wanted Harold back home, she would have denied it in public but admitted it in the privacy of any upstairs room at home. What may be thought by a Siptac in bathroom or bedchamber would be unthinkable in a kitchen.

Susan was another matter.

* * *

While she was unknowingly coming centre stage in Joy's thoughts, Susan was sitting alone in her gloomy kitchen, struggling with relationship problems of her own. Her low key date at the Happy Fireside's opening night had not gone well for her. It had been unpleasant enough to be sitting on a high stool in full view of everyone. But, inattentive to her and unable to hold his own with the heckling crowd, Harold had fallen well short of being an ideal escort – neither romantic nor protective.

Her thoughts hadn't quite reached a stage where she wanted to be free of him but they were on their way in that direction.

A light knocking sound drew her back into the practical present and she walked through the house to open her front door. If there was one person she didn't expect, this was the one.

Joy entered the house without further invitation and walked on into Susan's kitchen.

"How nice to see you, Susan. Such a pleasure. I was just thinking about you. You and Harold perhaps I should say. I suddenly realised we hadn't talked about him yet and that set me thinking – does Susan know? I just couldn't stay sat there and do nothing, assuming it would all turn out right for you if I didn't tell you. Of course it might do but, suppose it wasn't – all right, I mean? My conscience said to me 'Joy, you have to tell Susan; that poor innocent woman mustn't be kept in the dark a moment longer'.

So here I am."

Susan stared at her visitor, wondering what this was about. She had no illusions about Joy. The woman was a bundle of trouble and best avoided but, now, here she was on Susan's own home ground and evidently about to say something poisonous, intending grief for someone, presumably her. Susan prepared herself to show no emotion whatever came.

"The thing is Susan, Harold has a problem with women; especially old women, like yourself. He isn't to blame, it's the way he was treated by his mother. And of course, as you know, she was locked up."

Susan forbore to point out that Joy was no spring chicken herself and she certainly didn't know anything about Harold's mother, locked up or not. But, if Joy had expected her to rise to that bait, she was disappointed. Susan stayed silent, staring as rudely as possible at her visitor.

"I won't stop for coffee, thank you."

"No, you won't. Is that it? Did you come here to tell me anything about your husband – as if I'm interested in him – or just to waste a bit of my time? If you have something to say, say it because you've said nothing yet."

This wasn't the Susan that Joy had expected. Giving as good as she got and showing no concern at all about forthcoming Harold revelations, she gave every impression of genuine disinterest. Perhaps, the relationship was already over? Joy decided to let matters rest as they stood for the moment. She had probably done enough already, and there would be plenty of opportunities to pour more acid on the corroding relationship if necessary.

"Well, I'm glad we had our little chat, Susan. Bye for now!"

* * *

Returning to her window at the village hall, where she could monitor most of the residents' comings and goings, Joy fell to thinking about Chris Downe who had been entering her thoughts quite a lot recently. Nice to be described as cute – impertinent of course, but one must forgive these handsome young men for their outbursts of longing.

She was just wondering if she might buy a little cap – the sort that high quality professional kitchen staff sometimes wear, when Harold came into sight leaving the Happy Fireside on his way to lunch at home with Susan. Joy hurried out by a side door, in time for him to find her wandering slowly, apparently on her way to the village store.

"Oh, Harold, I'm so glad we chanced to meet. Can you spare a moment after your lunch with dear Susan? Any time, say two thirteen?"

Years of habit cannot be wholly overwritten by a few nights of illicit bliss and Harold could no more refuse that invitational command than he might have made a proposal of marriage to both the Crabbe sisters at once.

2:13 pm prompt and Harold presented himself as instructed. He was rather less cheerful than he had been that morning; Susan hadn't been welcoming and he hadn't eaten.

The Siptac house held a pleasant aroma of baking. As Chris might have said, Joy was looking quite cute, even without any additional headgear, and she was a good deal more welcoming than Susan had been a couple of hours earlier. She didn't suppose he wanted anything to eat, but there was a cottage pie going if he liked to try it. Moreover Joy found she had made a few too many apple puddings and she really didn't want to throw one away. But space was short and…

So Harold got his lunch after all and two apple desserts with a pot of tea to finish.

"Now, Harold, I have a little job for you…"

* * *

And Susan got her thankful freedom from the man with the troubled fancies about old women and the mad mother which his wife had dreamt up for him.

Chapter 24

Conspirators.

The air was motionless on a bright December morning. The night had been exceptionally cold. A light snowfall from the previous evening was lying on the ground all ready for play. Half a dozen warmly dressed children were trying, with little success, to make snowballs with snow too cold to stick to itself and throwing handfuls of white fluff at one another while screaming with laughter at their efforts.

Perhaps DCI Cardler had caught the children's happy mood because he was unusually cheerful as he parked his car in the village hall car park and walked to his friend's house. Police work had triumphed, as it always would in his view. Guesses and hunches were all very well – and the Chief Inspector was almost as good at imagining as the next policeman – but you couldn't catch crooks and get them up before a Judge without solid evidence. Don't even try.

"Morning Detective Chief Inspector. Just in time for coffee."

Cardler sniffed. The warm, inviting kitchen had evidently been cooking something good.

"And I could murder a breakfast if there's any going."

In fact there was some going and he fancied a second round of bacon and toast himself.

He knew the man by now and didn't expect to get anything out of his visitor until there was nothing left on his plate, so he didn't try.

"I suppose you know that demanding a bribe isn't legal? Do

you want more coffee, toast and marmalade, a whole fried bison?"

"Yes I do know that, and I also know it's an offence to offer a bribe. I'll have the coffee and toast. Might fancy the bison later, though."

He got round to it eventually - after draining his cup and carefully scraping the last smear of marmalade on his final scrap of toast.

"That's better. Not a large meal but it'll last me to lunch. – My treat today. Well, you were absolutely right. Mr Jo was there that day. At least he was handling your car at some time – I guess that's as far as his defence lawyer will have to go in meeting us. But I can't see a Court disbelieving our case that he was there the day Jo died. His Counsel's going to have an awkward time of it explaining how he got his prints on the inside of your car door otherwise. Pity we don't have the bottle he brought with him complete with his fingerprints on it, always assuming that's how he was going about it."

"Have you found him?"

"Still no success. He got away on the day and he's had plenty of time to bury himself anywhere on the planet by now. We'd keep up the search but there are no leads. The address we have for him is a rented London flat. His landlord never met him – all done through a big, faceless letting agency – and he doesn't seem to have been back there since some days before the murder."

"Did you find any other prints?"

Cardler was suddenly cagey.

"None that matter."

"I didn't ask that."

"Very well, if you must push: your prints were there, of course, and you won't be surprised to know we have them on record – a murder case involving your wife. And I'm sorry to have learned it – you had the worst possible deal with that."

He said nothing on this but:

"No other recent prints?"

"On the same door as Mr Jo's. A woman, name of Sally Redfern. Ring a bell?"

"You bloody well know it does. How do you come to have her on record?"

"We don't."

"Are you going to explain?"

"No."

And that was all he could get from the man. But for some reason, he felt slightly comforted. Perhaps it was just the mention of her name.

Later, they shared a lunch at Jack's. In the darkening afternoon he walked back with Freddie by a long circular route. When they reached home, he went straight to his office and sat in her chair to tear himself apart again for what remained of the day.

* * *

It is the ninth of December. Another meeting is taking place at the Hart and Sceptre hotel and Chris Downe is making a report to his two mistresses who, on this occasion, happen to be sitting together on the deep settee. They are drawing furtive admiring looks from a waiting group of six prospective diners, half of them women. The fact is, except in the privacy of her sunny garden where only Siptacs peer, whether casual or smart, Sally always dresses with conscious perfection and looks a million dollars; Greta achieves the same result but, with her, it is simply her natural self. Today their hair is down and their clothes are casual – that is to say casual as in the word catwalk.

A little of their glamour has at last rubbed off on their consort, who has bought some decent cord trousers and a couple of tweed jackets to help him overcome his growing feeling of inferiority at these weekly affairs. He looks much smarter now – exactly like a farmer wearing his best clothes and longing for his overalls. But he will get over that. In time he may even be able to move away from the colour green.

It is difficult to see how they would manage without him, or how Chris could in turn meet their need for information, if he didn't spend time fishing for it in his friend's company back at

Coldstow. Not for the first time, Chris is having qualms about what he has been doing. Split between his wish to help both the women (and his friend) on the one hand and a guilty feeling of disloyalty, he is constantly fighting with his conscience.

The two women know this, and they sympathise, but they know, too, that Chris will be made whole when Greta is free to sort him out. In the meantime, he must be kept on a short lead.

"They've been dusting fingerprints on his car, or whatever it is they do these days. They seemed interested in the rear doors, although, police being police, I doubt they stopped there. I had a word with our Chief Inspector friend. More accurately, he had a few with me. He wants to check out some of the prints. As ever, it's being done on the quiet – our Sherlock isn't to be troubled. The man's getting as protective of him as we are."

The older woman spoke:

"My fingerprints will be on one of the car's back doors, inside and out. Greta; what do we do to help?"

"I think you'd better give the Chief Inspector another call."

Chris continued:

"You know, I'm getting upset about all this. Sometimes I wonder why the secrecy? I wish we hadn't started any of it. I'm being disloyal to him – we all are."

There was a long silence before Sally spoke:

"Dear Chris. If anyone wanted a loyal friend, they couldn't find anyone better than you. We both love you for being exactly what you are. You have no guilt to bear; that's partly what we're for – to carry that burden and leave you free of it. We're each of us one another's protectors and, in time, healers. Take comfort from that. Now, let's have lunch – I'm hungry."

* * *

Cheri and Sam were standing in the Happy Fireside's car park, facing the pub's open doorway and looking at a sign above the entrance:

'Licensees and Proprietors Cheryl D'Arteur Wyke & Samuel Repplington.'

"Well Sam, it shows we're here to stay. Should have done it sooner but there's been so much else to attend to. Quite enough even without the Siptac woman."

"I didn't know you were a Wyke. I've heard the name before but I can't remember where."

Cheri changed the subject:

"Now, Sam, I have something to say to you. There's to be no more of your philandering. Remember, you're mine and I don't allow anyone to take from me. You're not much of a catch but I'll sort you out and you'll be the better for it. And you can start by keeping your distance with the kitchen staff. I know there's history there. It's to stay history. And, while I'm about it, don't forget where the money for all this came from. Now we can go back in and have breakfast. It'll be a good one; Lily's on duty this morning."

Sam hadn't expected that little lecture. The woman had an uncomfortable ability to see into his thoughts. Not being a particularly honest person himself, her frankness quite disarmed him.

"No, dear. Whatever you say. No more kitchen staff for me. – Only a joke! Anyway, having you, what else could I need?"

"Mm, I'll take that as I think you meant it. And one other thing: just remember I love you, faults and all."

They went back into Cheri's pub where he carefully avoided looking Lily in the eye when she brought in their breakfasts. She left the dining room with a huge feeling of relief and returned to the kitchen where Chef was starting her daily routine.

"She's told him, bless her. Thank goodness for our new employer. She's going to be a winner."

Chef said not a word but she didn't stop smiling for the rest of the morning. Cheri's Happy Fireside pub was settling down comfortably under its new regime.

Chapter 25

Puzzles and Dreams

Meals eaten together at the Happy Fireside or Jack's were a frequent occurrence for them. He was finding it easier now to confide in his friend about the progress, or lack of it, with both Jo's and Filly's deaths. This sharing did not however extend to his personal problems, either past or present. As to the past, Chris asked no more questions about his life before Coldstow, respecting his friend's evident wish to close that book for good.

Present troubles were another matter. Of course he said nothing of it, but he was plainly tortured by the loss of Sally, and Chris was finding it ever harder to stay silent about the private meetings in that comfortable hotel lounge fifty miles away.

They were standing in Jack's saloon bar one lunchtime, both saturated and trying to dry out by the pub's newly lit log fire which was kippering them in clouds of steamy smoke.

It had been raining heavily – typical Coldstow weather at almost any time of the year, but unusual for the recent autumnal weeks when there had been so much sun. They had both been working outdoors through the morning; Chris on the sort of jobs that cows make humans do, he investigating a muddy area around that sinister group of skips and containers at the edge of the village car park.

He felt in his coat pockets and passed something to his friend.

"Take a look at this, Chris. Any idea what it is? And – any comments?"

"This" was a flat backed, polished purple stone; it looked like a

piece of dress jewellery.

Chris took a surprisingly long time to examine the little item, then:

"I've seen this, or something like it before now. Quite recently I think…"

He stopped speaking suddenly as if he had caught himself saying something he shouldn't and abruptly changed tack.

"Well, whatever it is, where did you find it?"

"By the overgrown area where Filly's body was found. It was almost buried – looked as if someone had trodden it in. But before that happened, it must have been pretty obvious to anyone who was actively looking for it, or even if they weren't."

Chris seemed uninterested.

"If you've finished showing off your rubbish collection, I'm ready to eat. Let's order; I'm starved."

He wasn't fooled; that stone had significance for Chris. He had guessed that it would.

He returned to his office later that afternoon and began work. Four hours later, he took Freddie for a night time walk through the village and out onto the straight road that runs along the high ridge between the valleys of the rivers Crayne and Foxe. After a long day of rain, the night was perfectly clear and full of brilliant stars. A near-full waxing moon bathed the surrounding countryside in its soft light. He felt as if he might go on walking in that magical world and in the same dreamlike state for ever. All he had to do was lift and set down first one foot, then the other and planet Earth would spin smoothly past beneath him.

* * *

On the following morning, he drove over to Elcester and met again with Steph, the nice young Western Press archivist. It was always a pleasure – and the tea was good. This time he took Freddie in with him by way of a treat for both girl and dog. Steph liked Freddie and Freddie liked both Steph and her sandwich box.

"I'd like to see all the photos that were taken on the day the vicar was killed. And I'm also after a couple of library pictures you might have. Can I use the same office?"

Yes, the photos were his to look at and he could have the same office for as long as he wanted.

"Have you found out something? If you have, I wish you'd tell me; I'm really keen to prove myself here and a scoop all of my own might get me away from the office and out reporting."

"You'll be the first to know. Well, the first newsperson anyway."

"Promise?"

"Absolutely. By the way, do you know why the Western sent a reporter and photographer to Coldstow that day? – It surely wasn't likely to be newsworthy."

"Probably someone told us about it and made it sound like a big deal. I can look into it if you like."

"Please. And if that was the case, see if you can find out who."

Apart from a pleasant hour taking his cheerful young assistant, and ever-hungry Freddie, out to lunch at a local pub, he spent the entire day at the Western's offices, leaving at five with some half dozen further photographs and a thoroughly stuffed dog.

"Thanks for coming. It can be boring here at times. I'm going to get a dog like Freddie when I can afford it. I'd never be bored then."

"Yes you would. If you get another like her, you'll spend your life shovelling biscuits down her gullet and dealing with the consequences at the other end. Believe me, there's nothing more tedious."

His phone rang just as he reached home. The voice was familiar but he couldn't place it at first.

"Oh, hallo Steph; nice to hear from you. What's up, anything interesting?"

"I've got the information you wanted, or some of it anyway. It's lucky the Western's an up to date paper with really good records. Someone rang the front office about the vicar's do in Coldstow, saying it was a big event and worth covering. At first we thought it was just a try-on to advertise some village fete but we didn't want to miss out if it was more than that."

"Thank you. I guessed that much, what I'd really like is a name."

"I don't have that, but you may be able to work it out. We do know the incoming phone number; it's one that's been used before, by a woman who gives different names – she's got a bit of a record with us as a troublemaker. The number's 07867 6*****. Is that any help?"

"That, my dear young ace reporter, is even more than I hoped for. I'll take it from there. And I owe you another lunch."

"With Freddie, please!"

"She wouldn't allow it any other way."

* * *

His cleaner had taken occupation of the entire house, as cleaners do, and he was quite incapable of thinking; vacuums and wide open doors don't allow it. He grabbed a bottle of milk and walked across to the office with the dog. The silence and comfort of the room soothed him and the pleasurable task of making a mid-morning coffee set him at ease, or, at least, as much at ease as his damaged mind could ever achieve.

He sat in her chair and looked out over the tops of his trees toward the far, sunlit hillside. The view was unusually clear. A blue and white tractor, leaning awkwardly to one side as it ran along the furrows and followed by an energetic swarm of white gulls, was half way through ploughing one of the larger fields. He watched as the rich brown area of bare soil grew larger at the expense of the shrinking stubble. It was a mesmerising scene; apart from the tractor, just so had those fields been worked for generations. He let his thoughts drift into the past, imagining a team of shires with their ploughman as if taken straight out of an eighteenth century oil painting…

His coffee went cold, he daydreamed, dozed, then slipped into deeper dreams in which his mind busied itself with sorting through things it had lacked time to address while awake.

The ploughing scene in the old painting diminished into

the background making space for a stone-built church in a rural village. Evidently a morning service had just finished, the congregation was leaving and their elderly vicar was speaking to a few people by the church door. The scene altered and came alive. Suddenly the village was Coldstow, the time, the present day and the little group came closer, almost filling the foreground. The vicar's friends were now clear to see. The two oldest, a man and a woman, were similar in appearance and spoke in the same gentle, cultured accents. The other two were young women of much the same age, but very different in manner and appearance. Apart from the older pair, there was no obvious similarity between them, save that all four wore clerical collars.

The vicar himself seemed to be changing. In the ludicrous way that dreams have of moving along without explanation or apology, he became Joy Siptac, of all improbable people.

The phantom Joy opened a small bag she held in her left hand and tossed its contents over the clerical group as if it were confetti thrown at a wedding. But this wasn't confetti; it was torn pieces of white paper covered with odd bits of writing and coloured scribble.

The last brief scene as he came out of his dream showed Joy reverting to become the vicar again and a look of horror on the old man's face.

* * *

Its job done, the tractor had gone from the large field, leaving the gulls to their feeding windfall. He looked at the office clock – two hours gone; the cleaner would have left by now and he had missed saying goodbye and thanking her. Freddie was wandering around and squeaking; he took her outside to relieve her suffering and returned to re-heat his coffee and drink it as he stared sightlessly from his window. And all the time that dream, having survived his waking, was running around in his thoughts.

He could make nothing of it, yet it seemed his mind had got hold of something that he needed; it just wasn't prepared to make it easy for him, but then it never did.

Skipping lunch, Freddie took him for one of her favourite walks; out along the grimy lane away from the village centre, down to the river Foxe, now unseasonably shallow after the long dry period, across the ford and onto a stone track that climbed through oak woods on Chris Downe's land. A mile further on, the woodland changed to dreary Forestry Commission plantations of spruce and pine before the trees gave way to open moorland.

After the dark conifers, the bright clear afternoon sky and a brisk northerly wind tolerated no more inward thoughts. Gorse was flowering brilliant yellow, as it always does somewhere throughout the year, and the wide views all around were as uplifting as ever. It had always been a place where he could clear his mind and that day was no exception.

He sat down in the heather, passed a few biscuits to his starving shadow, then lay back and stared into the sky. After cloud watching for ten minutes or so, he slipped back into thinking over his earlier dream. Throughout his life there had been occasions when he sensed things without knowing how. He had always mistrusted and resisted the power, but he could never ignore it, and now here it was again. He knew the signs.

Save for the tiresome Siptac, the people in his dream had all been clerics. If one of them was Fiona, it had to be the young, dark haired woman; so the other was Greta. Who were the older two? Did they matter? He was sure they did; it had been a very simple, one might almost say, economical, dream. It surely had nothing to offer if half the characters were redundant. He turned back to his sky watching for a few more minutes and slipped into another daydream.

He was sitting with Chris and Cheri in the Happy Fireside; she had been looking at the photographs from Greta; what had Cheri said? Something important, but unremarked by him at the time, about identifying people. Something like:

"These two by the hall door are church people."

And they weren't just in that picture, they were in another, more private, photograph.

With a sudden slight thrill – the sort he would get with the first inkling of the solution to a very difficult crossword clue – an idea came, one that he had to pursue at once before it disappeared like an extinguished flame.

He rose, straightened his stiff spine and legs and turned back homeward. Freddie followed, disappointed that they weren't going to finish the circular walk but perhaps comforted by the thought of reaching food that much sooner.

Back in his office again, he spent another hour thinking and staring at the view without seeing it.

Caught up in the material evidence, he had almost overlooked the most important aspect of all; the characters of the people involved, their natures and their frailties. It would be difficult without knowing them personally, but not impossible. Crockfords might be a starting point, biographies, Who's Who .... It was a massive task and there were at least four people involved. He should have done all that at the beginning.

As ever with such open-ended research, he found himself being led up one tributary after another; the openings proliferated as he dug deeper. The scale of the task was enormous but he waded on through a maze of uninteresting, and repetitive, material, noting each small nugget of genuine information as it came.

He spent some time enlarging and image enhancing some of the photos got from the Western Press offices. Again, and yet again, he returned to those few documents and pictures he had taken from the vicarage at Sideleigh on the day he first met Greta.

He set the purple ring stone down on his desk and glared at it long and hard, asking himself what it had to tell him that wasn't a lie. Yet again, he realised that this, too, told a true tale of people, and therefore, something of the murder itself.

* * *

The following day he continued where he had left off the previous evening. This time the work was easier; he knew what he was looking for and he had what he needed before midnight; the history of a devout and gentle man and a spiritual woman, a husband and wife who died too young, a troubled child and one other. The picture was complete.

Relieved to complete his work, he avoided the temptation of her chair and went to bed where he slept a rare dreamless sleep.

✶ ✶ ✶

'johnthesolicitor@hmail.com

Hi John. I hope you're resting at last.

I could do with some help, as if I didn't owe you enough already.

Our little village has problems; no, that's the understatement of all time; it's seething with spiteful troublemakers and foul with their crimes.

A rare friend here asked me to investigate the death of her sister – I'll explain when we meet. It's been a dreadful job, but I'm nearing the end of it now.

I need some evidence to be sworn. The several witnesses are willing and I've drafted their statements. Would you draw up the affidavits and administer them? You'll need to stay here for a couple of days, or I can book you into the hotel in Larkston.

John, if it's a job you don't want to take on, just say. I have no right to ask any more of you.

Stay well, old friend.'

Chapter 26

Shared truths; pain and love.

They were standing in the vicarage study where he had first spoken with her. That was the day she had decided to trust him; it seemed the right place for what was coming.

Greta was looking older. The last few days had weighed heavily on her and he worried that what he was going to say would drag her down further.

"Well, my Sherlock, you have learned it all? I am sorry for your toils but you will recover."

He had rehearsed this. A set speech carefully worded to clear all doubts but avoid pain. Now he couldn't remember it. He stood still and silent, looking into her eyes, trying to read what she was thinking and wishing she had never given him this miserable task.

"Would it be easier, if I told you that I already know everything; that you cannot hurt me with the truth?"

He sat down to think. Here again came the same old question: why ask him to enquire into what she already knew?

The last mists in his clouded brain cleared, as if she had simply reached into his mind and set everything in order for him. At times she was almost frightening. He stayed silent, thinking about the whole of it as he had never done before. The people in the photographs, the killing done by someone who was either insane or completely uncaring of being caught; the obvious ring stone that must have been placed at the scene at a later date; the altered church notice and someone asking for a cleric's address.

And she had given him the task because he hated injustice and, most of all, the thought of innocent people falling under suspicion - suspicion near impossible to extinguish. Did she know his own history? – Being Greta, almost certainly.

There was another aspect too. One that affected him directly. She had said as much to him before – he was chosen not only to help others but for the repair of his own broken mind. A wrongly accused person, unable to clear his name and now finding the strength and skill to face and resolve that same problem for others.

He looked at her, it seemed that she read his thoughts as if he spoke them aloud in that quiet room.

"Yes, now you understand my friend. Do you want me to tell it?… I think it is better coming from you and if you have any part of it wrong, I shall correct you."

He had the strange sensation that they were merging together in that quiet and spiritual room; two minds becoming one. He was losing the power to manage his own thoughts, stepping across into her world; yielding to her completely and with no wish to resist.

"It is my task. I will tell it. I think it is a story of two children who lost their parents when very young; they were taken in and cared for by a loving uncle and aunt – probably their mother's siblings."

"Correct, although they were not just taken in: the children were adopted, and they were greatly loved. Go on."

"For no obvious reason, one of the children wasn't good. The other was a golden child; loving and kind. I suspect she had second sight from birth. That would have endeared her to adoptive parents who were themselves quite spiritual – a kindly bishop and his adoring sister who both loved God unquestioningly."

He waited to allow her to speak again but she said nothing.

"As time went by, the behaviour of the troubled child became more distressing. Age did not improve her. At some time, not long ago now, she told her guardians that she felt called to serve God. Innocents as they were, they believed her. The old Bishop helped her career and she became the vicar at Sideleigh.

I suspect there were hiccups on the way; things that hurt the old boy and his sister but they bore it all, believing Fiona was what she pretended – essentially someone who loved the God who was the centre of their lives.

But Fiona said and did things in public that were ever harder to bear. Then one day, out of the blue, the uncle received an email - a letter perhaps, or more likely, I think, a photograph; a picture of a notice on a village notice board.

It was about a foolish public meeting that Fiona had arranged to stir up a little trouble and gain publicity for herself. The Bishop would have been upset by that but what broke him was, toward its end, the notice said that she did not believe in God and that was something he couldn't bear.

His adoptive daughter; someone he had reared and loved; a child that hurt him all her life yet he always forgave her and believed in her fundamental goodness. And, of all things she became a cleric, then publicly renounced, even derided, his religion.

And there, at last, was the motive which had eluded me and left the police struggling with impossible suspects. Means and opportunity had been clear but not the reason."

And then he spoke of the matter he had been determined to conceal from her. Concealment was impossible now; Greta would allow no secrets or lies. He was powerless to keep anything from her.

"What the Bishop did not know was: that particular part of the notice was a forgery by someone else. Perhaps Fiona didn't believe in the Bishop's religion but, whether she did or not, those weren't her words and she did not write them."

Greta stared at him, horrified.

"Who could do such a dreadful thing - and why?"

Silently, she asked herself *"Do I want to know?"*

He read her thought.

"No, Greta, you neither want, nor need to know. It was no one in your world and I'm certain it wasn't meant to cause the harm that it did."

She sat very still, wanting him to be wrong but knowing he

could not lie. He continued, gently, with his story:

"From that point on, you know more than I do. But I'll describe it as I believe it happened. I think there was a discussion between the three of you…"

"I was not part of that. They made the decision and they planned how it was to be. Then they told me about it, quite openly and…"

"Let me go on – it's my report to you and I know why you involved me. I have to complete my task as you do; we are bound together in this; and, by telling you, I share your burden. That's how I want it to be.

To the Bishop, and probably his sister as well, Fiona had become an affront to God; she was a rogue animal loose in a precious and fragile world. There was no intention or wish to conceal what was in effect a ritual killing. The place and time were fittingly chosen to match her infamous notice. The weapon I don't know, but I suspect it was something which had a divine significance.

I think the Bishop had no qualms about being caught and punished under the law, yet he wished to carry out the final judgement that he believed was right – his suicide was to be an apology for the wrongs that had been done to God.

But he wanted to ensure, if possible, that, after his death, no one else would be accused of Fiona's killing, and certainly not found guilty of it. I suspect he didn't want to leave a confession to be read after his death; that would have brought more painful publicity for his Church.

That, at last, was where you came in; you engaged me to prove your uncle's guilt. Not to pass the evidence to some policeman but as future insurance to protect other possible suspects and, hopefully, never to be used.

I wondered if there was another reason for my involvement – to help me put my past to bed. – I'm not sure it has done that."

"Yes, my dear one, that was one of the reasons you were chosen. That and because you, too, have some power of second sight. Do not mistrust it; it can never harm you, of all people."

"I think my damage is beyond repair; time will tell; and that's something I cannot foresee."

For a full five minutes they looked at one another, her kindly thoughts reaching out to support him, he receiving them as dry soil takes in welcome rain.

He returned to finish the task in hand; he felt exhausted, tired beyond reason. It was hard for him to speak now:

"Greta, I'm giving you my report in this case. It also contains evidence: documents - letters, notes, print-outs, photographs - and affidavits by me, by Chris Downe, Western Press staff and by two others that I shall not name in this room. All, or any, of this can only cause you pain; I suggest you leave the case unopened. Please let me bear the burden for you. Just place it somewhere safe; in time you will be able to destroy it, unseen, in the knowledge the contents are no longer wanted.

While I'm about it, I give you back his ring stone. I know you all had similar rings - I see you're still wearing yours. It has no value as evidence in the murder. It can't have been dropped at the time, or the police would have found it as easily as I did. I wasn't fooled by it but it told me much about your family, none of it bad. I don't know what was used to end Fiona's life, or where it is; that piece is missing from the puzzle."

"I know both those things and we shall each keep our knowledge to ourselves. That is what he wished."

He said no more for some time. Again, they sat silent; sharing their thoughts, as those who are so gifted will.

"I love you, Greta. Never forget that."

She replied in a whisper, almost unheard.

"How could I?"

* * *

After he had gone, she sat down at the old desk and started to write in her graceful, scholarly hand. She wrote a simple letter, yet unlike any that had been written in that room before, or, hopefully, would need to be written there again.

'*Dearest and kindest Father,*

I have completed my task. All is well. As well as it might be.

He has done his work for us exactly as you hoped. It has been painful for him and I wish he might have been spared that. It seems we are all of us bound to suffer on our roads to recovery.

I trust he will now have a peaceful life, but I fear for him.

My love as ever - and forever.

Your own Greta.'

Chapter 27

Four Meetings.

The three conspirators are meeting in that nice hotel lounge again. It is getting very close to Christmas. As ever, the warmly lit Hart and Sceptre has been generous with both its decorations and its heating. A vast and perfectly presented tree dominates the entrance lobby and every public room has been tastefully and carefully decorated. For those inside, the slightly dreary street scene has been relegated to obscurity. But several passers-by who look in through the windows are tempted to enter, if only for tea and comfort.

It is a hair up and casual smart day for the women; it isn't clear to Chris how they know in advance of every meeting what the dress code will be. They certainly don't tell him.

Greta looks tired, but she has just been thinking of another gathering, and hopefully a happy one, that isn't so far off now.

"Almost time for him to meet his friends, to learn he is not alone, and has never been since this started. Of course his heart knows that already; he just won't listen to it."

As ever, Chris immediately began to worry.

"That's a day that needs careful handling. You know how he retreats in himself. We started this stay-in-the-background approach for reasons I've forgotten now. I suppose it seemed right at the time; now I wonder if it wasn't all a mistake. Instead of helping his confidence, we may have done just the opposite."

"So what do you suggest, Chris?"

"I've been thinking about it. Suppose we simply send him

an unsigned anonymous invitation to come here on the day. He couldn't just ignore it and, when he arrives, we'll be here to welcome him and he'll see Sally and they'll be…"

He subsided into stammering silence and blushes. The two women looked at one another in disbelief.

Sally spoke.

"That's a very good idea, Chris. If you like to write a letter along those lines, we can leave everything in your safe hands. Greta and I will be here on the day and we'll organise lunch and tea."

And from Greta:

"Just let us know if you need any help, but I don't suppose you will."

Sally looked at her and they both smiled – the double meaning clear to them and entirely missed by their bright red escort.

Soon afterwards they said their goodbyes by the visitors' parking area. The women waved him off and, as soon as his car had disappeared, without a word, they promptly returned to their comfortable lounge and ordered coffee enough for an hour's discussion.

"I do love him so; 'He couldn't just ignore it' indeed – that's exactly what he will do. There never was such a complete innocent. If we left it all to him our Sherlock would simply disappear and never be seen again."

"I wouldn't let that happen, Greta, not under any circumstances. If this business has done any good at all, it's taught me to fight for what I want. I used to give up easily, but no more."

"So what's your idea? I was sure you had one."

"Simple, I shall treat Chris' plans as if they weren't happening. And I'm not waiting for his meeting just to have everything blow up in our faces. I shall do exactly what you would do, my second sighted one."

"Wonderful!"

It wasn't until Sally had been driving for an hour that she realised they had understood one another perfectly without need for words.

* * *

Handwritten letters were rare in his post. Apart from Christmas, not more than five in a year. He recognised the writing on most and shredded them, unopened, unread and without compunction. It limited the pain.

The writing on this envelope was unfamiliar. Neat and without character, it told him nothing. He feared to open it but decided he must. Nevertheless he couldn't bring himself to do so until late that evening, when he took it with him to his office. Mail had no place in his home – he had set that rule when he started to work for himself. It was one of his few good decisions.

The envelope implied the content would also be handwritten, but it was typed in bold:

'A meeting is scheduled for 10.30 am on Friday 6th January at the Hart and Sceptre Hotel, High Street, Dartstock.'

There was nothing more. He turned the page over – white and blank. He studied the envelope, giving it a ridiculously thorough examination – nothing. As ever, when one hopes for a legible, informative postmark, there was just a smudged blur of wriggly lines – no place name, not even a date.

He thought about it for a while. Either it was a scam or a mistaken address, but neither made sense. With a sudden lurch of his heart, he wondered if this was one of his painful children deciding to hold a surprise party after years of hurtfully ignoring him. He definitely wouldn't be going.

A moment's further thought and he dismissed that explanation – both children had seen their parents as thick servants to be used until no longer required, then cast aside; they weren't going to change now.

That train of thought was a well worn route down into suicidal depression. He clawed his way out of it, like a man desperately climbing a slippery wall, and returned to the problem in hand.

No, he had decided. Even if this was a genuine invitation, it was too peremptory, unnecessarily mysterious, manipulative. And, if there was one thing he hated above all, it was being controlled by others.

He ran the letter and its envelope through the office shredder and turned back to the work in hand, which, just now, was to sit in her chair and dream a little while he played with her papers on her desk.

Much later he woke sufficiently to go to his bed where he struggled with sleeplessness, and half waking nightmares, until it was time to start a new day by attending to Freddie. Just so had he passed too many of his recent nights.

* * *

"I've got to be away next Saturday - have to see a man about a cow. Could you call over to the farm that day and deal with a delivery for me?"

"Of course. What time of day and what is it?"

"Might be any time late morning up to, say, four in the afternoon, and it's a new trailer."

"Fine. I'll go over to the house at ten and stay there until your plaything arrives. Anything else wanted?"

"No, that's fine – thank you."

He thought Chris looked unhappy – not his usual self at all, but he hadn't noticed it when they greeted each other.

"You seem troubled. Can I help?"

"It's nothing; a small personal matter that's all."

They went their separate ways.

* * *

"He won't be coming; I tested him. Asked him to be at my place for the whole of that day and he agreed."

There was silence at the other end, then, just:

"Dear old Chris. I'm not surprised."

"For goodness' sake, Sally, don't let this go, not now. You mean more to him than even he realises. It's gone wrong in the past because the silly beggar doesn't read his messages and, this time, I'll bet it's much the same thing; he's afraid of people. We've made the mistake of being too mysterious."

The line went dead. Chris thought for a while and realised with a sick feeling that he had just spoken to the wrong woman. Well, he could try to put that right and, if he couldn't, then he must spend the rest of his life cursing himself for the fool he was.

Greta received his news as if it was too obvious to tell. She seemed almost indifferent and Chris wondered if she cared at all. Surely he wasn't that bad a judge.

"Thank you for telling me, Chris. I shall look into the matter. And don't blame yourself. He is an awkward man to help. But we knew that."

"Are we still going to meet even though he isn't coming?"

"Of course."

She ended the call and poor Chris was left to spend the rest of the day kicking himself while, some miles away, their favourite DCI was being drawn into a little reluctant subterfuge.

* * *

5th *January – two more meetings*

Cardler wanted to see him again; no explanation, just a phone message from some faceless police sergeant at Elcester stating time and place – eleven am at the *"green place where you've met before"*.

The detective was sitting at a quiet table in the Green Witch's reception area – not a very private place and he assumed this wasn't about either Jo or the vicar. But he was wrong, Cardler started at once:

"You've finished your investigation, then?"

"What investigation's that? I thought we'd put Jo Downe's murder in the box marked **'Case as good as solved; no further action unless Mr Jo turns up – or maybe Dave, late of the**

Happy Fireside pub.'"

"As far as Jo's concerned, I've got a potential suspect for attempted murder with a case that no court would convict on, short of an outright confession, and another potential candidate for a manslaughter charge, again without enough evidence to make it stick. – All we can hope for is charging two publicans with illegal manufacture of alcohol, and we've got to find them first. So I'm talking about Fiona Abbot, not Jo. Now, what's your line on that?"

"Are you asking a layman's opinion?"

"I'm asking someone with a brain."

"That's a compliment, thank you. Exactly what do you want me to say? And is this on or off the record?"

"We're meeting here, aren't we? This isn't my office. And what I want is your opinion on who killed the vicar and why."

"I'd like to help but I can't see how without letting someone down. I'm not doing that."

"Let's try this: I'll tell you what I think and you can say if I'm anywhere near the truth; if you prefer you can just nod or shake your head."

"Ok, but this meeting isn't happening and I'm just an outsider who's a good guesser; nothing more."

"Agreed. First off: motive. Fiona was treading on toes with her public antics; something she said or did - said most likely - pushed someone too far. Are we nodding or head shaking?"

"Half a nod; it was more a case of something that someone thought the vicar had done."

"Second: motive again; it was done to punish or shut her up."

"Half a head shake; it was a cleansing."

"Three; the place and time were the opportunity – there was something significant for the killer about that. And whoever did it wasn't bothered about being caught; that means it was love gone sour or maybe some high moral issue. I don't go for the soured love idea; there doesn't seem to have been a lover in the background. That leaves morals. And a vicar might easily upset a religious fanatic. People were voicing their views that day."

"Half nod again. The word fanatic's too harsh and at that I've said as much as I dare."

"Ok. I'm done. You can tell your white lady we've reached a dead end just now and I'm assigning staff to other duties. But the case stays open; is that clear? And don't assume you know everything; it may be I know something on this that you don't."

"Clear. Are we lunching today?"

"Another day. I'll have a coffee and leave you to your steak pudding."

They chatted together over their drinks and the DCI left just before lunchtime.

"I forgot to mention: by way of apology, I've booked lunch for you in the dining room. A bit solitary perhaps but you won't be alone - Freddie's included in the deal. I recommend the steak pudding for her too."

Steak puddings and dining with Freddie indeed! He was left wondering if Cardler was having a mental breakdown. Turning it over in his mind he decided to have his lunch at the Green Witch anyway but it wouldn't be in an empty dining room. He walked over to the saloon bar and sat down at a small table where he could look at the pub's still attractive garden and out across a series of little valleys, to a washed out view of distant straw coloured hills and the light mauve open moor.

He found a menu and ordered another coffee; Old Amber didn't mix with hot drinks. Back at his table he fell into a reverie about what Cardler had said. What did the man know about Filly's death that he did not? And why was he passing a message back to Greta through him?

Out of his sight, a car drew up close beside his in the Witch's car park. It was in fact very close, so close that he wouldn't be able to open his driver's door. – Why do people do that when there's plenty of available room?

He could make no sense of Cardler that day. Perhaps for that reason, or simply because he was very tired, his mind wandered, and he dozed. Meanwhile someone left the Witch's adjacent empty dining room and quietly entered the saloon bar.

His menu fell to the floor, waking him suddenly. Embarrassed, he looked across the room to see if the lapse had been noticed. It seemed not, but he sensed there was someone he hadn't yet seen, standing behind him a little too close for comfort. Whoever it was, Freddie was getting excited, and that usually meant trouble.

There was something familiar. He supposed plenty of women used that scent. He wanted to turn round and look but, of course, this was just his wretched mind playing its games. He didn't need another disappointment; no one, except Cardler, knew he was there and she was somewhere far away, living a happy life with new people and free of him. He felt slightly tearful and a little angry because of it.

"You've dropped your menu, Sherlock. I can't leave you alone for one moment before you go to pieces, can I?"

She sat down at his table without looking at him and hunted for something in her bag. Open-mouthed, he couldn't take his eyes away from her. The hunt went on so long that he recovered enough to speak.

"I was just testing to see if you were alert; that's what menus are for."

She was busy doing something with her eyes.

"And I thought you were calling attention to yourself; it looked like a pass to me. Sorry if I misread it Sir; shall I leave now?"

At last she looked at him.

"You haven't changed; a bit thinner but the same old curmudgeon - my dearest curmudgeon. Now, are you going to answer me at last? If you won't admit you love me, I shall just stick to you like a burr until I wear you down completely. You'll have to say it in the end, because I shall keep embarrassing you with loud and public demands for love; you of all people won't be able to stand that."

"Oh, well, if you put it like that. I love you. Now, can I have my menu, please? I want to order lunch. You can eat too if you want. My treat."

"Animal! Of course I want to eat. - You and lunch."

* * *

6ᵗʰ January – yet another meeting

They had arrived a little early as arranged. Both of them stood looking out onto the main street. It was raining; there were fewer pedestrians than usual and the bare trees did nothing now to cheer the familiar scene. Even the visitors' parking bay was empty; their cars discretely left in a side street.

Inside, the hotel had replaced its Christmas decorations with vases of cheerful flowers. Its warm lighting was switched on everywhere to close out the drab winter day, but Chris was unhappy, fearful of what was coming. He thought of how it might be. Perhaps Greta had done nothing and the day would collapse into pain for all of them. Or maybe their friend would arrive but be upset, angry even, to discover he had been fooled by the few he believed to be his friends.

The more Chris thought, the worse it all seemed. Meaning to help and thinking they were being clever, they had met in secret, discussed him behind his back, tricked him and still expected him to be pleased to see them here; to be praised by him even. Put that way, everything they had done seemed base and shameful. His heart was beating hard; he wanted to leave; to go away and hide. But he could not; what they had started they had to finish.

Greta looked at her watch.

"Nearly time for the actors to play out the final scene."

Chris wanted to know what she expected but dared only to ask:

"Isn't she coming today? I was sure she would. I can't bear the thought of only one of them being here."

"My dear and so innocent Chris, I think it is about time I took you in…"

But that short speech would have to wait until later. One more person was arriving - no, two people. They were laughing.

* * *

EPILOGUE 1

Extract from an obituary in the English Church Times dated 21st January 20**

The Right Reverend Ernest George Morgan Abbot,
Bishop of Middleton.

It is with great sorrow that we report the death at the age of 83 of Bishop Abbot on the fourteenth of last month.

Much loved and respected by the many who knew him personally and the numerous people who had been helped and inspired by him, the Kindly Bishop, as he was commonly called, was responsible for so many good works within the Church itself and in the wider world...

We have learnt that our Kindly Bishop died quietly while at work in his office. Apparently his demise had been expected but the exact cause has not been made known. He leaves behind Juliet, his sister, helper and constant companion through life, and their adopted daughter Greta. Both Juliet and Greta were with him on the day of the Bishop's death. Sadly, their other adopted daughter, the Reverend Fiona, predeceased him last year.

The world is a darker place for our loss.

RIP

EPILOGUE 2

Extract from the Western Press newspaper dated 17th May 20** beneath a photograph of the smiling couple:

We take great pleasure in reporting the marriage between Greta Morgan Abbot of the Vicarage, Sideleigh and Christopher John D'Arteur Downe of Downes Farm, Coldstow on Saturday 13th May at St Mary's Church, Coldstow.

Greta is the daughter of the late Ernest George Morgan Abbot, Bishop of Middleton. She has recently been appointed Vicar of the parishes of Sideleigh, Ewer, Spattersleigh and Coldstow.

Christopher, a local landowner and farmer, is the only surviving son of the late Albert and Kaye Downe and the last in line of that well respected Larkston family.

The wedding was attended by some two hundred people, about half of whom were local residents from the Larkston area. Those present included a remarkable number of high ranking clergy, including three bishops, which we venture to guess is probably a record clerical attendance for Coldstow's modest church.

The only event that did not go quite to plan on their happy day occurred after the couple had left for their honeymoon when two onlookers were arrested by detectives investigating the sale in the local village store of alcohol on which excise duty had not been paid. Miss Rene Crabbe and Miss Louise Crabbe were taken into custody and later released on police bail. It is understood that police were acting on a tip-off by a local resident who was herself charged with the offence of wasting police time. According to police sources, the informant has given a number of different names in the course of a long history of similar incidents.

Elcester police have issued a statement to the effect that at least two further arrests concerning the illegal manufacture of alcohol for the purposes of sale are anticipated in the near future.

We are asked to point out that neither Ms Susan Smythe nor her partner, Mr Harold Siptac, had any involvement whatsoever in the foregoing police matters.

(Reporter Stephanie Wyke)

* * *

www.ingramcontent.com/pod-product-compliance
Lightning Source LLC
Chambersburg PA
CBHW061646190726
48289CB00006B/1762